THERE'S NO SUCH THING AS HAPPY ENDINGS

AARON LONG

THERE'S NO SUCH THING
AS HAPPY ENDINGS
· AARON LONG ·

For anyone who's in need of a pick me up.

FALL

RANDALL

August 19ᵗʰ 8:00am

My junior year starts in less than two hours, and I must start the year off with a secret. Unlike the past, I got to keep said secret to myself. Except for that time, I couldn't keep it in any longer, so I told the guy I was crushing on, and his ass told me he just couldn't handle it and left me standing alone with my thoughts. Junior year is the pre-game before senior year. Everyone thinks senior year is the year that counts but really its eleventh grade.

We've had two previous years to screw around, get a few B's here and there, and keep our GPA intact. Starting this year, I have so many AP classes my head may explode. This is the time where things really get sketchy. I have zero time for failings grades, and I also have no time to be sitting in the doctor's office.

I wore all white today for two reasons. The first: I really love going against fashion norms. The second: I need to be noticed this year.

I spent the entire summer befriending people on social media I never said a single word to. I also joined so many social clubs, and I even made time to respond to this rich kid' invite to his ridiculously over the top party this weekend.

"Randall. We need to get you a match—" Dr. Rickards, who also happens to be my birth mother says. She spends much of her time sugarcoating everything. She can be the definition of a strong black woman, but when it comes to me, she's the complete opposite. It's been eight years of dealing with this, you would think she would have developed her two fronts. The doctor front and the I didn't feel like raising two kids, so I gave you away front...if she would just lead with her second front, ruining my day would be an afterthought by now. "Randall, I want you—"

"I have cancer." I focus my attention to some bright blue cancer sucks poster hanging behind my mother's head. After a minute or so, I check back into the conversation and notice birth mom and adoptive mom are quiet. It's almost uncomfortable in here. My adoptive mother tightens the grip on her purse straps. "How about this... just say, we need to find you a bone marrow match as soon as possible." Dr. Christina Rickards sinks down in her seat while Maria Turía Garcia Price, my mother, begins to pace the room.

"Randall." She pauses. "It's getting harder and harder to tell you these things. I just got you back in my life." Dr. Rickards finally straightens up.

"Look, it's so cool. Trust me. You can give it to me straight. You said without a match, I have at most a few years and some change to live, and with it, we'd continue fighting until I'm finally in remission. This is my third time fighting and each time, I pulled it out...have faith when you talk to me."

Dr. Rickards is speechless.

"To be clear, you didn't get him back. He's still my responsibility." My mother pauses from her pacing.

"...I pay the tuition at Crestview." Dr. Rickards jabs right back. "Not to mention, I just added him to my insurance." My mother's body tremors as she sits back down, she immediately sinks her chin into her chest.

"Wait.!" I pull my shirt back over my head. "Money can't buy me and remember you offered. You wanted Shauna and I to remain close. Didn't want me to fall behind. Another person to have my back when things got tough for me."

Dr. Rickards groans. "My apologies Maria."

My mother nods, then goes back to fake looking at something on her phone.

"Moving on, Randall, we need to get you on a treatment schedule...Right now I have you down for once every week after school—I want to get on top of this to prevent it from getting worse."

"Why can't we do it on the weekends? Or better yet, before school? What if I make friends...more friends? I also can't be late to work again. The place is about to close for a bit and all though I'm well liked in that place, they will fire me."

"Do you really want to give up your Saturdays…for four hours getting treatments? Or Sundays? Who would Shauna binge watch that little liar show with?"

"There's twenty-four hours in a day…we'd find time—"

My mom grips my knee. "For once I agree with Christina. You're doing the one day every week plan…after school." My mom quickly types something in her outdated iPhone. "End of discussion."

"Well then. Let me put this in the system and I can have someone bring you" Dr. Rickards checks her watch, notices she's running behind on something, and starts throwing things in folders. "…I'm sure your job can handle it if you're a few hours late." Dr. Rickard's grips her fancy doctor lady purse then stands hovering over me. "Randall, when you come back this week, I won't be here…so please stay in your seat the entire time. I really don't want to hear about you skipping any treatments. You need this…it's the only way—"

"I get it. I'm gonna keep that shit in my arm…even though it makes me cold, I never feel like eating the next day, it's boring…I could on and on about my dislike for Chemo…Plus, why does it take four hours for treatments. I'm sure there's a fast forward option…ooooh! I'll take that option—"

"Randall. Sweetie." My mom calmly says.

"Yeah, mom?" I force my paperwork into my backpack.

"No more jokes please." My mom grabs her things. "Let's get you to school."

"Fine. No more jokes…but, you have to admit that a fast forward option is hella ideal."

"Sure. Let's go before we miss the Ferry." My mom helps me put my backpack on and I begin to follow her out the door. "My boy is a junior!"

"How about I go on my own?" I don't not make eye contact.

"Are you sure?" Maria Turía Garcia Price cries for three reasons. The first: When I share exciting news with her. The second: When we receive bad news. And the third: When I try to be a big boy. "I don't mind. You know my boss doesn't mind me being late." She follows up.

"Te amo. I got this! Promise. No other junior is gonna have their mom taking a million photos of them." I motion for my mom to get her annual first day of school photos. I give her five minutes of my time before I look at my watch to check the time for the ferry. Before my mother can coerce me into taking more photos, I give her a kiss on the cheek and head for the exit. "nos vemos más tarde."

"Cuídate!" She yells as I rush to catch the ferry.

9:25am

I live in Westlake, an island north of Seattle. I never quite understood why they even call the island Westlake. My mom said that it was a spelling error, and the Seattle people kept the name. I also go to school in Crestview—a rich bougie ass neighborhood in Seattle.

It takes me about an hour or so to get from Westlake to Crestview by ferry and the entire time I'm sitting on the ferry, I'm wishing that all the spoiled rich kids just drown (not really).

I get tired of them posing for selfies in my line of view, they're also always so loud, and soon as the boats docks, I always ask myself, why do these idiots ride the ferry if many of them already live in Crestview? All these stupid rich kids have to do is walk or ask one of their other equally rich friends to give them a ride to school.

"Brother!" Shauna yells. She's waiting for me as I get off the ferry. I greet her and we start the very short walk towards school. Distance from the ferry dock to Crestview is literally ten minutes by foot.

"Hey." I nervously give her a hug back. "What's up?"

"Are you embarrassed by me?"

"What! No! I'm still getting used to this dynamic of us." It's only been eight months since my mother forced me to tell Dr. Rickards that I knew about her relationship to me. Shauna and I had already known one another from work. She was the only person there that looked like me.
Shauna and I are both black, and rock our natural hair. Shauna is just louder and prouder than me. She got to live in an all-black household, while I got to grow up confused. I was fourteen when I realized I wasn't of any Mexican descent.

"Ok. Don't worry, I didn't tell anyone that we're now siblings." Shauna devilishly grins.

"I don't care if you did."

"...so, you won't mind that I told Sarah...I gave her a ride this morning...that's the only person I told. Promise." Whenever Shauna grins, I know her ass is up to no good. "Promise."

"Shauna, I don't mind." I'm examining my schedule realizing that I have a half day schedule on the A days of the week. "Fuck! I didn't even have to be until ten o'clock."

"Language. Mr. Garcia." Principal Pendergrass says. It looks like he's been letting his mustache grow while we've been away. The way he keeps caressing it should be illegal. "Also, good to see you're doing well."

"It's Price. And thanks so much." Shauna and I, cross the threshold into Crestview High. "He couldn't be more obvious." I mumble. "So annoying."

"Oh, my goodness. He knows?" Shauna slaps me on the back so hard I'm thrusted into some random persons locker. "Shit...I'm sorry. I know you're fragile."

"No worries." I brush the dust off my white shirt. "I'm feeling amazing though. Get me a donor and I'll be doing even better." Shauna doesn't like my jokes about having cancer, so I keep telling them even after she begs me to stop.

"Randall. Please."

"What? I wasn't going to say anything ignorant...or how do you say it...ignant?"

Shauna lets out a deep breath. "I'm just happy you're fine. I don't think—"

"Nope. Please don't sound like your mother." I walk a little bit ahead of Shauna. Her long strides catch right back up to me.

"What do you mean?" We finally arrive to the junior wing of Crestview. It's in the most run-down part of the school. We call this part of the school The Castle because it's nothing but Gothic Era chic down here. It doesn't match the recently modern upgrades that was done to the school. Juniors are the only ones who must share lockers because the school administrators are too lazy to force our student government to fix it up. "Randall, what do you mean?"

"She takes forever giving me news. What she told me today wasn't even bad news. It was the same news she told me last week...and the week before."

"What did she tell you?"

I'm hesitant.

"Randall." She shoves. "What did she tell you?"

"The same news she told me last week." I grin.

"Randall! I'm not going to class until you tell me what's going on." I arrive to my locker, and she blocks me from turning the lock. "I'm not moving until you tell me what she said."

"Fine." I pull my water bottle from my bag as if I'm about to give her some gut pounding news. Taking a sip, I realize how over the top we both are...so I accidentally spit the water out on Shauna. "Shit. I'm sorry." I can't stop laughing.

"What's so funny?" She asks.

"I didn't mean to make you nervous." I have to breathe a bit before talking. "She told me that they're having a hard time finding me a donor. Then we set up my treatment schedule, then I made a few jokes and walked out. Fin."

"That's all?" Her eyebrow starts to wrinkle.

"Yes. Promise." I give her my best puppy dog eyes before I send her on her way.

"Ok. See you at lunch."

"Sure."

11:00am

My first day is getting off to an amazing start.

I used to always think that me being sick for most of my life was a bad thing and that it was probably the reason why I am so delayed with a lot of things. But I've been kicking school's ass since finding out I was sick again last school year.

"Randall!" Jason calls out. He's another black student that goes to Crestview. We always feel the need to greet one another even though we aren't actually friends. The only thing that ties us to one another is my mother working for his mother.

"Hey, how's it going?" I hold out then immediately pull back my sweaty hand.

"I'm so stoked that you rsvp'd to my party!" Jason's smile brightens up an entire room. At one point, back in middle school, I got goosebumps and a chubby and all this dude said was: hey, what's up?

"Yeah." I say while biting my lip. "I'm trying to be a little bit more active this year."

"Dope!" Jason inches closer to me. "Hey." He nudges my left shoulder. Jason's nudge sends tingles up my entire arm. "You should come over a little bit early to help me set up."

"SUREEEEE!" I awkwardly say. "I'll probably forget though, so don't hold me to it."

"No worries just thought I'd extend an invite. Since we're pretty much almost… slightly…kind of friends. I love your mom." Jason throws his satchel back over his shoulder. "Well, see you around."

"RANDALL GARCIA PLEASE REPORT TO THE MAIN OFFICE." The loudspeaker announces.

"What did I do?" I groan.

I genuinely have no idea how to even get to the main office. I've never had a need to go there. Unlike most teen movies or television shows, the main office at Crestview is not the place you go when the principal summons you there.

The main office at Crestview is used for all of our clubs, student government, and media. Basically, the main office is our schools glorified co-working space for student run clubs to feel important. Principal Pendergrass and his team

I spent fifteen minutes speed walking and asking random students how to navigate to the main office, only to find out that the main office is not in not in the academic building. Now, not only did I miss lunch, but I'm also sweating crazy.

"Hi, I um—"

"Mr. Garcia" A chick with red hair greets me.

"My last name is actually Price. But, whatever."

"Oh, I'm sorry I will fix that right now." The girl who still has not introduced herself grabs her glittery pink clipboard to make the correction. "Done. Randalll Price. Apologies. Well, let's go."

"I don't even know your name."

"Oh, silly me." She pauses. "My name is Rebecca. I'm a junior...well, technically a junior. I tested out of everything except math, I run the theater club...correction, I am the student president of Theater...Mrs. Chambers is our advisor." Rebecca continues walking down the rainbow-colored hallway.

"I'm sorry, why am I here?" I ask.

"Oh, silly me." She randomly laughs.

"I thought I was in trouble with one of the student government folks...you know how they like to pretend like they're the authority around here."

"We were so shocked to see that you signed up for theater over the summer. I wanted to meet you officially. Last school year, we had one or two classes together and you never spoke a single word in class. Mrs. Chambers and I were taken aback when we saw the name Randall Garcia...shoot! Price. It's Price. Randall Price...We were so shocked to see that you signed up. "

I was aimlessly signing up for any and everything over the summer. I was in a horrible mood one day. Dr. Rickards blindsided me by forcing me back onto a strict treatment schedule. I felt like a prisoner and wanted to take some kind of control back.

Then, later that same evening, I was scrolling on Instagram and saw that a former crush now has a boyfriend and a gang of friends. So, I found myself on the outdated Crestview High website signing up for all the clubs I thought would make me the most friends. My sad little finger was just auto filling my name to everything.

"Cool. So, am I in?" We finally reach the end of the very long hallway and the loud lights outside of the theatre room greets you forcefully.

"I'll let you know in just a moment." Rebecca slams open the door to reveal a black box of a room that was so my former aesthetic. "You have to meet everyone."

"That's fine." This black box of a room is bursting with happy energy. There are photos of famous actors on the wall. I am a bit shocked to see so many photos of people of color. It's an amazing sight given today's world. "Wow, this place is so cool."

"Thanks. All of the former theatre clubs have spent years putting their marks on this place, now it's our turn." Rebecca pulls back the curtain and the room immediately comes to life with people. It's as if they were waiting for her to give them the command to move. "Everyone, we have a new prospect!"

"Hey, everyone." The gang of people begin to form a massive circle around me. "Oh God, I hope you all don't want me to sing."

Rebecca starts to laugh. "No. We're getting ready to greet you. We do greetings a little different than your typical Theater club. "Ready everyone?"

Rebecca jumps into place, bows her head, and begins saying: "I'm Rebecca. I am from Mark and James. Two gays, one white and one pale. I am from morning coffees and late-night chocolates, but deep-down addiction may try to take me."

Wow, I that was deep. I hope they don't want me to go that deep.

The next person to go is Martin (She's a girl): "I am from a cheese farm and hard work; disrespect may get you hurt." Martin stops for a moment. There's a sadness in her eyes. We lock eyes for less than a minute. "In my future, I will be from Broadway."

The last person to go is a guy named Abiyram. This dude is extremely tall, he also has a short bushy haircut, and harry potter rimmed glasses. He starts off, "I am Abiyram, I am from Hebrew reciting's, Jewish values, but Christian living. He pauses, then inhales, and lets out, "I am from holding it in and let God conversations, I am from childhood trauma no crying to your mama, and thank goodness, I am from Crestview Theater, my pride and joy where my ride or dies stay."

"That was...you guys were...that was everything!" I'm snapping my fingers uncontrollably.

"Thank you. Do you think you can do it?" Rebecca asks.

"Becca." Abiyram interjects. "It's his first time here."

"We're doing things a bit different." Rebecca reaches for both my hands, but instinct is to immediately put them in my pockets. "Where are you from?" She asks, her hazel eyes widen which allows me to notice how tired she looks. "Let us know."

"We can wait if you want." Abiyram says.

"No. No, I'll go."

"Perfect!" Rebecca rejoins the circle, grabbing hold of Martin's hand, Abiyram keeps his free hand on his chest. "Oh, Randall...don't try to be perfect. We put you on the spot. No need to tell us your entire life."

"Trust me, I'm not." I hear Abiyram snicker just a little.

I take a brief second to allow my brain to determine what version of my story we want to tell these people. I take a bunch of deep breaths then let out: "I am from Christina Rickards; she gave me up to Maria Garcia Price and Baxter Price. I am from Westlake, the only place that has my heart. I am from weekend telenovela binge watches with my abuela. I am from a long line for champions and fighters. I am from can—" I clear my throat. "I am from happy and sad moments, because sometimes that's life." I was so moved that I felt that I wanted to share my secret with this group of strangers. Then it dawned on me, that rich kids love feeling guilty about things they have no control over. I would rather gain their friendship organically instead of gaining it because they all think I'm going to die soon.

"That was great Randall!" Martin cheers.

"Yeah, amazing." Abiyram grins. "You're a natural."

"Thanks guys."

"Randall, we'd love to have you apart of the team—if you want?" Rebecca pulls me in for a hug. "We'd be honored to have you. Practice starts in a few days. We hope you'll join us. Please say you'll join us."

"I guess it's a yes." The circle closes in on me. Everyone giving me hug after hug. I can feel the love radiating through everyone. I have never felt so welcomed. I want to remember this moment for forever, even when the bad times hit.

BRANDON

August 19th 2:00pm

My day started off like shit and will undoubtably end up the same way. I don't know who I thought I was manifesting a great day last night. I told the fucking universe that today was going to be a great day. I even wrote that shit down...twice. Once in my notebook and the second time on a sticky note I placed on my bathroom mirror. Pearl Jameson (my mother) ruined my manifestation.

My mother used to be a great mom, then my dad died, and she just stopped caring. She went from cooking breakfast and dinner seven nights a week to only caring about her new husband's needs. *Parents honestly suck.*

"Brandon! Are you listening?" Principal Pendergrass snaps me out of my daydream. "I really do not want a repeat of last year with your attendance."

"Sorry sir. Didn't set my alarm." The truth as to why I showed up to school less than five minutes ago mostly has to do with Pearl. She gave my car keys to Sam and made a big ordeal when I told her to force her husband to come back home. The three of us got into a major argument and after about twenty minutes and countless calls from my best friend, I snatched my keys out of Sam's hand and stormed out the house. I needed to clear my head, so I sat in the school's parking lot hoping for security to catch me, so I could give them a reason to make Pearl even angrier than she already was with me. "iPhones fucking suck."

"Language, young man." Principal Pendergrass rubs his temples furiously. "You are an excellent student—you could be at the top...if you just came to school on time. What can I do to help you? You can trust me, Brandon."

Can you get rid of Sam Jameson for me?

"I'm good. I just forgot to set my alarm, got tied up playing guitar and it slipped my mind that school started so early." Pendergrass chuckles a little. "I promise I won't be late the rest of the year."

"Should we have a meeting with your mother?"

"Why? So, she could bring her husband and the two of them threaten me in front of you and you just sit there and look confused." Pendergrass is speechless. "Nah. Don't call her. We don't want me to drop out, right?"

"Listen." Pendergrass intertwines both of his hands then tilts his head to the left. "Your mom and dad…" He clears his airway. "Your mother and her husband only want the best for you. We've spoken about this."

"Bull. Shit!" I stand. "No, they do not. They don't even care if I—" I stop myself. If I said that she doesn't cook for me or even cares if I eat, then its CPS visit number five. Crestview can't have them driving through our prim and proper neighborhood again. "Look, don't call anyone. I can make a promise that I'll be on time."

"Brandon." Pendergrass takes a long loud gulping sip of his water, before telling me to take the rest of the day. He also thinks I'm going to come back tomorrow with a better attitude.

"I most certainly will not have a better attitude tomorrow." I attempt to mumble.

"What'd you say?" Pendergrass grabs my bookbag strap.

"I said, have an awesome day, sir!" I regather my things and leave his office.

Right before I can leave the office, I walk pass this guy who's dressed in all white, he's having a heated discussion with Sarah Hayes, our resident valley girl. She's the worst, all she talks about is the money she never earned. She's also the only person in this school who abides by the technical dress code policy we have set in place. Her blonde hair has been bleached so many times its basically white.

"...I'm sorry you chased me down...I cannot change your work schedule for Wednesday. We need you. We're about to close for goodness sake." Sarah writes a very large red x on this kid's paper and turns her back to him. The boy dressed in white doesn't even move. "Randall! I am serious, I am not changing your schedule. What's so important?"

Randall stutters.

"Well—"

"I have to help my mom; she needs me to help her at one of the houses on your street."

"Oh, how sweet—"

"Sarah, don't even say what you're thinking." I interject. Sarah tends to downplay your entire existence without even meaning to. "He obviously has a good reason to not want to work at your dump—just give it to him."

"Randall...fine. You better be on time every other day you work up until close for reno."

"You got it." Randall gives her a hug before racing out of the office. "Thanks guy I don't know." Randall takes off.

Shit. Now, I'm stuck with Sarah. I should have run behind Randall. "How are things Sarah? How was your summer?"

"Fine. Spent the summer island hopping in Greece with all of the Grecian Gods, Goddesses, and Those who identify as they. They loved me in Greece."

"Sure."

"Anyways, what'd you get up to this summer Brandon?" The downer in me wants to start from the beginning. I could be like, oh, as soon as school let out Sam punched me in the face which caused me to lay low for a few weeks until the bruising went away and then my mother prevented me from presenting my demo tape to a guy that could've changed my life. "I know you did something fun." Sarah is all smiles like she really cares about what I'm about to say.

"Oh, I stayed in the house and binged Outer Banks four times. It was epic." Sarah's smile disappears entirely. Which causes me to laugh. "Shit. You actually care about my summer plans."

"Brandon, you're not funny. We're friends. I care about all of my friends. I'm also super excited that I ran into you."

"Oh God, what did I do?" Sarah pulls out her phone and presents me a blank screen. "What am I looking at?"

"Oops. There's a video…" She's having a hard time getting her face to be recognized by her phone. "Goodness… yay...awe...I locked myself out again." She restarts the unlocking her phone game again. "There! Got it."

"Look, I have to go."

"No! Not before you take a look at this." She shows me a video of my best friend Kelly and I singing a cover of a Lady Gaga song. "Oh, cool. Now, can I go?"

"Wait. You should perform at Taverna." Sarah sticks a card in my hand.

"I should?" I examine the card.

"Yeah. We're having a show sometime soon and I think you should make yourself a part of it. This video has so many views, let's get some more eyes on you. If you practice day and night, you'd be ready for one of our re-opening shows. I'm serious Brandon. You're a great singer."

"I'll think about it."

"If you think too long…you know what, I'm just gonna put your name down and if you change your mind…which you won't...just let me know." Sarah ends up being the one to escape this conversation.

"I'm not going to do it." I'm sure I whispered this time.

Sarah about faces and leaps back in my presence. "Brandon, you have to do this. Look, just stop pass one day and you'll see for yourself. I promise no tricky business." After a few seconds of rolling my eyes, I oblige. "Yay! Just stop pass any time after school."

"You got it!" I hold up my thumb.

"See. Brandon…" Principal Pendergrass startles me. "I'm happy to see that you're making friends this early in the school year." I glare at him before leaving the office. "I'll check in with you tomorrow. My office at 9am."

"Sure thing! See you at ten!" I say as I head out of the administrative office.

2:45pm
Getting home early is the worst.

I have to be subject to Sam's unwarranted advice and if I don't listen to his advice, I'll have to hear about it from my mother when she comes home from her imaginary job. Today, on Sam's World of not-so wonderful news, he's talking to me about how I could be of better use to my mother.

Our kitchen is the homeliest part of our house. It's my favorite part of our old Victorian. When my mother and father were together, they really took their time perfecting it. Sam and I remain distant because the kitchen island has to be the length and almost width of a football field. Each time he moves his pasty white body, I inch even closer to our back stairway. I miss sneaking down those stairs to scare my dad, I loved that he pretended to be jump. Sam truly sucks.

"Brandon, you should allow your mother access—"

"No!"

"You raising your voice towards me?" Sam pulls out his cellphone. "Do I need to call your mother? He flicks his fat fingers up and down the screen until he gets to Wifey. "I'm not joking, I'll call her."

"Do. It." I turn my back towards him pretending to search for a snack in our oversized cabinets that should have never been painted green. Sam's way of erasing the memory of my dad. "You can't make me give up a single cent of the money my dad left me."

"All she needs is a signature." The tone Sam uses makes my face grow sour. He says it as if he's saying they're going to commit some forgery shit on my shit. "Who knows, she might even let you bring that fag over."

"And on that note, I'm out of here." I grab a pack of Pop Tarts and sprint up the back stairs. My speed causes me to almost knock down the photo of my dad.

"Where do you think you're going, we're not fucking done talking." I can hear Sam charging up the stairs. It dawns on me that Sam's world of not-so wonderful news is never this exciting. He's never this involved in the happenings of my day, life, or finances. "Brandon, you son of a—"

"What's going on?" Pearl meets me at the top of the stairs. I scoot pass her and try to make my way to my room. "Brandon!"

"Yes." I turn, drop the Pop Tarts, and fold my arms immediately. "He started it."

"I don't want to hear it."

"You never want to hear it. I was minding my own business in the kitchen then he started with me, telling me I had to give you access to my money." Pearl turns her back towards me and places her index finger on my upper lip. I remain still because Peal has too good of aim, I would never make it to my room without some kind of object following me in the doorway. "Can I please go?"

"No." Sam says.

"Baby, I got it." She gives Sam a kiss because he's offering his lips to her. I immediately turn away. "Brandon, why can't you just behave for once? Your dad—"

That does it.

I face my mother who if glares could kill, I'd be on my last leg with life.

"No! My dad nothing! He's rolling in his grave at you. Ever since you brought him in this house it's been turned upside down. I liked it so much better when you two snuck around, because at least you were fucking here. Look at our house, it's so dark now. There used to be light at every inch of this place, now there is nothing but darkness. You let this ass of a human—" Sam tries to grab me by my shirt. I step back causing him to fall. He will not ruin my dad's favorite plaid shirt. "I only have twelve months left in this hell hole and I only have nine months until I get what dad left me. We'll be out of each other's space by then. I WILL NOT be giving you or him access to anything dad left me. Now, I'm going to my room." I brush pass my mother and when she tries to grab my arm, I snatch it from her. "I'm going to Kelly's tonight."

"Brandon, you better not leave this house."

"What's the point? You don't care about me."

"Brandon. Please don't take me out of character today. You are not leaving this house."

"Whatever."

"Brandon. Stay in your room the rest of the night, I don't want to see your face until morning."

"Fine." I give in. Today has already been a shitty day, there's no need for me to make it even worse by causing her to take my door of the hinges...again.

RANDALL

August 21ˢᵗ 10:45am

My favorite class is English. Books and writing are my thing. For
the Junior/Senior reading it was a list of fifteen books they
expected us to finish by the end of the summer. I finished them all
by July.

     I had time to read while I was trying to keep myself away
from sick people and germs. All I would do in my sulking time was
read a book. Reading helped me escape my current world. I didn't
have to worry about my mother overworking herself just so she can
feel like she's being of good help to Dr. Rickards. I didn't have to
worry about my job and how I cannot wait to quit. I got to stay in
the mindset of all of the different characters I read about. I related
the most to Hazel and Gus.

     "Everyone." Mrs. Chambers, the AP English teacher gets
the class's attention. She has her hands on both of my shoulders.
"Randall Price will be joining our class."

"Hey." I wave. Of course, everyone keeps their heads down. AP students are always so damn serious.

She tightens her grip on my shoulder. "He's a junior who's tested amazingly…despite—" I shoot her a look. "Despite an already hefty course load. Let's be nice to him."

"Thanks. Mrs. Chambers." I shoot her a look. She is one of the few teachers that knows about my diagnosis. She's always trying to baby me like I'm disabled or something. Anyone with any kind of disability whether seen on unseen will tell you babying the person is not the move. "I'll take my seat now."

"Why don't you go take a seat next Brandon or Abiyram…raise your hands so he knows who you are." Walking to take my seat is the most awkward feeling ever. AP classes are known for low enrollment. The quietness of the class makes the sounds of my loud old ass shoes stand out.

"Randall. So cool that you're in this class." Abiyram smiles. I didn't want to point out to him that he still had his retainer in. "It's going to be cool."

"Yeah." I am so horrible at conversations with humans. "Sure." Abiyram's smile disappears, and he turns away. I want to fix this very awkward moment, but I feel like that'll take too much energy. He'll be alright. *Right?*

"Everyone, grab your notebooks, we're about to discuss the book…no! let's partner up…find a partner and let's get to discussing." I turn to Abiyram, I guess my lack of conversation has him having doubts about my ability to dissect a story, so he asks the random person sitting in front of him to partner up.

"Wow." I whisper.

"Randall...Brandon is available." Mrs. Chambers walks back to her desk. "Get close you two."

Brandon hides his face completely behind his backpack. "Hey, I guess we're partners." I sit in the open seat next to Brandon and scoot very close to him.

"Before we begin, who's read *A Little Life?*" Mrs. Chambers asks. All ten of us raise our hand. I don't want to pass judgement on this Brandon character, but I know he didn't read the book.

"So, did you read the book?" I ask Brandon.

"Yup." Brandon goes back to twirling his pen around his finger. "I got through it."

"So." I tilt the book he's pretending to look at down. "What'd you think?"

"I didn't like the book" Brandon blurts out and everyone in the class turns to look at the both of us. "It was too long."

"Well, you can discuss this with Randall." Mrs. Chambers goes back to monitoring the room.

Brandon sinks back into his seat. "This is so stupid." He mumbles. "Group discussions is so depressing."

"I get it. I don't usually like discussing books either. But maybe we can dissect why you hate this book so much." Brandon shoots me a death stare. "Or not...What specifically did you hate about the book, though?"

"The length. Like, come on. A 1000 pages for dude to be like he loves other or some shit. I was over it. Don't get me started on the style of writing."

"Valid." I say. "I can agree with you, the book did feel long winded, but it was told over time—the author couldn't just cut to the good parts or emotional parts. She wanted us to know enough about everyone, their stories, and relationships—"

"I like what you two are doing" Mrs. Chambers turns our little moment into a class time moment. "What do you all think about the ending?" The room grows quiet. "Let's not all speak at once." Brandon covers his face with his bookbag leaving me in the eyeline of Mrs. Chambers. "…Randall, why don't you get us started?"

"Umm…are you sure?"

"Yes. I like the conversation that you and Brandon were having." Brandon's olive skin somehow becomes red. "Go on, we won't bite." Mrs. Chambers is pleased with herself.

"Well—" I start.

"I thought it was fucking wrong as hell." Brandon interrupts. "Jude didn't have to do what he did, we spent hundreds of pages rooting for these characters—Jude and Willem specifically, and then Jude does what he did…just selfish." I disagree with Brandon. "Like, Willem died…sad as hell…but the dude made a promise to…uh—"

"Harold. He made a promise to Harold." I help.

"Yeah, he made a promise to Harold that he wouldn't go off the deep end and then he goes and does what he just said he wouldn't do. To me, it just proves that Jude was selfish."

"No." I say while shaking my head.

"Oh, this is getting good." Mrs. Chambers takes a seat on the edge of her desk. "What is it that you disagree with, Randall?"

"I don't think Jude was selfish. We spent decades with these dudes. We got to know them over time and in that time, we got to know the bond between Willem and Jude. They were almost like each other's anchors. Jude suffered from PTSD, he suffered a lot of traumas, trusting people wasn't something Jude was known for. Willem was his safety net—his reason for attempting to be better. When Willem randomly passed…cause let's face it…it was hella random for the author to kill Willem, Jude didn't have his anchor anymore. Jude wasn't a complex kind of dude. He harbored and held on to everything—"

"That still doesn't give him the right to do what he did." Brandon interrupts. He throws himself forward causing his hair to fall out of place. I can see the green in his eyes very clearly. Brandon gets a quick glimpse of me and for a quick moment we're both quiet.

"Have you ever loved someone so deeply that you would do anything for them, you'd be there for them every single day, sleep on their floor, help them be better, stay with them through everything, even after they've just threatened you or fought you…I'm not talking about a family member…I'm talking about a person. Have you ever wanted someone and once they were gone or abruptly left your life, you just wanted to end it all, too?"

Brandon is quiet.

"Randall posed an excellent question." Mrs. Chambers says. "Brandon, have you?"

"No. No, I haven't."

"So, we shouldn't call Jude selfish. His backstory and his mindset were all very well explained. We were just never told his true reasons for why he ended it all. The author never said that Jude ended it because of his love for Willem—it can however be implied."

"So, I'm valid in saying he was selfish for killing himself, right?" Brandon finally cracks a smile.

"Sure. But, since you've read the book, you know Jude and his mindset...he wasn't selfish in nature...he was very stubborn in that he didn't want to seek help for himself, but when it came to Willem, he tried to be about it, so it's safe for us to assume that Jude couldn't hold on to his life because his anchor wasn't there. If the author had written it in the book that Jude got help or at least sought after it...no, we still can't call someone who commits suicide selfish. It's not up to us to decide that."

"And, with that, class is over. Awesome work you two." Mrs. Chambers is the first to leave the classroom.

"Hey, Randall." Abiyram taps me. "That was really amazing! See you at rehearsals."

"Yeah, thanks."

"So, let me ask you..." My back is towards Brandon which causes his voice to send shivers down my spine. "Have you ever loved someone so deep that you wanted to end it all?"

I am speechless. I try to slide all of my belongings into my backpack.

"Hey, I took a look at your schedule…you have lunch next, so do I. No need to rush. So, have you?" Brandon smells like a very expensive cologne—it's not too musky and not too strong. There are hints of wood and vanilla. "You called me out, how about I do the same." He smiles.

"No." I take a beat. "But I came close to it."

"Damn."

"Yeah, I misread the situation by telling them about my situation and got my feelings hurt big time."

"Human's suck." Brandon smiles.

"Yup." I grab my backpack and head for the door.

"Wait up! A bunch of us are going to get ice cream, I worked at this ice cream shop…well, it's not really an ice cream shop…there's just ice cream there and I got paid to scoop it…anyways, do you want to hang with us?"

"Cool." I say.

"I'll wait for you after last period." Brandon says.

Then it hits me, I have my first treatment today after school. "Shit! I forgot I have to help my mom at one of the houses she cleans."

"Oh, no problem…if it doesn't take long, I can give you a ride and wait—"

"No! I mean, it's okay…this usually takes four hours or so." I pull at my shirt collar, which to anyone who knows me knows that is one of signs when I lie. My dad used to clock this action at least once a week—especially when it came to taking those dry ass cancer curing pills.

"Damn. I hope you're getting bank. No worries, dude, next time." Brandon tosses his backpack onto his shoulder.

"Yeah." I say.

"Well, let me see if I can sneak off campus to get some lunch and make it to my next class on time. Plus, there's some chick waiting for you." Brandon takes off, looking Shauna up and down. "Later, dude."

"See you around." I say.

"Finally, we've missed five minutes of lunch." Shauna says. "I really have a lot of shit talking to do with you."

"Fun." I say with sarcasm.

RANDALL

August 21ˢᵗ 7:00pm

"Today must be Groundhog Day" I say under my breath. Sitting back in this hospital room, in the same seat, with the same four kids—who all smell like skittles. "They have to do something about it being so cold in here." Not only does our fancy little chemo room feel like an ice box, but it also resembles one too. The room is painted Blue with childish white clouds plastered across the four corners of the room. Our seats were white at one point in their existence, now, they're just a pee yellow kind of color. I can admit they are comfortable as hell though.

"Randall, I think you're almost done." Joseph says. He and I have been riding the treatment train on and off together since we both were eight years old.

"Welp! Looks like I'm going to head on out." I am pushed right back into my seat by Nurse Jaqueline, the resident fun police in the pediatric ward of the hospital.

"Randall, your body must've been thirsty." Nurse Jaqueline jokes. She looks like a middle-aged Cindy Lou Who—seriously. She has a very obnoxious ponytail in the middle of her head that accompanies three uneven braids on both sides of the disheveled ponytail. "I can tell you are not in a joking mood…one more hour to go…then I'll call your mom." Nurse Jackie takes another look at my machine and then makes her way to another patient.

"You mean Dr. Rickards or my actual mom?"

I've just stumped Nurse Jackie.

"My mom is still working…I know how to call a cab or something—"

"Noooo." Nurse Jackie drags.

"Yessss." I also drag.

"No. Your…Dr. Rickards told me to call her when you were done, so we could have someone pick you up."

"And, I just said I know how to get home just fine."

"Randall!" Our going back and forth has made her poke her newest patient, a very pale girl with a scarf on her head.

"Ouch." The girl screeches. "That hurts!" The girl snatches the needle from Nurse Jackie's hand. "Pay attention!"

"Randall." Nurse Jackie clears her throat. "I will be informing your mother about this…both of them."

"Wait! I thought you were going to change the channel." I yell. Nurse Jackie finishes her nursely duties then rushes off with the remote. For three hours, we have been watching Family Feud reruns on the game show channel, and as badly as I need a good laugh Steve Harvey's voice became annoying at hour two. "Well, this truly bites."

"My name is Bella...by the way." The girl with the scarf on her head says.

"Huh."

"My. Name. Is. Bella." She slowly repeats. "I didn't want you to describe me as some girl with a scarf on her head." I smirk a little. "What's your name? Even though I just heard it."

"I don't mind repeating. It's Randall."

"That's a little boys name." Bella forces herself to laugh. With each *Ha* she coughs. "Sorry. I have cancer." She smiles causing everyone in the room to burst out into laughter. It takes me a minute to catch on before I join in on the joke. "I have minimal lung capacity...pretty much, I'm losing control over every part of my body internally."

"Damn. That's so messed up." I say.

"I know but imagine my banging new body in the next life." She realizes that didn't sound right but still chooses not to correct her statement. "I'm going to be able to do cartwheels and cheer without feeling like my lungs are going to fall out of my mouth while I'm upside down." Bella checks the imaginary watch on her arm. "It's going to be *soooo* amazing to look at a clock or calendar and not stress about the little time I have left."

"Yeah. That's cool." I say. Honestly, I feel like I'm just supposed to acknowledge what's she's saying—it's the right thing to do. I've never encountered someone being so upfront about the realities of cancer. Most of the other kids that sat in her seat when they passed on, we would just tell ourselves that they either switched clinics or got better, when in reality we knew they died. "I think I like you." I grin.

"Are you a believer?" Bella asks.

"Believer, in what?"

"God, silly." Bella reaches for her bag on the ground and pulls out her pocket bible. "You've seen one of these before, right?"

"Yeah. We have one in my house…used to read it all the time…well, I'd have it read to me."

"Nice. Its good both of your moms introduced you to some form of religion."

"Wait. I don't have two moms…well, technically I do, but my mom—the one I live with and have lived with for sixteen years she's strictly into man meat…Dr. Rickards—the one who pushed me out…I don't really know much about her…other than she's loaded and she's trying hella hard to be in my life."

"Oh. I'm sorry for assuming." Bella pulls another bible from her bag.

"No worries. It's confusing…just like my cancer diagnosis."

"How so?" She asks.

"You see, I have leukemia and I've been fighting—this time, for close to a year…I read somewhere that I'm supposed to be way sicker than I actually feel, I'm supposed to be in the hospital like full time—"

"Wait!" Bella forces herself forward. "Are you hoping for the other shoe to drop on purpose?"

"No…maybe…I don't know."

"Randall. You can't do that."

"I guess I've grown to being pessimistic when it comes to my battle with cancer. This is my third time getting this disease, and today makes it treatment number thirty-three in terms of these lousy chemo treatments. Radiation is another long-winded story. That also means I've wasted one hundred and thirty-one and a half hours fighting this very fucked…messed up disease."

"Woah. That's a lot of time." Bella says.

"Yeah. That's five days spent in the hospital and we're only counting Chemotherapy hours. The hospital has made me not hope for anything from this…I guess…life."

"Can you make me a promise?" She asks.

"No. We just met." I say.

Bella stares blankly at me.

"Yeah. Sure, I'll make a promise to you…girl I just met."

"Excellent. The promise is for you to start living. The cancer in our bodies is going to continue to do what it wants to do. There's no need for us to worry ourselves."

"Yeah, I guess you're right...I've been partly trying to do that anyways this school year. I guess I just need more time in this new mindset to fully flush my pessimism away."

"You're going to pull through this." Bella says. "I feel it in my heart of hearts. You're going to survive. This is just part of your story."

"Yeah. So are you...we're both—"

"I'm not too sure about me pulling it out." Bella throws her blanket over her legs.

"Come on Bella, what happened to living in the now?"

"Randall, I am. My tumor I'm pretty sure is inoperable. It hasn't shrunk in ages. I'm doing chemo for my dad. He thinks that by forcing me to do these treatments that he's buying time with God to answer his prayer." Bella wipes a tear from her face. "I want to tell him that I believe that God has already answered his prayer."

"Wait—"

"No, I'm not giving up if that's what you were about to ask. I'm just being real with myself and my body."

I am speechless. Nothing I am thinking can possibly make Bella feel any better.

"Randall, one day soon, you should meet my dad—"

"Randall." Shauna interrupts.

"Hey!" Nurse Jackie appears out of nowhere to remove the needle from my arm. "Let me guess you're my chauffeur?"

"You guessed it." Shauna smiles.

"Randall, take my number. Let's plan to meet up and continue our conversation." Bella tries to slide her little green bible in my hand, and I immediately gather my things to go. "Talk soon."

"Take care of yourself, Bella."

8:45pm

"Randall, your pizza is going to get cold." Shauna ignored me telling her to just take me home so I can just sleep this chemo hangover off. "Don't make me look like a fat ass."

"I am not in the mood to eat, right now."

"Why? Are you feeling sick?"

"No. Today was my first treatment in a month. This is how I usually feel after."

"Didn't they give you pills or something?" Shauna takes a huge bite of pizza.

"Yeah. Chemo pills." I say. "It's not a chemo hangover cure. Just pills helping to fight my cancer."

"Well, what do you need me to do?" she asks.

"Stop forcing me to eat."

"No worries. I'll make this entire pizza disappear." Shauna shoves another slice of pepperoni pizza down her throat. "I have no gag reflexes."

"You shouldn't say things like that out loud." I say.

"Why not?"

"People will think you're easy and try to be all over you. I don't know how to fight…so don't bring those kinds of problems over to our table."

Shauna laughs causing some her pizza bits to land on my face. "Let's switch topics." She takes one more nasty bite out of her pizza. "What were you and that girl talking about?"

"Her name is Bella."

"So." She finishes chewing. "What were y'all talking about? Convo seemed tense."

"She's up in the air when it comes to surviving her cancer. She wanted me to stop being so pessimistic about everything and to just live without question."

"Awe…you know she's right, though?"

"Whatever." I lay my head on the very dirty table.

"No, Randall I'm serious. My mom would always say to think about a time before… when things get hard…just think back to the moment before the bad thing happened…you have to do that."

"I've never had that—"

"Prince Island." Shauna brings up. My mom was able to afford to send me to a boarding school my freshman year of high school and part of my sophomore year. That place was like Disneyland to me. "You had one free year of not having cancer."

"I guess." I say. I try not to think about Prince Island too often. That year was my favorite year, no constant poking, no chemo hangovers, I hadn't thought about my disease once. Present day, it's all I ever think and dream about. *I just want it gone.*

"Well, I'm telling you that you need to just let this all go and fully allow yourself to be free. You said this was going to be the year where you actually lived...so do it. No more sarcastically joking about your diagnosis. You're living from now on." It's so easy for everyone to tell me what to do, but the majority of the people in my corner have never faced what I am going through.

"Fine. I am going to allow myself to live, I'm going to be as happy as I can allow myself to be. No more sulking, no more sarcastic jokes...if I can help it...I'm just going to do it."

BRANDON

August 22nd 5:30pm

Sarah's family bar Taverna, from the outside, is for an acquired taste. This place is butt ugly. The place stays crowded with people, though. The majority of the people that come to their lounge are all hipsters that live all throughout Seattle and neighboring cities and islands. People spend that hour-long ferry ride from Seattle to experience the ambiance of this place. Taverna is a staple in Westlake.

When you first walk in, you expect for it to be as ugly and simple as the outside of the building, but when you walk in, it's a hipster's paradise. They've forgone traditional tables and chairs and there are just rugs, pillows, and small ottomans lining the space—almost like an outdoor concert set up but inside. All the different kinds of lights, all varying in length and style—I can admit are my favorite part of the entire place.

"Brandon!" Sarah rushes up to me from behind. "...I didn't actually think you'd show up when I offered."

"Are you making bets on me?"

"Yeah, cause you're flaky." Sarah grabs me by the arm. "Come, let me show you around." Sarah pulls me to the center of Taverna, and she forces me to spin around. "Tour done. Did you want to test out the mic system tonight?"

"Dude. You don't waste any time, do you?" I say.

"Nope."

"Let me just get a feel for your place." I take a moment to envisions how this place is ever filled with people. "Wow." I hesitantly say.

"Pause." Sarah places her finger on my slightly sweaty upper lip. "Have you ever performed in front of people before?"

"Umm...yeah...wait...define performed in front of...does YouTube count?"

"No, it doesn't count. People on the internet love our edited versions of ourselves...people need to hear you live."

"Well, no one has let me perform anywhere...plus, my mom would never go for that." At the beginning of summer Kelly had written both of our names down for us to do this showcase in town and my mother was all for it, then the day of the show she caused us to have a major blow up and she forced me to stay in my room. I couldn't even see my best friend kill it. We both could have gotten managers that night. "My mom and her husband will definitely lose their shit...when'd you say she showcase was?"

"It's in a few months. You can practice here; we're about to close for some renovations soon but if you ever need the place, you got it."

"That's so nice." I say.

"Do you want a snack or something…I mean you're about to get to work…I can at least feed you before I force you to work."

"I'm so confused…work?"

"Yeah, if you tell your folks that you have an actual job, that should get them off your back, right?"

"Hopefully."

"Well, then, let me go get you some paperwork so your mother can sign it so you can be here late at night—"

"I'm not bussing no floors, or making drinks, or cooking. I can be the door man or something. I'm horrible at manual labor."

Sarah laughs. "Brandon." She pulls me closer to her. "Your job is your music. This is what you're going to be doing. We can even fake some paystubs, so this all looks legit to your mom…she'll never know when this place closes. We just need to get you ready and able to perform in a few months."

"Ok. Great!" I say.

"Is that alright with you?" Sarah asks.

"Yeah…why are you doing this?"

"Because more than one person has to make it out of here by chasing their dreams." Sarah smiles before heading off to get me my forged documents.

I can't help but to smile from ear to ear, I borderline want to shed several tears. Sarah has not been someone I would have ever wanted in my corner because she can sometimes be shallow or all about herself. I can now see why her friends stick around—this girl genuinely cares.

"Brandon. My mom is running the forms off, and I put an order in for some French Fries and other goodies, why don't you go to the bar and get something drink."

"Gotcha." I stand for a moment pretending like I saw a bar when I walked in here. This place is an explosion of hipster decorations it causes the bar to get lost in this place.

"It's over in the corner behind the bookcases." Sarah says from her end of the large room.

Who has a bar behind a bunch of bookcases?

"Wow." I loudly whisper. The bar area of this place is now the best part of this entire space. I am all smiles when I see all of the greenery that is hiding and mixing with the bookcases. There are vines and flowers partly going up and down the bookcases. I go in a little further to see that the bar is its own stand-alone fixture. A simple wooden rectangle and three pendant lights gently lighting this place up. "How is this place so cool?"

"Hey!" Shauna says. "Didn't know we were open on Thursdays." She scans me up and down.

"You aren't. I came to check the place out." I am still admiring the design of this bar area. It is the coolest thing I've ever seen.

"Oh, well, do you want something to drink?" She asks.

"Yeah. Do you have Ginger Ale—"

"We don't have anything the outside world has. We have craft juices, and stuff."

"Craft juices?"

Shauna hands me a menu. "Lean closer." She immediately lines the bar with small paper cups. "I'm only going to pour the ones I think you may like—"

"Shauna, I forgot the last thing you asked for…Brandon? What are you doing here?" Randall has two bottles of pills in his hand.

"Hey Randall, what's up?"

"Randall. Why do you keep walking around with my drugs?" Shauna stops pouring my little shot drinks and snatches the bottles from Randall. *Girl has some long arms.*

"I work here." Randall approaches. "Are you getting a job here?"

"Technically. Need a cover to tell my mom. When I'm out late." Randall has the most endearing smile.

"Oh, cool." Randall goes behind the bar with Shauna.

"What's your job in this place?" I ask. "What are you known for?"

"Being late." Shauna interrupts.

Randall shoots her a look. "I mostly only work on show nights. It's all I can tolerate. I help the artists with their green room requests, and also whatever else Sarah may need me to do."

"That sounds like an easy enough job."

"You would think so…but we all know how Sarah can be." Randall says.

"How can I be?" Sarah comes up to the bar with a tray of snacks. "Don't be quiet now." She slides the tray onto the bar and Shauna immediately gets to eating. "Randall, I didn't know you knew anyone besides Shauna and I…and now the theatre kids."

"You're seriously in Theatre?" I ask.

"Yeah, it's a long story." Randall quips.

"So, Brandon before you eat any of this food, are you going to sing for us?" Sarah asks.

"Nah." I say.

"Why not?" Sarah asks.

"Because." I say.

"Because, why?" Sarah pushes. "You have any amazing voice."

"Can I tell you something?"

"Sure."

"My dad recorded that video of Kelly and I singing. He was the only person that really ever encouraged me to do it. I had that video for two years…that was the last time I sung any kind of a song for any kind of audience. My dad was my champion for everything I wanted to do or be in life. He never questioned me or asked me any questions. He was proud of me genuinely and I was proud to call him Dad. Then he died and I lost the urge to do anything even close to my music. I sang because my dad believed in me."

"I'm sorry for your loss." Randall says. He places his hand on my forearm and he lets it linger. "I can relate. Maybe, we can become your new support group." Randall taps my arm. "I'll push your ass on that stage myself if I have to."

"Thanks dude. I'll count on that support."

"Brandon, I'm sorry if you feel like I pushed you—" Sarah says.

"No! You didn't push me. I'm ready to get out there. I know my dad would be so proud to see me doing this."

"You miss him a lot, don't you?" Sarah asks.

"Yes. Cancer fucking sucks, man."

"Your dad died from Cancer?" Randall asks.

"Yeah. He had pancreatic cancer and fought for a year before it...you know—"

"Shit. I just remembered I left I my phone in the breakroom." Randall abruptly runs off from the table. "I'll be right back."

"Oop. I forgot I moved it so I could charge my phone..." Shauna takes off behind Randall. "Don't eat all of the fries...Sarah!"

"Are they?" I ask Sarah

"Who, Randall and Shauna?"

"Yeah." I say.

"Oh, God no! Randall is gay...well, he doesn't have a label. Shauna is boy crazed out of this world...and I know you didn't ask about my preferences...but I'm sure I like chicks."

"Cool." I go back to staring down the hall Randall ran down.

"Wait! Do you have a crush on Shauna? Y'all would make a very unusual pairing, but weirdly I could see it."

"Nice, you think that...and, no, I don't have a crush on Shauna."

9:27pm

"Dinner was hours ago." I'm in the house less than five seconds before my mom starts with me. "Your father and I waited for you...we had things to discuss." Pearl finally steps out of the way to allow me to step out of my shoes and place my keys on the foyer table. "Brandon, I am getting so tired of your disrespect—"

"What disrespect...I texted you and told you that I was going to be late."

"And I told you check with your father to see if that was okay."

"So, you wanted me to go to his gravesite and hope for a whisper? I mean because dad is dead, and he's been gone for two years now...did you forget that?" Pearl doesn't like that I turned my back to her. She's following closely behind me. If I were to let one loose, she'd catch all of it. "I don't want to argue tonight—"

"Brandon!" Pearl pushes me causing me almost to fall down the stairs. "Get back here!" *Get back here* causes Sam to appear. It's like he loves inserting his two cents in my life. He's trying too hard at this parenting thing—we don't need him in our lives, I just wished my mother saw that.

"No." I rush up the stairs to barricade myself in my doorway. Pearl and Sam will not bring their chaotic energy in room causing me to be up all night. "This isn't an argument. I'm seventeen, I hung out a little later on a school night—"

"You think that makes you a man, boy?" Sam says while pulling my mother behind him. "Your mother wanted you home for dinner."

"Enough." I sternly say gripping my door. "I'm going to bed. I don't know what you two are on, but I am not going to be the punching bag tonight. I'm sorry I didn't call, I'm sorry I'm such a fuck up, but for goodness sake, can Y'all please just lay off of me."

"Brandon, I want to deal with this tonight. I don't want you to think this is alright."

"Mom. Enough. Please. I cannot take it anymore."

"Boy!" Pearl grabs Sam by the arm.

"Not tonight." Sometimes when my mother just caves in, I almost wonder why she even started with me to begin with. I'm always tempted to tell her to blink twice if she needs me to call a crisis helpline, then she does some shallow bullshit, and it makes me want to write her out of my life all over again. "We'll discuss this in the morning."

"I bet you don't even remember, do you?" I pull my phone from my back pocket.

"What?"

"Dad died on this day two years ago, and you didn't even try to be nice."

"Oh, Brandon...I'm—"

"No." I push her hand away. "I'm going to sleep."

"I love you." She forces.

"Yeah, I know." I close my door on both Pearl and Sam. "You don't fucking love me." I whisper. "This is not love."

10:00pm

Before I go off to bed tonight, I hear my phone vibrate on my desk. I was so close to not giving in to my technology addiction, but something in me told me to at least see what it is.

"Hey, Sarah gave me your number."

"Who is this?" I already knew who it was, I just couldn't let him know that I knew.

"Randall. We're in AP Lit together." He responds.

"Oh!" I accidentally press send. "I meant to say, Oh! Cool, it was nice chatting today…and the other day." Randall leaves me in suspense with the speech bubbles.

"Yeah. Same."

"Are you going to Jason's party tomorrow?" I bite my nail in suspense of waiting for Randall to respond.

"I was planning to, are you?" He responds

"Cool."

"Shauna is going out of town, so I don't know if I'll be around for long though."

"She's not your only friend, dude." It takes me a second to press send, I wanted to make sure I didn't sound too creepy. "You can hang with me." I follow up.

"You wouldn't mind?" Now, I take forever to respond. I don't want Randall to be scared off by my promptness. "Don't leave me in suspense." He follows up.

"Yeah, of course!"

"Cool man." I am in the middle of typing out, I can pick you up if you'd— then Randall follows up with. "Have a good night, see you tomorrow."

"Same. Good Night." I spend a few more minutes going over the texts between Randall and I almost studying them. "Thank you for today, dad." I kiss the photo of him, close my eyes and hope for a better day tomorrow, like I do almost every night.

August 23rd 8:45am

My home is my lifeline.

My mother spent the past sixteen years making this home an actual home. The energy of my home makes it hard to be away from it sometimes. I cherish my time spent here. When I found out I was adopted I used to think that my reason for wanting to be here so bad stemmed from me being given up, but I think it's because my mother has always made feel like I was hers from birth. My mother can make even the most unloved feel loved.

"Randall. Your Abuela wants to see you off before school." When my abuela moved in with us after my dad died, that's when life truly became complete. "Get out of this bed." My mom snatches the blanket from over top of my head and notices the full pill bottle sitting on my windowsill. "Oh, Randall. You're not taking the pills?"

"Mama." I sit up to give me more time to lie. "I have been taking the pills. That's just the new bottle. Remember Christina gave me a few…"

"Nice try. Papito…you have to take the pills if you're going to ever feel better."

"That's the thing…I do feel better." I lie. "I was just admiring the fact that I didn't wake up with any body aches this morning." I lie again. "I've been feeling a lot better since starting the treatments again."

"Randall." The way my mother says *Randall* she's knows that I've just said some bullshit. "If you take your medicine, you'll feel way better."

"Alright. Fine. I start. You have my word."

"Sure. It's your body. I'm just your mother. Now, hurry up before your breakfast gets cold."

9:00am

My abuela is blasting Selena early in the morning. *'Como la flor'* usually gets me pumped in the morning but I have a migraine that is so obnoxious. I walk into the kitchen with the hood to my jacket (no jacket attached just a random hood) over my head and sit expressionless at the breakfast table.

"Randall baila conmigo." My abuela sways her hip right into me causing my head to throb even harder. "Come on. Let's dance."

"I'm going to be late." I groan.

"Listo?" My mother asks.

"Grandma, I have a headache." Speaking in English is the quickest way to get under my Abuela's skin. "I'm going to—"

"En Español." My abuela demands.

"In English." I say. My headache is not allowing my brain to switch languages right now.

"Randall, what's…" My abuela kisses my forehead. "Oh, papa."

"What's wrong?" My mother joins. "Are you feeling well? You're a little warm."

"Got a slight headache…plus, I slept wrong. I promise I'm good…that's all. Promise. I swear."

"Oh, okay! Have a great—" My abuela shoots my mom a look. "Que tengas un gran día." My mom kisses me on the cheek then sends me on my way. "Oh, Randall!"

"Yeah."

My mom hands me an orange and granola bar. "Te amo."

"Yo te quiero más."

"Impossible." My mother blows me a kiss as I head out the door.

12:00pm

"Guys, we have to talk about the play." Rebecca pauses. She makes someone hold her drink. "As you all can see Abiyram has fully committed to the play." Abiyram stands up to show off his newly shaved head, he also looks like he hasn't slept in days. Or the fact that we're missing lunch…on pizza day. *WTF*. "We want this kind of commitment from you all."

"What specifically are you asking?" I ask what everyone in the room might have been thinking. "Can you not speak in riddles?"

"Ok." She pauses. "Well, I want you to cut your hair."

"Like, all the way off?" I ask.

"Yes." Rebecca has this sinister smile on her face. "I think you would look so cute with a shaved head. Don't you think?"

"This isn't Broadway." I stand to be at the same eye level with Rebecca." We're also doing 'Fiddler on The Roof' …how did you conclude that we should cut our hair?"

"I get your concern." Rebecca says.

"I'm not cutting my hair." I say.

"Randall."

"Rebecca…I'm serious, I am not cutting my hair."

"Why not?" She stomps.

"This isn't some elaborate stage production; I shouldn't have to cut my hair for a school play. There's no way Pendergrass signed off on this. I am not getting rid of my hair for you and that's final." Truth is. I lost my hair. When my hair fell out last year during the treatments, my mother and the nurses at the hospital gifted me with a wig. It resembled my former puffy bush. It made me feel like my old self. I've have grown attached to this head of hair. It sucks that underneath it, the progress my hair has made, will fall out all over again.

"I understand. Maybe this is something you can think about."

"I thought about it…and I cannot cut my hair." I grab my things and head out of the theater room. "I'll see you all later."

"Randall. Dude. Wait up." Abiyram catches up to me. "What's going on?"

"I just cannot and will not cut my hair. I don't want to make a big deal because it's just hair, but I am not invested enough in this to cut my hair because some chick told me to."

"I get it." He pauses. "I only did it because…" He takes a deep breath. "People here think I'm too feminine with my hair growing out, and I got upset and chopped all my hair off." For a second, I thought this dude was about to tell me he had cancer. It wouldn't have made me tell him my secret though. "I kind of regret it now."

"Shit. Dude, I'm sorry."

"No worries." Abiyram looks me up and down. "She'll get over it, just give her a day or two, then come back to practice. Take it easy in the meantime"

"Amazing. Later Abiyram."

"Hey Randall." Abiyram calls out.

"See you at the party tonight?"

"Yeah. Of course."

"Great." Shauna appears out of nowhere and bumps into Abiyram. "We can chat more tonight at the party if you want."

"Of course, I look forward to it."

August 23rd 7:00pm

Who the do I think I am?

My brown hair is now a dirty blonde—I let Jason and Kelly talk me into dying my hair when we got bored setting up for the party. I took an entire hour to tell myself that it complements my tan skin, even though I know it washes me out. This is why I personally do not like seeing mixed race kids with blonde hair. I feel like our skin tone lies so close to the middle that any drastic thing we do to our appearance is immediately a new talking point for people.

I throw water on my face one last time thinking I may come up from the mirror looking different. I give myself a smirk in the mirror then head out of the restroom to go find my friends.

"Brandon. I think I like your hair like this. I can finally tell that you're mixed..." Jason says. "Shoot! Not like that...wait, did I offend you?"

"No. It's no big deal." My race is a touchy subject. When people have questions about my race, I always keep it *my mother is black, and my dad was white*... "I'm cool. You're cool."

"Why'd you do that thing, though?" Jason asks.

"What thing?" My voice goes into a high pitch tone. "I have no idea what you're talking about."

"Yeah, you do. Whenever you're uncomfortable your upper lip twitches...kind of like it is now. It's cool to be uncomfortable talking race with me. We're in the same boat dude."

"Are we?"

"Yeah. Did you forget?"

"I think I did."

Jason takes a beat. "Well, my mother is black, and my stepfather is white...he adopted me when I was three and he's been the only dad I have ever cared to know." Jason's stepfather is also a billionaire that basically built Crestview.

"It's different though. If you were to get pulled over, it may go a different way before they find out who your parents are. If I get pulled over, the likelihood of things going left currently stand at zero percent. I pass for white every day and I guess I'm second guessing my hair color choice and who I am as a person—I was so not trying to look like that dude."

"What dude?"

"You know, like every other dude that walk the halls of Crestview."

"*Ooooh*, I get it. You wish there was a way you could make yourself look mixed race? Or be someone else."

"Yeah. Exactly!"

"Wait, you seriously wanna be someone else?" Jason places his hands on his hips.

"Yeah. That's what I'm saying…or that's how I feel currently."

"Follow me." Jason grabs me by the arm. He leads me back to the restroom. "Hey, sit. Look in that mirror."

"What are you doing?" I ask in confusion. Jason covers my head with a towel that smells like eucalyptus. "I don't think I like this."

"Just go with it. KELLY! Could you come here a minute."

"Kelly? Oh, No." Jason pushes me back onto the toilet seat. "Brandon, just go with it. It'll be worth it. You need this."

"What's up?" Kelly's groggily voice says.

"Just be here." Jason demands. "Ok, Brandon are you ready?"

"No."

"Oh well." Jason snatches the towel from off my head. "What do you see?"

I'm forced to stare at myself.

"Come on dude, what do you see?" Kelly pushes.

"Me."

Jason pinches my cheek. "Wonderful."

"I don't get it."

"The only person you should see when you look in the mirror is you. You don't need anyone else's opinion of how you should define yourself. You are Brandon Marciano. You're not Brandon Mixed-Race Marciano, nor are you just black or just white...bro... that's what makes you, you. Everyone else is taken." Jason uses all his might to push me closer to the brightly lit vanity. "There's no need to want to be anybody else or freaking look like anyone else. Just let life do its thing. Identity is an ever-evolving thing, you're not going to come into your own overnight. It starts with talks like these to yourself."

"How'd I get so lucky in the friend department?" I tap my tears away.

"Dude, you know I'm here for you, right?" Kelly puts his hands on my shoulders.

"Yeah, yeah, of course...I know you are."

RANDALL

August 23rd 7:50pm

I can't remember the las time I went to a party or left out of my house on purpose this late at night. The new me wants to take advantage of every single opportunity someone throws my way. So, if all of the cool kids are going to a party...I will be at that same party holding up walls with other kids.

My mother spent a good part of the afternoon interrogating me. She was mostly questioning Jason and the sanity of his parents. She wanted to know why they let him spend thousands of dollars on parties that could never end at a reasonable time. When Jason turned sixteen his parents spent thousands on him, and literally invited everyone they knew to the party. It started hella late and wasn't over until three in the morning—I saw this all on social media over the summer.

The downside to traveling to Jason's house is catching the ferry all the way there. Crestview is like another country when you live on a damn island.

I'm greeted by Bill our trusted ferry driver dude. He kind of resembles the dad from Cheaper by the Dozen. He's always in a hurry, so it's a shock to see him waiting for me, and even helping people with wheelchairs board the ferry.

"Price!" Bill screeches.

Bill has the voice of a tween girl.

"Hey, Sir." I quietly say back.

"How have you been? Long time no see…well since I last saw you four hours ago." He cracks himself up. "You have some nice friends." He says before helping me aboard.

"How so?"

"Well, there was this fair skinned kid with the brown hair or blonde hair. He waited for two ferries back at the view." *Brandon?* I don't say anything. I'm letting this discovery sink in. "I told him to go enjoy the party, and I'll wait on my way back to the lake." Bill isn't a nice human on a regular basis.

"Thanks." I take my seat behind Bill.

"Don't thank me. If it weren't for the face that kid was making—" From here I zone out. I mean, sure Brandon and I have been around each other on more than one occasion now. And, sure we've technically had a handful of meaningful conversations the past few days, but I didn't think we were at the waiting for each other part of the friendship.

All of my fears of going to the party melted away, the minute the ferry left the dock.

8:45pm

Arriving at Jason's party, I forgot how lovesick teenagers are in Crestview. It's non-stop tongue action the minute I walk through the door.

God, I want someone. I think.

At this rate, I'll take love in any form.

All I want is to be kissed by someone. Similar to Simon, in Love Simon. I want someone to kiss me on a Ferris wheel. I want them to get chills the minute our lips lock. I know its desperate for me to want love to come in that form, but I have to at least hope for it. I just have to. It'd be the perfect happy ending to this shitty ass year.

Being two years away from eighteen and never being in true love, is not the plan I had for myself when high school first started. All that dude had to do was love me back.

"Hey." Brandon approaches me.

"Hi!" I grab hold of my shirt collar. I notice a very gaudy chandelier hanging over my head. I also notice that Jason's house has to be at least four stories high. The staircase seems to continue on for forever. Its way bigger since the last time I was here.

"Glad you came." He says.

"Yeah." I go in to give him a hug. I don't know what it was for, but I felt obligated to hug him. The hug also felt…natural. Brandon and I spend a few minutes staring at each other. It's awkward. "Thanks for waiting for me at the dock. Bill told me. That was really nice of you. Also, nice hair. It's cool. It genuinely looks good on you."

"Awe, thanks dude! I had a small conniption earlier about it…I'm good now…and it's no problem. I wasn't sure if you knew how to get here walking."

"My mom works here." I say.

"Oh…I'm sure you told me, I just forgot."

"She's the maid…she's like the big maid in charge of all the other maids." I joke.

"So, you've been here plenty of times?"

"Yeah." For some reason, I never noticed how muscular Brandon's body is. He has on a button-down shirt that shows off his arms. I'm sure he's wearing the slim-fit version of my shirt. Not that he'd ever shop at Old Navy on purpose. He seems like a Banana Republic kind of guy. "Jason probably doesn't remember this…but, he and I were friends back in primary school. He got popular in middle school."

Brandon and I briefly run out of conversation.

"Wanna go get something to drink?" Brandon offers.

"Yeah. I'm craving coke." Brandon laughs. "Shit." I say softly. "I didn't mean coke like the nose kind, I meant coke, as in the cola kind…"

"You're good dude. I knew what you meant." Before we make it to the kitchen, Brandon pulls me into the theater. Jason has an almost full-size theater in his home. It even has that old popcorn smell.

"This isn't the kitchen." I say.

"I have to say hello to some people…that's cool? We don't have to go in if you don't want to."

"Yeah. It's fine. Don't change for me." Brandon gives me a smile before he continues leading the way.

"Hey guys, look who it is." Brandon holds my hand while he spins me around like I'm a trophy. I see a few other kids from school I've had casual conversations with.

"What are you doing?" I whisper.

"Are you uncomfortable? I can stop." Brandon's green eyes are piercing through me, I can slightly feel my heart skip a beat.

"No. I'm good. Let's sit." Brandon asks another kid to move seats so that we could sit next to each other. However, the way these seats are made, it's impossible to not be skin to skin. I guess I don't mind. I think. I can almost hear Brandon's thoughts that's how close we are. I can feel slight butterflies in the pit of my stomach. The butterflies make me smile sporadically and each time Brandon looks in my direction I have to turn my head. I can't have him knowing these smiles might be because of him.

Jason and Kelly wheel a snack cart in the room. "Randall, you came!" Jason yells. "Good to see you bro. Can I get you anything?"

"I'm good with a coke."

Kelly hands Brandon a bowl of snacks followed by my coke. Brandon motions for a bottle of water and it makes me lowkey self-conscious to be drinking my coke in front of him.

"No soda?" I ask.

"Nah, I break out like crazy from that stuff…that doesn't mean I won't sneak a sip of yours, though." He grins.

"Movie is starting." I whisper.

Brandon gets comfortable beside me. I can feel the warmth of his body on mine. This is the kind of warmth I need when I'm getting my treatments.

After a few awkward scans of the room, I get comfortable too.

While Avengers is playing in the background, I envision what Brandon's thinking about. My mind is wandering restlessly. Like, what if he's thinking what I'm thinking about? Hulk needing to GTFO before he ends up dead. Or what if he's thinking that the nachos that Jason provided for the party could've used some real cheese, and not the peanut scented vegan cheese he provided.

I catch Brandon smiling in my direction.

"You good?" I whisper.

"Yeah." He smiles. "I'm having a good time." He whispers. It sends chills all up and down my spine. Brandon then puts his arm around me, and those nervous butterflies come rushing back. I settle in. I'm enjoying it. It feels nice. I am enjoying this. Then, he pulls me in a little bit closer and I do not know how to react, I've never been in this situation—it's all too much for me.

"I have to get out of here." I'm forgetting to whisper. I break out of his hold.

I step over everyone's nice name brand shoes on my way out of the room. I slightly fall on a guy that smelled like every essential oil imaginable. I push Brandon's hand away as he tried to catch my fall. I'm moving so fast I stumble all the way to the exit of the theater.

"Randall, wait up." I hear Brandon call. I keep going. The music I was hearing, I can no longer hear. I continue moving aimlessly through Jason's house. I end up in the maid's kitchen there are no partygoers in this room. There's at least twenty people crammed in this room swiftly making finger snacks. I keep walking down a glassed covered hallway. I am looking for air.

My mind became too much for me. My thoughts went too far. I saw way too much with Brandon. Then I heard CANCER, so I immediately second guessed those thoughts because nothing can happen with Brandon because I won't be here years from now. Then, I guess I felt my chest tightening and I had to get out of there.

"It's hot in here." The glass covered hallway has a door all the way at one end of the hallway. It feels like it's taking hours to get there, my nervous virgin little feet are so heavy. "Finally!" I pull the door back and the kids that were sitting on the brick wall smoking weed scatter.

A tug on my arm keeps me in place. "Hey, you, okay?" Brandon is out of breath.

"Sorry." I sit in the middle of this courtyard. "I was getting hot in there."

"Understandable. Lots of people are claustrophobic." Brandon is staring at me as if he owed me something in this moment. "Was it me, though? I was sitting a little too—"

"No! No, you were fine. You are fine. So, very fine." Shit. "Not fine as in gorgeous."

"You don't find me attractive?"

"Yeah...you are..." I notice Brandon leaning into my line of sight almost like he wants me to slip up again. "You're an ass." I shove him, then we both fall backwards in laughter. We're laughing so hard. "Damn." The water sprinklers shoots me right in the face it scares me out of this moment.

"No, stay." Brandon pulls me back down. "Let's just enjoy this moment." Brandon lays back down on the now soggy grass. "It's not that bad, just look at me." Brandon grabs hold of my arm again to keep me in place.

"Fine." Looking at Brandon in pure bliss as the water drenches our bodies is amazing. The birds have gotten in on the action by chirping so loud causing the fireflies to dance around us. "We're going to be sick."

"So..." Brandon jolts his body up and heads right into the sprinklers. I have this habit where I listen to whatever people tell me to do. I run into the sprinklers with Brandon. I freeze this moment in my brain. His smile and his stares make my body heat up. I am most definitely not used to this.

"Come here." Brandon grabs both of my hands and intertwines them in his. "Imagine it's a slow song and just go with the moment." I lay my head on Brandon's chest and we just move about in a circle. My head on his chest I can hear how steady his heart is beating. Then, the butterflies turned into something else, and I started to feel things in the southern region of my body. "This is nice." He whispers. I catch a glimpse at the time on his watch and notice hours have passed.

"Wait, what time is it?" I ask.

"12ish."

"I have to get out here."

"Why?"

"I'm going to miss the last ferry."

"Stay the night here. They have an extra bed in their guestroom."

"Nah, I promised my mom I'd be home. I don't want her worrying about me." And, just like that we sprint towards the dock. I should've informed Brandon that running makes me sometimes throw up. That's the one exercise I don't enjoy doing. Jason's house isn't even two blocks from the dock, and I am winded. Jason has the privilege of having a private dock in the back of his backyard; a perk his family gets for basically building this town.

"Randall! Hurry if you're going to make your ferry." I am all gassed out. "You can just stay here and let me call your mom."

"Bill is going to wait." I say. Brandon ushers me the rest of the way to the ferry.

"See you later, I guess?" Brandon says.

"Yeah, you will." Brandon pulls me in closer to him. I could've sworn we were about to kiss or something right in front of Bill. Instead, Brandon hugs me.

"Thank you for tonight." I did not want to let go of Brandon. If I've learned anything from the movies—I have to let this grow. "Call you in the morning?"

"Sure." I say.

Bill and I both watch Brandon walk away.

"If you don't cuff him then I will." Bill says before sounding the last call horn.

Brandon runs back towards the dock.

"Randall Price! You fucking rock!" Brandon shouts. I'm too gun shy to yell back.

"Seriously, lock that kid down." Bill says before taking his seat behind his enclosed cell. I spend the rest of the ferry ride watching Brandon get smaller and smaller as the ferry picks up speed.

August 24ᵗʰ 2:32am

"If he left two hours ago, I don't see the issue in calling to see if he got home." Jason says. "I say go for it." Jason pushes my phone to my ear. "Do it."

"What if he went home and just crashed?" Kelly says.

"So." Jason scolds. "We're trying to go on double dates and shit…no shade, but I'm sure Brandon is done third wheeling." Jason gives me a wink then pushes the phone back to my ear. "Call that damn boy…"

"Just wait till the morning." Kelly interrupts.

"Why?" I ask.

"Because…" Jason covers Kelly's mouth.

"Did you wait to call me?" Jason asks.

"You were different…that Randall kid seems like he's always nervous or like he's holding his breath. Don't get me wrong, I think you two would be dope together…that kid seems like…" I hit dial to call Randall.

"Yay!" Jason grabs Kelly by the arm. "We don't have to be noisy…he's going to tells us everything anyway. We'll be downstairs."

"Hello." Randall answers.

"Oh, hey." I breathe a sigh of relief. "I was going to leave you a voicemail…just wanted to know if you got home okay."

"Yeah. I literally just got in. My mom and I stayed outside talking…she didn't want my wet body sitting on anything." Randall snorts. "Oh, that's so embarrassing."

"No, no. It's cool. I fart when I'm nervous." I hear Randall laugh. "Just kidding…it's actually a mixture of burping and farting…you should hang up now."

"I'll just keep air freshener with me at all times." Randall takes a beat. "Hey, can I Tell you something?"

"Yeah. Go for it."

"I wasn't running away from you tonight at the party…well, I kind of was…but it was mostly my own brain…I just had a lot of thoughts racing at once."

"I definitely get it." Randall takes a beat. For a moment we take turns breathing into the phone. "I haven't had that much fun in a while. Thanks, dude."

"No. Thank you. I had lots of fun too."

"Great…so, this may be a bit forward…" I lay on my stomach keeping the phone tight to my ear. "…and don't think I'm weird."

"I'm all ears…just to give you a visual, I have my right hand cupped around my ear." Randall takes a second to laugh at himself. "Sorry, you were about to say something."

"I can pick you up for school next week, if you…"

"Cool, I'll text you my address… Just don't laugh at the size of my house. It's very humble…it's also very big because I'm an only child, so I don't have to share anything with anyone."

"No worries…and I thought Shauna was your sister."

"She is. We have the same biological parents too. Just our mother decided to give me up instead of Shauna…short version, she got pregnant with Shauna and then a few months later got pregnant with me and just couldn't keep me…medical school and stuff." Randall pauses and I can hear him inhale. "My mom asked to raise me, and the rest is well…history."

"I'm sorry." I say.

"Don't be. I'm cool with it now. I actually like how I came up…how many kids get to say that they got to grow up in the kind of home I did. My mom loves me and so did my dad. I don't think if given the opportunity I would change it."

I remove the phone from my ear for a moment and slowly place it back to my ear. "Here's a visual for you…I'm smiling." I was so close to telling Randall about my upbringing and how I'm envious of his past and present. "I like that about you."

"What?"

"You look at the positive with everything."

"I don't have any choice but to… deja pasar la vida."

"What does that mean?"

"It translates to *let life pass*, but I tell myself to let life happen. My dad would always tell me that when I was younger. Along with a bunch of other philosophical stuff."

"He seems like a cool dude."

"He was." Randall says.

"Yeah. My dad was an amazing man too…I miss him every single day." I say.

"I'm sure he's proud of the person you are …I know he's smiling down on you every day. You have a guardian angel, Brandon."

"I hope so."

"Brandon, you have to believe it. I believe that my dad is the one that blows my candles out at night. I sit a candle in my windowsill, and I always forget to blow it out…to me that's my dad." I hear Randall take a deep breath. "…my dad died in a car accident last year…worst day of my life."

"Oh damn. I'm sorry."

"I'm good now…we're good now. It's like the universe kept his soul on this earth to give me comfort every single night."

"You're so positive Randall Price."

"Gee. Thanks so much…new visual…I'm laying on my stomach because I'm hella tired, but I don't want to hang up the phone yet."

"Then don't." I say.

"So, I won't." Randall responds.

"So…I'm turning to lie on my back because I have acid reflux." I take a moment to stop myself from smiling so hard my cheeks were starting to hurt. "Let's just stay up the rest of the night…wanna watch a movie or show together?"

"Yeah…what's that new one with Michael B. Jordan?" Randall asks.

"Please don't tell me I have to compete with that Greek god."

"You're good. He won't answer my DMs."

"I think I found it…sending you a link."

"Cool" he says.

I hear an older woman mumble *Randall. It's late, time for bed.*

"Brandon, I'll call you tomorrow. My mother doesn't want us to have any fun tonight."

"Wait!"

"Maria doesn't play…she'll take my phone."

"One more thing." I say.

"Go for it." Randall whispers.

"Wanna sneak and do this tomorrow night?"

"Yes…I'll text you when it's safe to call."

"Perfect! …new visual…my heart is happy…sleep good tonight."

"You too! buenas noches" Randall ends the call. I roll over and try to replay the entire night over in my brain. I can't remember the last time I smiled this hard.

9:00am

I slept at most three hours. I was in too good of a mood to go to sleep, so I spent the night staring up at the ceiling. I kept thinking about Randall and all of the new experiences I can't wait to show him and all of the new experiences I would love for him to show me. I even downloaded an app that teaches you Spanish.

My mom called me at five in the morning and thought she was going to ruin my night. I heard her out for the entirety of her yelling spree then I politely explained to her that she has to let me grow up and she rudely told me that I didn't have to live in her house and if I'm going to continue disrespecting her then I can get out. Not even that was able to penetrate my happiness.

"Damn. You're still smiling." Kelly lays an iPad in front of me. "Here's some of the pics from last night. I can't believe none of the neighbors called the cops on us."

"Yeah." I start scrolling through the album with Kelly.

"So, what did you and Randall talk about?" Kelly asks.

"Stuff." I say as Jason enters the kitchen. "We really bonded last night. At least I think so."

"Why all the doubt?" Jason asks. "When I went back to snoop, I heard you laughing. People don't laugh when they're bored."

"I guess you're right." I continue scrolling. "Randall is really a chill guy and I like that."

"And you're two so different." Jason says. "I think that's amazing. It'll keep you rooted... or grounded...whatever the word is."

"Yeah." I see a photo of me chatting with a guy I had a crush on freshman year. I keep scrolling.

"Food is ready." Jason says.

"Then what else happened?" Kelly asks while sliding a plate my way. "I'm invested."

"Nothing too crazy. He told me some personal things and I told him some too, then we were gonna watch a movie, but his mother stormed in his room."

"Speaking of mothers…did you call your mom back?" Kelly asks. "I don't want her calling me anymore. That woman is mean."

"Yeah. Long story short, I may need to crash with you for a bit. She's just going through some stuff…gonna let her figure out her issues. She'll be good in a day or so."

"I'm cool with it. My folks are always in the city, so it's no big deal." Kelly and Jason start savoring their waffles and egg whites. I am not that kind of cute eater. I get right to it. I take large bites of everything on my plate, drink some orange juice, then get back to taking my large bites.

"Hey, you got any more photos of me anywhere?"

"Yeah. I'm pretty sure. Some kid sent me some of you outside…they're somewhere in that folder." Kelly goes back to playing with his food.

It takes me a few minutes, but I'm finally seeing the photos I truly care to see.

There's a photo of Jason, Kelly, and I all laughing in front the bonfire that started the night. I email myself a copy of that photo.

Then I scroll pass a photo of Randall.

This photo makes me grin. It's a photo of him admiring the entryway. I can tell he thinks he's out of place. I send myself a copy of this photo as well.

Then there's a photo of Randall and I watching the Avenger movie together. We look good here. I look like I'm protecting him. My arm thrown around his shoulder. The way he accepts the comfort—I remember it giving me goosebumps.

All of a sudden, I feel a drop of water land on my forehead.

"Hey, you were daydreaming...again." Kelly flicks water at me again. "Can you promise us that you will take things slow. It's not cute when you get your heartbroken."

"I got you." I say.

"I'm not worried. I can tell you and Randall will become something. I just got this sneaky feeling. No one smiles like that from a photograph. Just be careful with your heart. Love works best in steps it's not actually zero to one hundred...there's so many steps in between." Jason says.

"I promise."

BRANDON

September 1ˢᵗ 5:00pm

I saw on the news that Washington was closing the beaches down
on Memorial Day. I'm not a big beach kind of dude. There's
something about sand and water that just doesn't sit well with me.
Then Kelly suggested that that we do something at the fire pit.
Which I am always down with. Anytime I can force myself out of
the house and hang out with friends sitting by the fire chatting—
it's a win in my book.

Crestview doesn't have any cool beaches. It's mostly lakes
and shit. Plus, all of the lakes have a bunch of rules that don't really
make sense. If you want to have some honest fun, we willingly
make that drive to Westlake. Since, Westlake is an island it has the
best views and amazing shorelines in all of Washington State.
People literally get engaged there like twice an hour during the
peak summer months. No joke.

"Brandon, did you invite Randall?" Kelly asks.

"Nah, I thought it could just be our usual hangout group."

"That now includes Randall. Don't tell me you're bored already?" Kelly hands me my phone. "Call him. Text him. Send him a smoke signal. Something, dude...or did something happen. What you do?"

"No. It's not like that. I'm taking things slow. Just don't want to seem like I'm smothering him."

Kelly tosses me some towels. "Dude, the past week, you two have only talked about school and you sat in his rehearsals for the play...one of those rehearsals you had to be there because I asked you to show up to help with the music arrangement. People building relationships do hang out outside of school, you know. Jump out there, my guy."

"I think you're right." I say.

"Then invite him." Kelly sits on his bed and stares. "I'm not going anywhere until I hear you call or text him...as a matter of fact." Kelly snatches my phone. He unlocks my phone then hits dial on Randall's name. "He answers quick...Randall! Brandon has something he'd like to ask you." Kelly throws me my phone then heads out the door. "Later. Meet you there."

"Hey! What's up?" I ask.

"Oh, Shauna and I were packing a bag to go down to the beach and stay until sunset. Wanna come with us? She just started seeing this dude and I don't want to be a third wheel. That's not cute."

"What if I told you that I was just about to invite you to the beach with me?"

"I would then have to ask you if you installed cameras in my house...the one you have not been inside of yet...Mr. Parks outside and wait."

"Hahaha. I'll come inside soon... but do you want to go to the beach with me?"

"Duh. I can meet you there if you want."

"Randall, do I look like the guy that's going to let his main guy walk to the beach...even though it's hella close to your house."

"Well, when you put it that way...sure. I'll tell Shauna I'm waiting for you." Randall says. I throw on my shoes, grab a jacket, and head out of Kelly's place. "I'll be waiting, Brandon."

"Dope. I'm literally on my way. Heading out the door now."

"Praying for no traffic." Randall says.

"Dope! New visual...I just hopped in my car, then I'm gonna pick you up a surprise and I'll be on my way. I can get there in thirty."

5:35pm

While I'm waiting for Randall to come outside, I see an older lady with red hair staring at me from the other side of the street. I wave at her and she takes this as her opportunity to cross the street. For an older lady she walks very fast.

"Hey!" Randall slides into my car. "I don't want to mess up my hair." I notice that he has something sticking from the top of his head and I go to reach for it. "I got it!" He pushes my hand away. "Sorry, it's just an instinct...did I get?"

"Yeah. And note to self, no touching your hair..."

"Young man, does Maria know you're riding around in this sports car?" The lady with red hair asks.

"Yes, Mrs. Potts. She knows where I am." Randall smiles when I know he's cursing up a storm in his mind.

"Who are you, by the way?" She asks.

"I'm Brandon. I'm his...friend." I can feel Randall's eyes staring a hole right through me. "We're close friends."

"Well...Brandon...you better be nice to him...I mean it." The older lady with red hair turns to walk away.

"I like her." I lie.

"She's harmless. She watches out for everyone on our street. She's everything. You think you're a music buff. Her house is a musician's paradise." Randall tugs one last time on his hair.

"I'd love to see it one day."

"Of course. I'll ask her if we can play around one day. I'd love to see you two sing. Now, that would be a show."

5:48pm

All eyes are on Randall and me when we show up to the beach. This time Randall doesn't pull back or retreat internally. He goes to find us a spot. Thanks to Kelly, he's already saved us a spot in the circle.

"There you all go! I thought y'all got lost on the way down the street." Shauna says. She is wearing a bikini top and shorts. Her hair is straightened so it covers a good portion of her chest area. "I would've hurt you if my brother didn't make it here in one piece."

"You got it." I say.

"Shauna." Randall says.

"Sorry, I'm a tad bit overprotective." Shauna sits back down next to her date.

Randall hands me a bottle of water. "I'm sorry she's so...you know."

"No. She's good. Always looking out for you." I say.

"Yeah. She's wears that big sister tag close to her chest." Randall smiles.

"That's dope. I wish I was someone's big brother, so we could be close like you two."

Randall nudges me. "Hey, you're older than me."

"Yeah, but I don't want to be just your friend and I definitely don't want to be your sibling." My heart starts racing. "I'm wanting to be more to you." Randall looks up at me.

"Okay everyone the sun is setting. Let's light this fire!" Kelly announces.

"Hey, come over here really quick." I lead Randall away from the group. "I've been wondering for the past week or so what this will become, and I just kept getting nervous because I've never actually been in a relationship with someone before. I thought...or think we're on the same page with everything—"

"You talk a lot…" Randall interrupts. "We're taking it slow, but I will reserve myself for you."

"You little devil. You took my moment." I grab Randall by his hand. "I swear I'll only move as fast as we both want. I'm not going to mess this up."

"And I'm going to do my part as well." Randall takes my other hand. "This is a two-way street…wow, my first actual…something outside of friendship." Randall pulls me in for a hug. "That's strange. I don't have any butterflies."

"Neither do I."

"Oh, look at us. Maturing." Randall lets go of me.

"Let's go back to the group." I take the lead, but Randall pulls me to a halt. "What's up?"

"I have something to tell you…you have to know this."

"I'm listening."

Randall takes a pause.

"What's up? Did I do something?"

"No! It's just…I have…I have…to really start looking at the weather. It's getting chilly out here." He smiles.

"Oh, I have a jacket in my car, I can go get it." I offer.

"Thanks. It's not that serious though, I'll be alright."

We retake our seats within the group. "Let's scoot close." I wrap my arm around Randall and we both get ready for s'mores. "Hey, can you guys pass the marshmallows?" I take a few out and place two on my stick and Randall does the same. We stare at one another before we place our sticks in the fire. "You ready?"

September 2nd 12:30pm

September 2nd,1938, is the day Abuela Carmela was born. Her real name is Griselda. She doesn't acknowledge that name because of obvious reasons. It got too annoying for her that people kept asking if she knew who Griselda Blanco was.

We couldn't celebrate her birthday how we wanted last year because we were all still grieving the loss of my dad plus, cancer treatments were a bitch this time last year, so she just settled for a nice meal, and we all slept in my mom's bed.

"Are you celebrating tonight?" Shauna asks as she angrily stuff random items into packing boxes. Sarah has us doing the job of a moving company.

"Yeah!" I say taping a box closed. "You're still coming, right?" I scribble *random* on one side of the box and push it to the side.

"Duh. I'd love to meet your grandma." Shauna says.

"When you come don't ask too many questions that I'll have to translate for her." I tape another one of Shauna's poorly packed boxes closed.

"Why not?"

"My abuela is more comfortable speaking in Spanish. But I don't feel like translating today. Keep your questions simple."

"Will do. I'll keep it simple and to the point." Shauna takes a moment to correct her hair. It's just a bushy as the wig I wear on a daily basis. "Quick question, you know you're black right?"

"Shauna!" I exclaim.

"What?" She jumps.

"I had no idea that I was black...wow, I'm African American" I start examining my caramel skin. "I truly am a negro."

Shauna laughs. "I just thought I should remind you. Anyways, I'm excited to meet your Abuela." Shauna kicks her last box towards me, and I tape it close. "Randall, I think we're all done little bro." Shauna examines our task lists. "Wait. How do Mexicans celebrate birthdays?"

With a straight face I say "Like most people...birthday cake. Music. Gifts. The usual dry birthday stuff."

"Who all did you invite?" She asks.

"You. Brandon..."

Shauna shoves me. "I'm so proud of you. You finally have boy toy. A fine one at that."

"He was happy to come too." I say.

"I'm sure he was." She winks. I throw the pen I had in my pocket at her. "What? I'm sure he cannot wait to...you know."

"It hasn't even been a week. Plus, I'm not doing that for a long time. I want to get through these next rounds of treatment before I think about anything in that nature."

"Understood. By the way, how is treatment going for you?"

"I honestly don't know. It's fine, I guess. I'm happy I'm not always tired anymore and that I don't have to fake my energy as much. I'll just be happy when cancer is behind me."

"Does Brandon know?"

"Hell no! And don't bring it up today at the party. No sad talk. I want to tell Brandon on my own at the right time. Once I know more about donor prospects and stuff."

"You got it. My lips will be sealed...that is your secret and your information...not my place." I give Shauna a hug. "Awe, love you too..."

"You guys should be cleaning, not gossiping." Sarah says. "You don't get paid for this. Back to work." She taps her watch.

"Actually, we do get paid for this." Shauna showcases her piles of completed work. "As you look around this place, we have cleaned it from top to bottom and packed just about every single thing that could fit into a box." Shauna walks out of the back are and we follow. "We were waiting for more tasks, by the way."

Sarah holds her hand to her chest as her cheeks turn a rosy color. "I am seriously shocked. I appreciate all that you've done."

Shauna turns to sarcastically say. "Oh. My. Goodness. Sarah Hayes gave us some gratitude."

"Yeah, I must be sick or something." Sarah stares at Shauna. "I guess you guys can leave early. Doesn't make sense to keep you another two hours…"

"Peace!" Shauna does not give Sarah the opportunity to change her mind, she heads for the nearest exit. "Randall let's go! Let's go eat!"

"Have a good one." I wave goodbye to Sarah. "See you at school tomorrow."

2:40pm

When we arrive to my house, my Abuela and mother are dancing on the porch, their music blasting. My mother is dancing off beat and that still doesn't stop her from doing the bachata by herself. We invited the majority of our neighbors that we've known for years, and they are getting in on the action as well. They're all slow dancing to *"Paloma Negra"* by Jenni Rivera.

Anyone who knows that song, knows it's not quite a lovey dovey slow song. It's also not the song to slow dance to. *Ya me canso de llorar* translates to *I'm tired of crying*. *"Paloma Negra"* I think it is a song about fighting for your lover—making them see that you're it.

"Ya no se si maldecirte!" I sing. I join my mother and Abuela on the porch to finish our performance. *"Tengo miedo de buscarte y de encontrarte!"* I belt before being pulled into a hug from my abuela.

"Oh, mijo!" She tightens.

"Hi Grandma." My grandmother looks stunned. I slipped up. "I mean Abuela."

"María, qué está pasando? Who the hell is this grandma lady?" My abuela plucks my forehead.

"Lo siento mucho." My Abuela truly hates that we're so Americanized. "My mind it's…never mind…I don't think you ever got to meet Shauna."

"Yes. Randall talks about you and that Brandon every single day." My Abuela forces Shauna into a bear hug. "You smell good mija. What is that?"

"Umm…I actually forgot to put on deodorant so it may just be laundry detergent and sweat." My abuela lets go.

"Ella me gusta mucho. I like you very much!" She kisses Shauna on the cheek. "Now, where is this Brandon you keep talking about?" She pronounces it as *Brrrandon*.

"He's on his way. Remember he lives on the mainland."

"Well, tell me Shauna…is this Brandon gorgeous?"

"Abuela! That boy looks so good…muy delicioso." Shauna fans herself. "That is how good he looks."

"Let's go inside." My mother tells us. "Everyone! Join us around back…"

"Hey! Sorry I'm late." Brandon shows up a bit flustered. I am so happy that his dirty blonde hair has finally settled in, it looks really good on him, I like that it's more shades of brown than blonde now. "There was a lot of traffic."

"No worries! Get in here." My abuela grabs him by the wrist. "So, you're the boy my boy talks about every single night."

"Yeah." Brandon is grabbing at his collar. "That's me." I hand Brandon something to drink when we reach the kitchen.

"What are you? If you don't mind me asking." My abuela asks.

"I'm mixed. Black and White."

"You're half black?" Shauna and my Abuela asks.

"Yeah." He grins.

"I just thought you tanned well." Shauna jokes.

"I actually do." He winks.

"Let's eat everyone!" My mother announces.

We head to the backyard, where my mother has a full spread of all my abuelas favorites. The long table is lined with foods I haven't had since…last week possibly. We have empanadas, plantains, all the fixings for the best tostada, there's beans…we love beans…especially with rice. It's even more special when I look and there are *Leche Fritas* there.

"Shut up! Lecha Fritas are the shit." I say in excitement.

"No. Not until you eat something else first." My mother slaps my hand.

Leche Fritas would have to be one of my favorite desserts my abuela has ever gotten from my great-grandmother. It's made from flour, milk, and sugar. You cook it until it forms into a dough, you then portion it off, fry it, then top it with a glaze, and cinnamon. My abuela adds a little nutmeg during the holiday season. They're so delicious—especially, while hot.

"María, let him have just one." My abuela slips me one right in my mother's face, I don't even hesitate to take it. My mother glares at her then jolts her eyes right to me. "Especially, with what he's going through." My mother's heart sinks.

"Mama!" My mother whines.

"El no sabe." I say while darting my eyes in Brandon's direction. "Aún no le he dicho."

"What's going on?" Brandon whispers.

"My abuela wants to start this off with dessert first. My mother doesn't." I lie.

"Oh. I really need for that Rosetta Stone disk set to come in the mail." Brandon jokes. "It's probably too late for me to learn Spanish anyway."

"No, it's not." Shauna interjects. "I feel like I'm part of the family. Randall speaks Spanish so much; I'm starting to comprehend most of what he's saying." Shauna shoots me a look. "It's such an amazing language."

"Maria didn't even want Randall speaking Spanish when he was younger…then she started letting me watch him more and more." My abuela pauses so she can laugh. "Randall's first Spanish line was "Paco, toma tu mierda y vete."

"What does that mean?" Brandon asks.

"Paco, take your shit and go." I say. "All my abuela watches are telenovelas. That's basically how I learned Spanish." Brandon grins. "My mom said I would say that to her at least once a day when she needed me to do something around the house."

"That's funny."

"Yeah. She got tired of me cursing in Spanish, so my dad and mom started speaking more and more Spanish around me and now I'm one hundred percent fluent."

"And on that note lets the dig in." My mother passes the me the enchiladas and I go to town. We spend the rest of the evening trading stories about my upbringing. Brandon mostly enjoyed the food. A lot of it he's never tried or had before. I had to keep translating for him because when my mom and abuela get comfortable they forget all the English they know and it's only Spanish.

"I love your family." Brandon whispers.

"Thanks."

"I don't think I want to go home. They're perfect." Brandon says.

"Oh, Brandon! You're a part of the family now." My mom says. "You are welcomed here as long as we're here." Brandon smiles then lets that information sink in.

"She's not joking." I say

"That's totally fine." Brandon grabs another empanada, and we continue our storytelling.

RANDALL

September 6ᵗʰ 8:15pm

After an already long week at school, filled with play rehearsals, getting to know Brandon, and trying to maintain total sanity, I did not want to go to my treatment today. The upside to coming today was the fact of knowing I only have ten more rounds of chemo. The treatment seems to be working. I feel so much better than I did months ago. My hair however disagrees, but I refuse to worry about that— it's just hair.

After treatment today, Bella's dad offered to take us for ice cream. He really thought it was a great idea to take us to get something cold after being cold for four hours. What the movies never tell you is that chemo makes your entire body so cold—like bone chilling cold. It takes my body a good two days to warm up. I run on my stored energy until the treatment starts to do it's kill them bad cells thing.

We arrive to The Ice Cream Shack. The last time I was at this place was two years ago with my dad. He let me get whatever I wanted that day. I had just come from a swim team tryout, and I failed miserably. It was like a cheer up snack.

"Hot fudge sundae. Good choice." Bella is admiring my ice cream tower. "Meanwhile, I got this baby ice cream cone."

"No. I was thinking of getting that…then your dad said it was on him, so I decided to splurge." I dig my spoon into my sundae making sure to get every bit of vanilla-banana-strawberry-goodness. "Oh, that was satisfying." I lick the spoon, then go in again. *Yes, I'm cold as hell…but it's freaking ice cream.*

"How are you though?" Bella asks. Her dad decides to take his ice cream to the car. "I feel like you're always asking everyone else in the chemo about themselves that I forgot to ask how you were. "Don't sugarcoat either."

"Oh, I'm good…I actually mean it. I feel good for someone with leukemia."

"I'm happy to hear that." Bella takes a lick of her ice cream.

"How are you doing?" I ask.

"I'm also fine. My dad pulled me out of school, but I am good."

"Wait. Why did he pull you?"

"He doesn't want me around so many germs." She places her ice cream down in a random cup that was left on the table. "How are you able to do it?"

"My teachers know. My family knows. They do all they can to sanitize and keep their colds and germs to themselves, but I don't really think about that stuff when I'm at school. I just make sure to keep myself away from people that are sick and stuff and also this isn't my first rodeo…my mother pulled me out of school once years ago and Dr. Rickards told her that it would make depressed—she reminded her about the advances in science…and how good the entire team at Westlake U was."

"Advances in science. Try pulling that on my dad. He believes prayer fixes everything— don't get me wrong, I believe it too, but I wish I could be around people all the time…like you."

I for once am lost for words. "Yeah."

"Anyways, on a happier note. I saw that you were going to be in a school play…fiddler on the roof?"

"Yup." I show her my finished sundae bowl. "I like the whole rehearsing process…it's the remembering choreography part that gets under my wig."

"But I bet you are so good in it."

"Oh, I'm the best." I lie. "I have the most lines." I lie again.

"I know you're lying." She grins. "Are you dating anyone? Or can you date?"

"Yeah. His name is Brandon. He's pretty dope."

"How did he…" I turn my head away. "Oh. He doesn't know, does he?"

"No. I'm waiting to tell him."

"Understandable."

"You're like the only person that isn't trying to force me to do anything."

"No offense. You don't have to tell anyone if you don't want to." Bella tosses her stuff in the trash. It misses and we both just ignore it.

"I don't?"

"God, no. It's no one else's business but yours. It's your life."

"Well, did you ever get around to tell your dad about your decision?"

"What do you mean?"

"A few weeks ago, you were on the fence about wanting to continue treatments. Where are you with that?" Bella picks at the paint peeling on the table. "Seriously, where are you with it? I won't judge."

"I personally don't want to continue doing the treatments. I just don't see the point. But I'm going to keep at it because the doctors are seeing some progress. It just doesn't make sense for me to quit at this stage in the game." Bella looks me in the eyes for the first time tonight.

"That's great. Some progress is better than nothing." I lay my hand on top of hers. "I'm happy you're keeping at it. That's really amazing."

"Yeah. Really amazing." Bella takes her hands from under mine. "It truly is."

"Like, just think about it. A few years from now, we're going to be happy living our young adult lives."

"It's only because I met you." Bella is giving me eye contact again. "When I would watch you in that chair just accepting the treatment and not fighting and letting that stuff enter your body. I got the hint that it wasn't because you didn't want to do the treatment, but because you want to hurry back to your life. I got inspired. Doctors saying, I was making progress was the icing on top for my motivation. I still wish I had something to rush back to though."

"You do."

"Oh yeah. What is that?"

"Your dad." I point to her father awkwardly eating his sundae in his car. "I know he wants you to live and not to give up. Living is the hard part and we're already doing it. All it takes is one day at a time. Every morning when the sun shines in my room, I thank the universe for allowing me to be here in this moment called life. I don't have time to give up…because that is too easy. People with cancer are already winners. We just have to keep showing up for ourselves, as hard as it may be."

"Yeah. People with cancer are winners." Bella reaches across the table to give me a hug. "You are a wise boy, Randall Price."

"So are you." I say.

"Okay you two, ready to go?" Bella's dad asks.

"Yeah, I'll show you a shortcut to my house."

BRANDON

September 6ᵗʰ 9:00pm

"Ok. Let's go over this one more time." Kelly says as his car comes to a complete stop outside of my house. "We're going in there to get the rest of your stuff. If your stepfather or mother tries anything, we're not going to feed into it."

"That's easier said than done." I stick my house keys back in my jacket pocket. "I am so not trying to get into any shit with the two of them."

"Look at me bro. It's me and you." Kelly pulls his key out of the ignition. "There's nothing left for you there. She's proven that she has given up on you. Why would you want to continue putting yourself through bullshit?" Kelly gets out of the car and sprints to my side of the car. "Get your ass out of the car."

"Dude. Wait."

"No. Let's go." Kelly reaches over me and unhooks my seatbelt. "It's time for you to be happy. How much sense does that make to be forming a happy relationship with someone, but you are purposely keeping yourself miserable in other areas of your life? That makes no damn sense. Your mom doesn't deserve you bro."

"But what if he leaves her?" Coming up with any excuses is a specialty of mine. I've been doing this to myself for so long, that its' become second nature. "I don't want to lose another parent. Who knows what she'll do."

"Dude. She'll finally get it together when she loses everything. It's not your problem to worry about her any longer."

"Yeah?" I say.

"Yeah?"

"Let's do it." I get out of the car and walk across the driveway to our front door. "I don't think anyone is home." I go to unlock the door and notice the top lock is locked which typically means they don't want company, or my mother wants to catch me coming home late.

"Even better. Unlock the damn door." Kelly demands. "I have to pee so bad." I finally get the door unlocked and immediately shut the alarm off. "Thank goodness. I'll catch you in your room—"

"I don't have to go up there. All my shit is right here." My mother has all of my clothes and other belongings scattered in duffle bags across the floor. "She even had the common courtesy to label everything. How sweet."

"And all of a sudden I no longer have to pee." Kelly starts picking up the bags.

"This isn't right." I sprint up the stairs to my room. "They painted the walls." I mumble to myself. "Where is my bed?" My room is empty. "Whatever." I slam the door shut and sprint to our back staircase and take the photo of my dad and I off the wall. "Forget them."

"Brandon! Let's get out of here." Kelly shouts from downstairs. I do as I'm told and head for the stairs. "Don't let this bother you."

"I'm not. I just thought I'd at least have one final showdown with my mom. I wanted her to tell me to my face that I was no longer welcomed in her home. I wanted her to make it official. I want her to look me in the eye and tell me…" It dawns on me that my father's clothes were in our main coat closet. "I have to check on my dad's things." I sprint to our main coat closet, and I almost rip the doors of their hinges. "No." I groan. "Where is his shit?" Everything of my fathers is gone. "That bitch."

"Hey. Let's get out of here." Kelly starts for the door.

"She's dead to me." I murmur. "She got rid of all of my dad's stuff."

"Oh man, I'm so sorry."

"I don't want anything to do with her ever again." Just as I say those words my mother and her husband walk through the door. "How dare you?"

"Brandon. You better watch your tone when you speak to me." Pearl says.

"We needed the space. Your father isn't here." Sam adds.

I walk right pass Pearl and Sam and grab as many duffle bags my hands could carry and Kelly grabs the rest. "You know how much that stuff meant to me."

"Brandon, know that when you leave out those doors—"

"Yeah, yeah…he can't come back. We've heard that line before." Kelly interrupts. He pushes me out the door and slams the door shut behind us. "Bro, you don't need them. They weren't good for you anyway. The universe is giving you so much more." Kelly pauses from hauling my stuff. "Hey, come here." He drops my bags to the ground and holds open his arms. "You got me. We've always been family." Kelly hugs me tight. "Don't worry about them, that's your past. Look at all the places you are going."

"Yeah." It's taking so much in me not to be irate and storm back through the house. I wanna to trash the place and make my mom see all that she's about to be giving up. My mother has proven time and time again that she doesn't care. "It's time for me to carry on." Had I stayed and argued I would have been giving her what she wanted "I'm choosing to be happy all the time." I unclench my fists.

"As you should bro. As you should." Kelly says.

"Let's go."

"Dude, I'm seriously kicking myself…we so could've walked. You live next door to me." Kelly is not even a two-minute drive from my house. "We're extra."

"Hey, I wanted to make a dramatic exit."

September 27th 12:00pm

"I dare you to go camping with me next weekend." I
challenge Randall. "A bunch of us are going camping next
weekend before the campgrounds closest to us close until Spring."
I take out my phone to show him a photo of our little cabin. "See.
Kelly and Jason rented a bunch of these small cabins."

"I'm down. I just have to ask my mom" Randall grabs my
phone to inspect the photo "…or we can ask her together?"
Randall suggests.

"I'd so be up for that. Moms love me…especially your
mom and Abuela." Every morning when I pick him up for school,
they both always make it a point to chat me up. So, I purposely
arrive thirty minutes early just to have our morning conversations.
"I'm even going to forward your mom the itinerary Jason came up
for this weekend."

"Itinerary?"

"Yeah, Jason loves to plan so he planned this whole day out. We have breakfast at a certain time, lunch at a certain time, and dinner…at a certain time…"

"Will we get to be alone?" Randall asks. "I don't want to spend so much time doing everything Jason has planned for us to do."

"Oh, yeah, of course. I promise we'll definitely get some alone time to just be us. I wouldn't have asked you to come if I didn't definitely have some fun things planned."

"Fun things? I'd so love to hear about all of these fun plans you have." Randall leans over the lunch table. "I'm all ears."

"Oh, you're sneaky…to bad I know how to keep a secret."

"So do I." He winks.

"Switching topics… I finally was able to get all of my missing shit from Pearl's place."

"That's so good. I think you need that positivity in your life." The night my mother packed all my shit. Randall called me. I ignored his call and he ended up calling Kelly. Kelly told him everything that had happened. I didn't pay too much attention to the conversation, and I never asked Randall what he and Kelly spoke about. "I'm happy you have a safe place to lay your head at night."

"Yeah. Plus, you can spend the night sometimes. My room is all set up." Randall looks away from me. "What's up?"

"Nothing…It's embarrassing…I'd love to spend the night at your place though." Randall forces himself to smile.

"You can tell me. Who am I going to tell?"

"No. I think I should just keep this to myself." Randall takes a sip of my water. "I promise this should be kept…"

"I'm a virgin too." I interrupt.

Randall's facial expression changes instantly. "Wow. Really?"

"Yeah. Your boy has never had sex with anyone. Not even a ghost." I'm now blushing. I can feel my cheeks getting warm. "I just never wanted to do anything with anyone."

"Yeah. Same." Randall adds.

"Plus, when you're gay there's so much you have to figure out…like who's on top and who's underneath. I was just not ready to decide that…what if I like both?"

"I can tell you've thought a lot about this." Randall says. "From what I saw on Degrassi, I'm pretty sure they said it's okay to like both…as in positions." The lunch bell cuts our conversation short.

"We'll pick this us after school?"

"I can't. I have a doctor's appointment…have to get my physical for this stupid play." Randall swiftly slides from our table."

"Oh, yeah. I heard some people complaining about that earlier." *I actually didn't.* It sounds like something Crestview would make student clubs do.

"Yeah. Rebecca sucks—"

"Brandon!" I know Kelly's voice from anywhere. It's so raspy and deep at the same time. "We're gonna be late to Chemistry. I know you wanna copy off me. Hurry your ass bro."

"I gotta get of here." I give Randall a kiss on the cheek then rush off to catch up to Kelly.

8:45pm

Performing in front of people makes me so nervous. I get even more nervous if there are people in the crowd that I know. I've been trying to for months to get on the Bookstore on Highland's list of set performers—I assumed I would be over my fears by the time they made their way to my name.

Out of nowhere the shop manager calls me while I was tuning my guitar and he told me that I had a shot if I could be at the bookstore within the hour. I immediately hopped in my car and raced all the way to Westlake for this opportunity.

"Brandon. You're up in five minutes." The manager Peter says. He's a very short red head who spits after he finishes his sentences.

"Cool." My nerves are rushing through my body. There is a girl reciting a poem who seems to have captured the audience's attention massively. There are so many snaps coming from every area of the room. "I can do this." I whisper to myself.

"Two minutes. Dude." Peter says. "Get yourself self together." It's going to take more than two minutes for me to shake these nerves away. "You're up." Peter pulls me by the arm and leads me to the stage landing. "Get up there."

On stage I have no idea how I should talk to the crowd. I take a deep breath with my back turned away from the audience. When I turn around, I blurt, "Hey everyone!" and begin to play my guitar. I start the intro to this cover of one of my favorite artists. I now have the crowd on my side. They love my impromptu guitar solo "This song is a favorite of mine. It's dedicated to a guy...I wish I wasn't so nervous to sing it to him." I begin to sing:

Let's dance when we're not supposed to be.
Can't stand when you're not close to me.
Damn, can't believe you notice me, notice me.
So, let's dance when we're not supposed to be.
Can't stand when you're not close to me.
Damn, can't believe you notice me, you notice me

I stop for a second. When you are on a stage you really aren't aware of the crowd. The bright lights are the only things you're fighting against. I'm taking in the audience. I begin to sway my body back and forth and encourage all of the couples to do the same thing.

Only thought I'd have you in my dreams.
Things you say leave me feelin' weak.
And those brown eyes of yours are all that I need.
And you whisper that I'm all that you see...

9:00pm

I finish my set, on top of the world. The audience cheers for a while, they don't hear Peter when he announces the next act following me. I walk off the stage, with the crowd still demanding more. I conquered one part of my fears. "Thank you, dad." I whisper. Now, I have to share it with everyone.

"Brandon. You want to perform here again?" Peter asks. "Or perform anywhere in general? My family has a place. Your crowd is definitely there."

"Yeah. Of course." I'm all smiles.

"Have you heard of *Taverna?*" He asks.

"Yeah."

"You should definitely hit my sister up. She manages that place with our mom, I'll put in a good word. I could definitely hear you headline the New Year's Eve show. Hit her up." I should have told Peter that I know his sister but I'm riding a high and don't want to bring Sarah into this night.

"I'll definitely talk to her at school on Monday."

"Cool." Peter and I shake hands before he steps away.

I waste no time leaving. "Hey, my car is a white BMW ticket number…"

"Brandon? Right?" I turn to face the guy and girl sitting behind me. "Remember me, we're in English together…Abiyram. She's Rebecca." Rebecca grabs Abiyram's hand and kisses him on the cheek. "We're also in the play with Randall." Abiyram says.

"Cool." I finally hand the valet dude my ticket number. He mouths Five minutes then sprints to go get my car. "What can I do for you two?"

"We loved your song?" Rebecca says. Her stiff hair doesn't move with her head. "I just loved the dedication to Randall. He's such a special boy." She smiles.

"Yeah. He is." Abiyram follows up. Rebecca glares at him. "I think it's cool that you're so proud to do this out loud."

"What is *this*?" I ask.

"Sing. In public. I'd be stupid nervous. By the way, where is Randall?"

"Oh, he had a doctor's appointment and wanted to rest afterwards. I had someone record it. Also, I gotta get better at singing in front of people I know."

"I understand that brother." Rebecca tugs on Abiyram's arm. "Well, I guess we gotta get out of here…and if you need us to put in a good with your crew about how well you sang tonight, we'll definitely do that."

"No need. This is my car pulling up." The valet guy finally arrives with my car. I pull out a ten-dollar bill and quickly hand it to the guy. "See you both at school."

"Take care, Brandon!" Abiyram yells.

"Cool." I say as I hop in my car and quickly drive off.

RANDALL

September 30th 3:20pm

"Guys, I really would love it you all catch on to the choreography. The play is in two months, and I am concerned." Rebecca has been pacing back and forth across the stage for close to ten minutes now. "Especially you, Randall. It looks like you have two left feet. I thought you were Mexican or Latin." Everyone in the black box stands still. Ironically, the poster of Zoe Saldana falls off the wall. "Shit." Rebecca covers her mouth. "I am so sorry."

"I'm not even Mexican." I go to my bookbag and grab my water bottle. "You just have diarrhea of the mouth."

"I'm really sorry." Rebecca coughs into her hand—not into her sleeve. She also has the nerve to try and hug me. I immediately move out of the way causing her to stumble. "What did I do now?"

"You just coughed into your hand." I point to the hand she just coughed in. "I accept your apology…can we get off of me now?"

"Sure. Let's take it from the top." The music director starts the music from the top and I do not know the part we are rehearsing because when it was initially introduced, I had chemo that day. I try to camouflage myself in the back of the room, but Abiyram pushes me forward and now I am back in Rebecca's peripheral.

"Randall." Mrs. Chambers calls. "Are you alright?" Mrs. Chambers knows about my situation, and she purposely goes out of her way to be awkward sometimes. "If you're tired, just have a seat." Everyone continues dancing and reciting their lines.

"Maybe Fiddler on the roof isn't for Randall." Rebecca turns to Mrs. Chambers. "He just doesn't seem like he wants to do it."

"Not true." I interrupt. "Why can't someone just have a bad day?"

"Randall, it seems like you're always having bad days." Rebecca grows an even bigger head and slowly approaches me with both her arms crossed. She makes each step in her Doc Martens known. "I do not think he's cut out for this play any longer, maybe you should just be a part of the club and not in our plays. Set dressers needs lots of help."

"Well, Rebecca, who are you going to replace him with?" Abiyram asks.

"Why are we talking like I am not in the room?" I ask.

"We cannot kick Randall out of the play." Mrs. Chambers states. "What is one of the most important rules of this club?"

No one answers.

"Rebecca, you should know what it is." Mrs. Chambers switches places with Rebecca at the center of the room. "Go ahead and recite it please."

"No one should be turned away; anything is possible in theater." Rebecca mumbles.

"Exactly! This means Randall is free to stay in this club for however long he feels like it. This also means he will not be leaving this play." Mrs. Chambers gives me a half smile before continuing. "Do I make myself clear?"

"Fine. Just do not say anything if he tanks this performance in a few months." Rebecca goes back to the head of the room and tries to call out orders for everyone. "It will not be on me if this play fails."

"Who said I was going to fail?" Instead of answering my question, she turns her back to me. "The human brain doesn't grasp anything in just one hour. It takes time and repetition."

"Randall. We will not be doing this right now."

"Whatever. You never want to talk when you're in the wrong…you do know that's not how you grow as a person?" Rebecca motions for someone to start the music. "Ignoring me will not get your point across." Rebecca then points to Mrs. Chambers to take her place. "I'm going to sit this one out because I will not hold this up for everyone."

"Start the music!" Rebecca yells. "From the top." Rebecca spins her finger, and everyone takes their place while I take my seat in the audience sitting next to Mrs. Chambers.

"I'm happy you stood up for yourself." Mrs. Chambers whispers. "It's really great to see it. I mean it, young man."

"Thank you. And can you stop making my thing awkward?"

"What thing?" She asks.

"You know the c-thing?"

"Oh!" She shouts. "I'm sorry, I had no idea I was making things awkward for you. I just thought I was—no, you're right. I was making things awkward." We both giggle a little bit causing Rebecca to shoot daggers right through us. "I'll stop."

"Thank you."

"No. Thank you." Mrs. Chambers adjusts herself in her seat. "You are going to win, by the way."

"Oh, I know I will. That's the mindset I go at this from." Beating cancer is one hundred percent in your mind first, and it's in your body second—don't let anyone say different.

5:00pm

"Hey, I apologize for Rebecca earlier." Abiyram is way too close to me. "She's just under a lot of stress right now. She doesn't know where to place her emotions most times."

"Why do you do that?" I ask him.

"Do what?"

"Apologize for Rebecca. She's not your responsibility."

"I get it. But she is my girlfriend." In the LGBTQIA+ rule book, there is one cardinal sin and that is, never under any circumstances out another possible member of the community. I do not believe that Abiyram is one hundred percent straight. So, I try my hardest not to show the shock on my face about him having a girlfriend…who happens to be Rebecca. "I don't want people thinking she's a horrible person."

"I don't think she's horrible. That red hair color is horrible, but she's not a horrible person. I just don't get her."

"She's, my girlfriend." Abiyram reiterates.

"Ok."

"I don't want anyone to think my girlfriend is this mean girl." He repeats again.

"Are you trying to convince yourself that she actually is your girlfriend? If so, I believed you the first time you said it."

"I just…I just…uh—"

"Randall." Rebecca says. I am wholeheartedly regretting staying behind after practice. "I've been looking for you all over this little box."

"Well, you found me." I smile.

"Can we talk?" She asks. "I have something I really want to ask you."

"Go ahead."

"Are you germophobic?" She asks.

"What?"

"I saw you in here earlier disinfecting, wiping the chairs, and I overheard you telling Mrs. Chambers that you didn't want to be around anyone that was sick."

"That may mean he's just cautious." Abiyram jumps in.

"So, are you—a germophobe?" She asks again.

"No. I just like being clean."

"Well, I can assure you that we're all clean. We come from Crestview. You're an islander." Rebecca doesn't cover her mouth this time.

"What are you implying? That I'm dirty because I live on Westlake. If so, fuck you." I text Brandon to see if he's done with his music practice. "You are so mean. Just plain rude."

"No. Randall. I am trying to run a serious production around here." Rebecca pulls out a piece of paper from her pocket. "You see all of these people that would kill to be a part of this play?" She places the paper in my hand. "That's a lot of people."

"I don't really care. Just like…calm down. You're being rude for no reason." Brandon finally responds and tells me to come to the music room. "I don't know what you're going through, but I am not about to ruin my day arguing with you. I actually like being in the play and I really enjoy the cast. You aren't going to find drama with me. It's so much easier to be happy than rude."

Rebecca takes a sit on the ground. She pulls Abiyram down to the ground with her. "You're right. I am not being fair. I am sorry."

I just look down on Rebecca.

"Oh, since I know you're about to go see Brandon…I saw you text him…tell him, that he has an amazing voice."

"Sure."

"I was shocked that you weren't at the bookstore seeing him perform. You two have been growing closer to one another lately. It would have been nice to see you cheering him on." I am not going to let Rebecca's shenanigans get to me. Although I am somewhat slighted that I am finding out about Brandon's performance. Rebecca will not get to see me upset.

"Yeah. It's not worth it to me to keep going back and forth with you. You're so angry today and I'm not going back and forth with you." I gather all of my belongings and head for the door. "Also, I knew about the performance. Just for your information." I lie.

RANDALL

October 5th 11:00am

"There is absolutely no sex on this trip." My abuela says as slyly packs a pair of condoms in my duffle bag while my mother's back is turned. "You'll get...wait, people usually say that you will get cancer if you have sex...but...I guess." My abuela shrugs. "How do I finish my joke mijo?"

I can't hold my laughter in which causes my abuela to let out a loud obnoxious whaling laugh. My mother remains stoic. "You two are something." My mother smiles. "Randall, are you sure you have everything?"

"Yes. I double checked." I say while sliding my phone charger into my bag.

"What about a coat? It gets really cold..."

"Yes. I have one."

My mother opens my duffle bag. "Donde?"

"Ok, maybe I lied." I grab my old beat-up jean jacket hanging from my vintage desk chair and toss it in my bag. "…now, I'm all set."

"I am making sure that you've packed enough…" My mother sees the condoms. "I'm making sure you have everything that you're going to need…shit, your port!" *Shit.* Is right. There are two most common ways to administer chemo, a lot of people who haven't been through this battle as much as I have go with the arm, it's easy comes with less questions and it's less intrusive—I however have a one that gets me the most questions and stares—it's in my chest. "How are you going to explain it to him."

"I don't know…I'll probably just say I had it since childbirth. Or it's a modern-day pacemaker…I'll figure it out. Don't stress me out before this trip. I promise to tell him."

My mother throws her hands up. "I guess I'll just have to take your word for it…back to packing. Do you have everything?"

"Yeah. Also, I'm pretty sure someone is going to have something that I'm missing."

"No. I don't want you using anyone else's anything. Especially since you're still doing the treatments…I do not know why Christina ever gave the green light for this trip. How can she say limit your circle and then say it's fine to go camping?"

Technically, Dr. Rickards just listened while I told her I was going camping with Brandon. She asked if it were in my backyard and my response was: *something like that.* I caught her at a moment where when she was in a hurry.

"We're going to have to rethink this relationship. I'm your mother and I should have final say. Ella no ha estado en tu vida." My mother takes a seat on my bed. "Yo soy tú madre."

"Mama. No one can your place. She just wants me to live my life. I can't be scared. I'm kind of over being afraid to live.

"And I understand that but you're sick. You can't keep doing what everyone else is doing. There's going to come a day where you are just going to have to stay still. Do you hear me, Randall? I will not lose you." My mom takes a deep breath. "Randall…"

"El no esta roto." My abuela interrupts. "Mija, he's not broken…listen, he's a child. Let him experience all of the things. It's just one night."

"Mama, él es mi hijo…that means he is my responsibility." My mom takes possession of my duffle bag.

"M. I'm going to be careful. Don't worry. I promise to check in often. It's okay if you call me. Call me a million times. I promise I won't do anything that will put me in danger." We ignore the knock on the door. My eyes are glued on my mother. I hate seeing her sad. When she worries it make me worry and it causes me to somehow take on her pain. Our bond is so strong.

"I know. I just…I just want to spend as much time with you that I possibly can." My mother caresses my cheek. "Te amo más que la vida misma." She kisses me on the cheek before handing me my bag. "Have fun." I head for the door.

"Oh! Mijo! Let me get the door. You go in another room." My abuela charges for the door ahead of me. "Your first sleepover with a boy we like." Brandon knocks on the door again. "Go in the kitchen."

"Abuela…"

"Baby, let me have this moment." My abuela pushes me in the direction of the kitchen causing me to drop my bag.

"This is so embarrassing." My mother laughs. Her cheeks are so rosy, I forget that I was supposed to be hiding in the kitchen. "My baby is growing up. Have fun okay. Do not worry about anything. Or me. Okay. Enjoy tonight."

I smile in acknowledgement.

"Brandon! Sweet, sweet Brandon!" My abuela introduces us to Brandon as if this is my first-time meeting this boy, I am legitimately but slowly falling for.

"Hey, everyone." Brandon gives me a wink. The crinkle on the side of his face gives me butterflies every time he does it.

"Hey Brandon. How are you?" My mother asks.

"Es-ta…muy…bi-en." Brandon nervously says. "…Did I say it wrong?"

"No. You said it right, just say it with confidence next time." I give Brandon a hug. "See. Watch. Ask me."

"How are you, Randall?"

"Está muy bien." I smile. "Confidence."

"I gotcha." Brandon pauses to a take look at my head-to-toe came look. "Love the outfit."

"No, you don't."

"I do. It's cute." He caresses my arm. "I love that you went all out for this—"

"Alright, you two. You should get a move on." My abuela hands Brandon my duffle bag. "And remember Randall...there is to be no sex on this trip."

"Alright, ma'am." Brandon sees the same wink I saw my Abuela give. "I'll go put your stuff in the car."

"Ok." I say. "I'll be right out."

"Randall."

"Yeah, mom."

"Please, tell him what's going on."

"I will. If there is a moment that just the two of us can have...I'll tell him. Promise." My mother frowns her face. "Mama, I promise to tell him everything. He will know by the end of this trip. I'll ruin our happy weekend with news that I have freaking cancer."

"All I'm saying is—"

"Mom! I get it. I will tell him. He deserves to know."

12:00pm

I have been feeling somewhat good. For someone who is in the middle of a rigorous treatment schedule, Junior year is full force, and Brandon and I are becoming a thing. I feel okay.

"Hey!" Brandon touches my knee. We've been driving for close to half an hour. "What are you daydreaming about?"

"Nothing." I lie. "I'm regretting not taking one last pee before we left."

Brandon laughs. "That's funny…because I too have to pee and there is no place to stop for like another thirty minutes."

"Damn." I eye the water bottle sitting in the cup holder. Brandon catches me glancing at the empty water bottle he demolished as soon as we got in the car.

"Dude, are you thinking about—let me pull over."

"No. I am not peeing outside." A few years ago, during my cancer free years, I remember this one time I had to use the bathroom really bad, and my dad made me pee on a tree. My mother witnessed this and told me that peeing outdoors makes the earth sick. That has scarred me ever since. So now, I make it a habit to always use the restroom before I leave the house even if I don't have to use it…or, pee in bottles. "Peeing outdoors makes the earth sick."

"What?" Brandon unhooks our seatbelts and unlocks the door. "Who told you that?"

"My mom."

"No way. Our pee is water…we're watering the earth."

I can't help but laugh. "Still not peeing outside though."

"Suit yourself." Brandon gets out of the car.

I sit for a moment. Making sure it remains clear for him to pee, but the thought of peeing on myself scares me out of the car. "Fine." I whisper to myself.

"Randall?" Brandon catches me staring at his equipment.

"*Shhh.* We're just peeing." I didn't mean to look. I just turned my head and saw his entire anatomy staring at me. "My bad. I didn't mean to look."

"What are you sorry about? Brandon finishes and then buckles his pants.

"*Ahhh.*" I fix myself. "I wasn't trying to look; it was just there. Just sitting outside of your pants wincing at me."

"You're cute. Don't apologize for something like that." Brandon grins. "Get in the car."

6:45pm

The last time I went camping I do not remember my dad and I roasting marshmallows. Maria Price would not have allowed us to ruin her backyard. I also don't remember being surrounded by people my own age. Growing up I was my own best friend. I didn't really have people who I could run home to after school and play video games with. When I started High School on Prince Island that was the best year and a half, I spent with people my age. It was also the last time I felt seen.

"Randall. You have to put your stick in the fire." Jason points out causing me to stop daydreaming. I almost forgot Jason, Kelly, Shauna, and her guy came on this camping trip with Brandon and I. "Oh wait, are you're allergic to Marshmallows? I know a lot of people allergic to random shit like Marshmallows."

"Nah. I was just daydreaming." I place my stick in the fire.

"Did I miss anything?" Brandon joins the rest of us, he wanted to change out of the jeans he'd been wearing all day.

"Nope. I saved you a seat." I smile.

"I like my marshmallows burnt as hell." Brandon says. "The burnt the better."

"Wait. Randall, your mom, does she even have marshmallows at your house?" Shauna asks. "When I was snooping, I didn't see one American thing in your cabinets." Everyone except Brandon looks to me.

"Wait. Randall, you don't eat sweets?" Jason asks. "I wish I could be like you."

"Yeah, I love sweets. Don't listen to Shauna—" I glare at her. "—My mom doesn't really buy a lot of snacks we get here though. I grew up drinking hella soda, but a snack to me are all the things my mother whips up from her childhood."

Brandon bumps me. "I can't wait to try more of your moms cooking. That party a few weeks ago was heaven."

"It was." My eyes linger on Brandon.

"I have a question." Shauna asks. "Since we're in the majority for once tonight, I want to know if you feel black, Brandon."

"I don't think we should talk race." I say.

"We're having a good night." Brandon says.

"I just wanted to talk about something deeper other than school stuff or neighborhood stuff or other typical rich people stuff." Shauna says. "…but if y'all don't want to talk about this kind of stuff. I'm totally cool with that."

"We can talk about this another time." I say. "Not today."

"I get it." She says.

"Cool…but to answer your question, I think we all feel black. We live in the United States." I take brief look at Brandon and use my arm to stealthy examine our skin colors.

"Truer words have never been said." Shauna says. "And on that note, I'm going to take my ass to sleep now." Shauna and her guy gets up from the group and go their own way.

Brandon places his arm around my shoulder, leans in and whispers: "New visual…us…down by that lake in ten minutes dreaming and making wishes." He whispers.

"I love that visual." Brandon and I are inches from kissing…or at least I assume we are. His head is so close to mine, but maybe that's just how he whispers. "Let's get out of here." *I am not whispering.*

8:00pm

"You know…I have never been a fan of staring up at the stars. It's something my dad and I used to do all the time. He would lay on his back with a blanket on top of him and I would lay on his chest, and we'd just stare at the stars and give them fake names. We spent hours doing that. After my dad died, I would lay in my backyard and stare into the sky…I stopped because it just wasn't the same anymore."

Brandon scoots and puts his arm around me. "I get it. You miss him, don't you?"

"Every single day. That old man is on my mind."

"Oh, I get it." Brandon nudges. "Every day something happens, and it reminds me of something my dad and I used to do." Brandon and I sit for a moment in silence. I guess we didn't want to continue to change the mood about talking about our dead dads. "This is nice. I'm happy you came."

"Me too. Is it also weird I can literally feel our relationship changing…in a good way?" I turn to face Brandon. "Most times when we're together it is like we've known each other for years and years."

"Right!" Brandon turns to face me as well. "I so agree." There's a tense energy that grows between the two of us. "But, taking things slow is the right thing to do."

"Yeah…of course. Totally!" I force myself to smile.

"Question for you."

"Yup!"

"Where is the North star?"

"Dude…Brandon, my favorite subject is English."

Brandon lets out a strange laugh. It's one part choking and one part laugh. "Well, in that case…let's imagine where it is."

"Cool." We both scan the sky looking for any star that could be our North Star. "Hey, what about that one?" I choose a star that is hella brighter than all of the other ones. It's also slightly bigger than the rest. "That's our star."

"Yeah. I agree. I love our little big baby star."

"That's our *Estrella*."

"Love it. Estrella."

"Picture this, months from now when you're away in college counting down the days until you see me…just look up and you'll see it…and when you see our star…picture me."

I wish there was some kind of way to permanently remember intimate moments in our brains.

In ten years, whether Brandon and I are together or not, when I get asked the question how my first real relationship was, I want to be able to recall this moment. Every simple moment I want to be able to remember. Detail for detail.

A few days from now, I'll be able to remember how Brandon looked while taking in all of this Westlake campsite. I love how he's admiring the nature while periodically looking back at me to see if I'm enjoying this moment as well.

A week from now, I'll remember how bad I know we both wanted to kiss one another earlier when we were around that campfire with Jason, Kelly, and Shauna. His piercing green eyes sending signals through my body—the kind of signals I believe I should be feeling for him, and I hope to God he has those same signals or urges.

A few months from now, I'll remember the two of us laying and looking up at the stars. Although we were mainly quiet, I still imagined his thoughts. I imagined that Brandon was thinking about all the ways he could make this night a permanent one. If only we didn't have young lives to live—him back in Crestview and me still here in Westlake.

In a year from now, if the chemo hasn't ruined my memories, I hope to remember the name of our baby star *Estrella* and how I honestly saw a twinkle in Brandon's eye and how he glowed when he smiled at me. *Yeah, I want to remember this moment for a lifetime.*

October 6th 12:00am

For some reason the stars shine brighter in Westlake.

There's more hope in the sky over here.

At 11:11 when I was deciding how I was going keep the night going with Randall, I wished to keep him happy. I asked the star wishing gods to please help me not saying anything stupid that would cause him to trail off and go find Shauna.

I envisioned a camping trip that was just our little moment. I didn't have anything special planned or in mind. I knew that I wanted to make lasting growing moments with Randall.

Tonight, I got the clarity that Randall is the right person for me. He's a first love writers of movies base their characters off of. That is one special boy.

"Hey, before we get to the good part of our story, I wanted to share you with this really old poem my dad and mom would recite to me every night before bed."

"Alright." Randall sits up and turns to face me. "Don't look so nervous." He smiles and it's almost simultaneous when a light shines across his face causing him to look so fucking angelic. "What? Do I have something on my face?"

"No. You're perfect." I inhale a moment. "This poem is everything to me." I begin to read:

> *Peace flows into me*
> *As the tide to the pool by the shore;*
> *It is mine forevermore,*
> *It will not ebb like the sea.*
>
> *I am the pool of blue*
> *That worships the vivid sky;*
> *My hopes were heaven-high,*
> *They are all fulfilled in you.*
>
> *I am the pool of gold*
> *When sunset burns and dies,*
> *You are my deepening skies;*
> *Give me your stars to hold.*

Randall is silent.

"What are you thinking?" I ask.

"Sara Teasdale." He says. "That poem is called *Peace*."

"Yeah! How'd you know?"

"That poem is…did my mom ever work for your family?" Randall has a concerned expression on his face.

"No. Your mom is an angel. I could never forget her." I say. "What's up?"

"She used to recite it to me whenever she or my dad had a hard day. It was like her prayer. The poem is about seeking and finding your peace. When my dad died and she was having trouble moving his things or coping with him not being on this earth, she'd recite that poem."

"That's freaking trippy. We have so many small and big commonalities. I got reintroduced to this poem since being on my own—I'm realizing the bigger picture. Peace is what I'm after. It's what I need."

"I believe you're going to remain at peace…and get everything you ever wanted out of this life." Randall runs his hand down my thigh. "You deserve the world, Brandon Marciano."

I look Randall in the eyes while holding his hand in place on my thigh. "I am starting to believe I have everything I ever wanted."

Randall leans in to give me a hug. His heart is truly racing. For a second, I think I felt it. We stay embraced. I feel his mind racing. "I wish I could pick up this island and move it to New York when you go. I just had to have been born a year after you."

"I don't have to go to New York, there are other colleges here—"

"NO! You're going to New York." Randall breaks our embrace. "New York is your dream. Plus, my dream school happens to be in New York as well. It's no Julliard, but it's either NYU or Columbia. Shauna and I both have those schools on our college lists."

"Oh, that'd be so amazing." I say.

"New York has always been my dream."

"We're going to make it a dream...just you wait."

"We sure are." Randall takes my hand. "Let's go to the cabin."

1:30am

I'm observing every ounce of Randall.

Randall doesn't know this, but when he laughs—it appears to me that he's forgotten all that he's been through. Randall's skin also radiates at night. His caramel skin complements the bitter orange candle lights in our cabin.

When Randall is smiling, laughing, or doing that nervous second guessing he always does, it makes me want to be a better person to myself and not take things so seriously or be in a hurry when it comes to life. He makes me want to fight through all that I'm going through to become better for myself and if I'm fortunate to get to fully love him—be better for him.

I used to have this recurring dream, where I am on a boat and the boat keeps crashing through wave after wave, everyone I know minus my parents keeps trying to save me only for them to be overtaken by the waves…I would have that dream every single night when things were bad with my mom…I haven't had that dream in weeks. The dreams stopped after that moment with Randall at Jason's party months ago.

"You're inspirational, dude."

"Huh?" Randall looks up at me. "How so?"

"I honestly have never tried to do anything to help myself get out of the funk I was always in, but for some reason what you said earlier clicked—it's like you're good at this helping people shit…my dad used to always tell me to worry about the people that stayed. He would always tell me that the life I'm living is supposed to be lived in the way that I'm currently living it."

"I love that."

"It clicked that I was taking in everything and staying in my head, but there's so much I have to be grateful for…" I stared at Randall, my eyes starting to water.

So, I kissed him.

I want Randall to know that I want this no matter how slow we take this. I am all in for the long haul. I'm will not give this up. For anyone.

"Look Randall, I know we just started whatever this is shaping out to be—

"I want this too. I want you."

"Good." Randall slowly reaches up back up to me for another kiss. This time I'm able to taste the mint gum he's been chewing for a moment now and the chocolate from our s'mores from hours ago. "You're amazing Randall Price."

"Randall!" Shauna storms into our room. "I need to sleep here."

"Why?" I ask.

"Because…he…wants to have sex." Shauna says quietly. Almost as if she's embarrassed to say it out loud. "He wants to have sex."

"Wait. Is he forcing you to have sex?" Randall asks. "Because then he needs to go."

"No…okay, I don't actually know if he wants to have sex…I just need to sleep in a room with someone that is not straight. I'm trying to keep my V card until at least Christmas."

"I don't think we wanted to know that." I interject. I grab a bunch of pillows off the bed Randall and I was going to share. Randall tosses her a throw blanket and I make a nice makeshift bed on the floor for Shauna. "Here you go." I say bitterly.

"Wait. You two are going to make me sleep on the floor?" Shauna looks offended. "Seriously, little bro…the floor."

"Yeah. You left your cabin. Why do we need to be uncomfortable?" Randall asks.

"Good point." Shauna makes herself comfortable on the ground. "Good night."

"I guess we should call it a night too." I whisper to Randall. "We got plenty of time."

RANDALL

October 6th 8:00am

Cancer aside, I have so many fears for my life. I have a fear of heights, I hate steep staircases, I hate clowns, I have a deafening fear of bugs (of any kind), I also hate thunder—it makes me remember the sounds from an MRI machine, and I definitely have a slight fear of falling too deep in love.

The morning my dad died. One of the last things he told me to do was to dive into love. My dad made it a point to pull me in for one of his dad hugs and he said over and over to not be afraid to fall face first and that's what I'm going to try to do.

"I snoozed your phone…sorry. I think your mom was calling."

"No worries." I check my phone to see Dr. Rickards had called me. "I'll be in the restroom taking this call." I sprint for the restroom and dial Dr. Rickards back. "Hey…sorry…I was sleeping."

"No problem. Randall, I actually already told your mom."
Dr. Rickards makes a loud gulping noise on the phone.

"Just tell me." I say.

"Based on the scans I saw before you left for you trip,
things are starting to look up. You're still not out of the woods but
there's no need to have you come in every week. I'm going to
adjust your treatment schedule to about twice a month, so we can
keep the Leukemia at bay. Just keep doing what you're doing, and
fingers crossed we'll have you a donor before spring."

"I don't know what to say."

"Say that you're going to keep on track. No missing
treatments—just a few left before we can take a break and let your
body try to heal."

I don't say anything because this is Dr. Rickards eighth or
twelfth time telling me this. Each time since I was eight after we'd
think I was on the mend; the Leukemia comes back with full
vengeance trying to take me out of here.

"...Randall I'm not joking. In order to beat this—

"Ok. Gotta go thanks." Brandon crashes into the
restroom.

"I just really couldn't hold my pee any longer." Brandon is
doing a weird pee dance in the doorway. "Can I?"

"Yeah. Of course. Go ahead." I take my phone into the
main part of our cabin. "I'm back. What were you saying?"

Dr. Rickards takes a little pause. "Randall, everything has
to be on point. I'm doing my best to find you a donor that is a true
match. I want you to win."

"I want to win too. You have my word that I am going to do all of the things the right way." Brandon comes out of the restroom. "I can do that."

"I do also want to set up an appointment with you...it would be so nice if we hung out. What do you think?"

"Sure. I'll send you my schedule."

"Perfect."

"Yeah...well, I have to go. See you soon." I hang up.

"Hey, sorry if I ruined your call back then."

"No. You were good. Just my doctor mom wanting to catch up with me at some point."

"Oh...cool...is it cool?"

"I guess so.

"On a happier note, let's go find some breakfast before we head home." Brandon starts to gather his things. "I should've taken my shower while I was in there."

"No problem." I say.

"You can take your shower before me if you want."

"No, Brandon, you go."

Shauna rushes through our cabin door. "Why didn't you two stop me from being dumb?" Brandon pays Shauna no attention and heads right for the bathroom to shower. "I somehow ended up in bed with a boy."

"Oh, no." I sarcastically say. "How was it?"

"It was fine. He just wanted to talk about life and shit. I entertained him and then we fell asleep. I woke up to this guy fixing breakfast for all of us."

"That's sweet. Brandon and I will be there shortly—"

"Wait. Brandon is in the shower, and you are still out here with me—" Shauna looks into my bag and throws me a random bunch of clothes. "—Get your ass in there with him."

"What! No. There's no chance I'm doing that."

"Why not?"

"You know why, Shauna."

"No, I don't."

"Yeah, you do. The entire fact that I have cancer." I get closer to her. "How do I possibly tell him without losing him?"

"I cannot believe you haven't told him that you're sick."

"Shauna. It's not that simple…I don't want him to think his time with me is borrowed. His dad passed away from this. I want things to be alright before I tell him anything."

Shauna throws her hands up. "Fine. You know best…I'll just say this—"

"I already know what you're going to say."

"Oh, yeah."

"Don't let someone else tell my story for me…your mom says it all the time…she sounds like my mother. I promise I am going to tell Brandon."

"Sure. I'll see you two for breakfast." Shauna saunters out of our cabin.

"Hey, everything alright with you and Shauna?" Brandon startles me. "Shit. I'm sorry."

"You are like a stealth angel." I joke. "You're going to cause my heart to jump out my throat."

"Hey…suggestion…why don't we get out of here early? I want to show you something. That's if you want."

"Yeah. I'm down."

"Perfect. I can pack our things if you want." I spend a second quick thinking making sure I don't have anything in my bag that will give my secret away. I take my toiletry bag with me into the bathroom to get ready.

"You're cute…I'll be quick."

10:45am

Brandon and I had intended on leaving the rest of the group and heading out early but somehow, he and I got sucked in by the smell of pancakes. We couldn't resist. I'm not a huge fan of bacon, so I slid my bacon onto Brandon's plate in return he gave me the remaining half of his scrambled eggs. We scarfed everything down, hugged everyone goodbye and got right on the road.

"Hey, is that too much air?" Brandon snaps me out of my minor haze. "I can roll the windows back up."

"No. This is fine. I love the smell of whatever ocean or lake that is." I stick my hand out the window and let my hand glide with the air, wiggling my fingers—assuming that each of my fingers needed equal amounts of air.

"We're almost there." Brandon turns a corner and instantly this area is familiar to me. I have never come to this place the way Brandon decided to come. My brain starts to tighten, and I get butterflies all through my stomach. "This place is so cool."

"Why did you choose this place?" The smell of this place overcomes me. "I need a minute." Brandon pulls into the parking lot of my father's family garden.

"What's up?" He asks.

I am quiet.

"Hey, did I do something wrong?" Brandon touches my shoulder. "Talk to me."

"This was my father's place." Brandon sits back in his chair. "Shit. I didn't…well, this island is pretty small, I should've known. I'm sorry."

"No. I know. There wasn't a way for you to know. I kept it from you." I press the unlock button on my door. "But I need to tell you something. My father's family took this place over after my dad died. My mother keeps me from them, she claims it's just too hard to be reminded of him when she sees them."

Brandon restarts the ignition. "Let's get out of here."

"No. It's been a year…show me what you wanted me to see, and I'll see if I got a story for you." Brandon takes a beat. "I'm serious. Pulling up here just shocked the hell out of me. I had no idea how attached I still was to this place. Let's make the most of it before we head back home…and never come to this part of Westlake again. Plus, thank goodness they're closed today."

"Alright then." Brandon gets out of the car first and he walks ahead while I'm still in the car. Getting out the car, I notice that the parking spot that used to be labeled for my dad has been taped over.

Brandon leads me through the Whirling Butterflies and through the Coreopsis.' He grabs my hand when we pass the dying Caryopteris'. I may know every inch of the place, but I want to see this place through his eyes. I want to see what it is that he was so proud for me to see. Brandon takes a quick look at his watch and then he tightens his grip and runs through the overcrowded garden. We make our way to the Black-Eyed Susan's and instead of rushing pass them we go through them to find a huge opening. Brandon pulls out his phone.

"What's up?" I ask.

"Just checking something."

"What is it?"

"Look up." Brandon stares up at the sky. "You see?" The sight of two meteorites passes through our view causing my eyes to light up. "That's so amazing." I was listening to a playlist in the shower and a commercial came on and said that around this time we'd be able to see meteorites from this exact location and we might even be able to see a little daytime reveal of the moon." Brandon lays on the ground.

"You seriously drove all this way across the island just to surprise me."

"Of course. Stars and space seem to be our thing now and I wanted to do something that was spontaneous and cool."

I give Brandon a kiss. The electricity in both of our bodies causes me to warm up a bit. "You're amazing." Brandon kisses me and before things can go a little bit further—Brandon gets up.

"Let's get out of here." Brandon smiles. "I wanna get you home. I know your mom is missing you like crazy. We'll have more moments like this. Not here exactly, but we we'll get more opportunities for more spontaneous shit." Brandon and I take our time leaving the garden. I am all smiles the entire walk back to his car. "Randall Price. You just don't know what you've done to my heart."

5:00pm

"You don't even know how bad I needed this trip. Being with you this weekend was everything and more." We arrive outside my house. We took every detour possible. I'm sure Brandon and I could have continued this weekend for as long as we possibly could but that's not reality. "Brandon, you're really good. I truly loved this weekend."

"Since we're giving compliments, don't get me started on what my thoughts do when you aren't near me."

"I have a good idea. My thoughts do the same." I say. Brandon leans in for a kiss and this time our lips stay connected for longer than a few seconds. It's as if we're seeing who can keep this game going the longest. *Can your heart skip a beat from a see you later kiss?*

I lose our little kissing game. "See you later."

"Have a good night, Randall Price."

"Same to you, Brandon Marciano."

RANDALL

October 23rd 2:30pm

The clinic where I get my treatments have finally gotten rid of the childish paint that covered the walls. I hate the bare white walls they replaced it with. The people in charge of the paint job didn't feel the need to put the posters that reminded us to power on and to push through back up.

Now, I have to actually pay attention to everyone in the room.

"Randall, you stare any harder you might get punched." Bella sits in her seat across from where I'm stationed and assumes the strapping up position. I am probably the only person here who gets their chemo through a chest port. The nurses have my hooking up routine down to a science at this point. I am also the longest running member of the chemo club. It sucks ass because that means I've seen the most kids come and go.

"I was just thinking about something random." The nurse checks my almost empty bag then steps away to go call my ride.

"Long time, no see. What have you been up to?"

"Oh, you know school, trying to date, and have an active social life."

"How is Brandon by the way?"

"He's good."

"What's really going on?" The nurse finally finishes hooking Bella up to her feel-good medicine. "Talk to me."

"Like, there's hella passion from both our ends—I know it. But the fact that he doesn't know about me…keeps me from wanting to do more with him. Sometimes I feel like because of this damn secret, his lust for me is greater than mine. I can't even use any descriptive language when we kiss…other than it makes my heart skip a beat and my hands feel all clammy and shit."

"That's descriptive enough." Bella makes herself comfortable, she motions for someone to help her place her blanket around her feet. "Kissing doesn't necessarily have to be the fireworks we see in the movies. Don't read too much into it. You're moving at the right pace, but if you're feeling like the cancer is what's holding you back from giving yourself to him, then you have to do what you have to do."

"So, you're saying I should tell him?"

"Randall, I would never tell you what to do. It's your story. No one should dictate how you tell your story. Also, it's none of his business. You're sixteen and going through something major."

"I get it."

"So, are you going to say something?"

"I don't know, possibly. I plan on inviting him over before someone else does. It's gonna go well. I know it."

"Your lips. God's ears." Bella sinks a little bit.

"What's going on with you?"

"Well, according to my doctor I'm doing fine. I'm starting to have a little bit of a life. Oh, and my hair is starting to fall out…like everywhere. That may seem like a bad thing, but before when I would do treatments my hair never fell out and I never had those sensations everyone in here is always bragging about…now, look at me. I forgot how rude Radiation was though. She's so disrespectful. Ms. Radiation is so disrespectful."

"That's great!" I give Bella an air high five. "Dude, that's so amazing! You honestly just made my day." I notice Bella's smile disappear as my excitement for her grow. "Why aren't you happy? I'd be over the moon."

"Nothing. Just it's been two years of no progress. Forgive me for not jumping over the moon. I'll get there in a few weeks if things stay the same way." Bella takes a book out her bag. "For now, I'm going to read a good book and pray these four hours speed up."

"Well, I'm happy for you."

"Randall! You are all done for today." The nurse unhooks me from the poison machine and hands me a piece of paper to give my mom. "Your ride is outside."

"Well, Bella on a happier note…we are doing alright… and that's a great thing."

"It sure is."

"...see you in a few weeks. We should definitely plan another get together...oh! You could come see me in the school play and maybe we could get some food afterwards."

"I'd love to be there. Send me the details. Take care...Randall."

"You know what? My doctor mother gets off in a few, I can stick around and ask her to give me a ride home. Shauna will understand."

"You didn't have any other plans?"

"I was going to sit in on the band rehearsals for the play, but we have a lot to catch up on. I haven't seen you in almost a month—"

"Randall?"

"Yeah."

"Go be with your dude. You don't have to worry about me. I'll be fine. See you soon."

"Alright then." I give Bella a hug and leave the clinic.

RANDALL

October 28th 3:00pm

Play rehearsals have been kicking my ass lately. I had no idea that you could get tired from reciting lines and pretending to be someone else. Today, we started to add more choreography to the play—with the expectation that words, and movements are supposed to happen at the same time and I'm currently feeling dizzy but there is a room filled with people and I do not want to make a scene. I don't want to show Rebecca that I lack the experience she keeps whispering to other people about. I do not want to give her a reason to delay or hold up rehearsals.

Plus, Brandon is also here.

Brandon and Kelly are organizing the music for our play and since the play is less than a month away, we've been working closely with the music folks for the past couple of days.

"Randall, you were late on one of the turns. Please try to keep up." Rebecca has stormed the stage. "Also, please try to keep your sweat off the stage…it will cause people to fall."

"Gotcha. I'll try not to look like we're doing physical activity." I sarcastically say. Brandon overhears and he's laughing. Rebecca doesn't like it though. "Can I go rejoin the group?"

"Sure. Take this though." Rebecca has some sort of towel in her hand, and she tries to reach for me to wipe the sweat from my forehead. "Let me help you out—"

"No. I'm okay. Don't do that." I swat her hand. "You don't have to do that…like ever. Just please Rebecca stop throwing me off." The bands that hold my wig down was squeezing my brain, so I temporarily took them out—had Rebecca continued her unwarranted help, my wig would have ended up on the ground and I would have been forced to explain my situation earlier to Brandon than I had anticipated.

"Alright, everyone! Let's get back to it—"

"Hey, Rebecca…since Randall isn't in this scene could I take him for a sec?"

"Whatever…have him work on his two left feet while you're away."

Brandon doesn't pay her any attention.

"What's up?" I ask.

"Just wanted to make sure you were okay. You seem a bit out of it." Brandon gauges my body temperature…without touching my forehead. "You're not overheated or anything, right?"

"I'm good. Just really shouldn't have signed up for this shit."

"Then quit."

"Brandon...I'm trying not to be a quitter...plus my Abuela brought this new point and shoot camera for opening night...I don't want to disappoint anyone...also, I can see myself as an actor. Actors don't quit school plays."

"I get that."

"Quitters never prosper...remember that." I feel a tap on my shoulder. "Yes." Abiyram has been sent to do Rebecca's dirty work. "What did I do now?"

"Rebecca wants us to go over the moves before our scene."

"Sure, give me a second."

"Fine. I'll be upstage whenever you're done."

"Ok. Sounds good."

"I feel like I should be jealous...so many people want your undivided attention...Randall...I don't know...you should've told you were an in-demand kind of boy."

"Oh, you didn't know...it's the quiet ones that you have to look out for."

"Really?"

"Yeah." I pretend punch Brandon in the chest. "You should have done your research my guy. I'm gonna be a lot to handle."

"Hey, Picture this...you waiting for me after rehearsals and then we could do an early dinner of some sort and who knows you could maybe...I don't know...spend the night."

"Brandon, that offer is so appetizing…but my mom and I made plans for after this."

"Oh, no worries—"

"Tomorrow…the day after that…and the day after that…and so on…I'm all yours. Whatever you want to do, just let me know."

"You know I am…I could still give you a ride home, right? You have time for that?"

"Yeah, of course…I'll come find—"

"Randall! You need to be upstage working on foot work. Move it!" Rebecca demands. "Please do not make me recast your role."

I look back to Brandon. "I'll find you after."

"Randall—"

"I'm going. Putting my dancing shoes back on." I join Abiyram on stage and he and I are going over my horrible foot movement. It takes a while before I actually start to get the steps down.

"There you go!" Abiyram steps away and lets me do the steps to all of my parts on my own. "See. You knew what you were doing this entire time."

"Thanks dude!"

"No problem." Abiyram gives me a hug. "Shoot. I'm sorry. I didn't mean to invade your personal space."

"Hey. It's alright. We're huggers. It's cool." Abiyram's dark skin turns slightly red. "Hey, it's alright." He retreats a little further away from me. "Dude, you good?"

"Yeah." Abiyram sprints to Rebecca's side. I go back to doing my steps on my own because once again, you cannot out someone if they are not ready to come out. I nod to Abiyram letting him know that he has me as friend whenever he's ready to have a chat.

"Looking good, everyone." Rebecca says.

"Thanks. Abiyram's a really great teacher." It was my entire intention to jab Rebecca by complimenting Abiyram in front of her. "You're good too, Rebecca."

"Gee. Thanks…now from the top, people!" Rebecca commands.

BRANDON

November 5ᵗʰ 7:00am

I can feel my pillow vibrate more than I like for it to. I see my mother's name pop up on the screen. My first instinct is to let it go right to voicemail. I do not need to take her negative energy with me to school this morning.

I answer. "Yes, mom. How are you?"

"Well, I could be better. Life could be better. You could be home with me and not that boy. We could be having meals together…but you're with your friend—"

"Look mom, if you called to argue—"

"No. I called to tell you that I'm divorcing Sam." *Holy fucking shit rockets.* On the outside, I'm pretending like I give a damn, but on the inside, I'm throwing myself the biggest party. I'm already thinking about how easier and happier our lives will become with Sam out of it. "We're going to stay together though. We have to." She just killed my high. My smile dissipates entirely.

"I'm confused."

"Your father and I just feel like marriage have become so mundane, why do we need a piece of paper to affirm our love. We have all we need in each other. Pearl and Sam against the world."

Just fuck me, right?

"That doesn't make any sense."

"Your father and I just feel it would be best for our family."

"He's not my dad. He's a fucking loser who uses my mother and you cannot see it."

"Brandon. I thought you would be happy for us."

"Mom! You need some serious help. You need to figure out yourself. After dad died you completely lost your mind." I can hear Kelly outside my door…or it could be Jason. I take a minute before putting the phone back to my ear. "You always forget that you have a son, It's always Sam before me. I haven't heard from you in weeks, and you think I want to be awoken with this news."

"Calm down."

"No. How can you love him more than me?"

"I don't love him more than you. He's just easier to tolerate."

"Wow. Are you serious?"

"Yes…I don't love who you have become."

"Well, who have I become?"

"Sam says—"

"Fuck what Sam says! What do you say?" If I squeezed any harder, I swear I would've broken my phone. "What do you say mom?"

She's speechless.

"Answer me!" I plead.

"Fine. I don't love you. Not right now at least. This is not how I raised you." I place my phone on my desk. I can faintly hear my mother crying and talking into the phone.

"Have a great life, Pearl."

"Brandon, wait."

I hang up.

There is a huge part of me that wants to cry so bad. I want my mother to love me the way she's supposed to love me. She went from proud of her child to someone I don't even recognize. The way that Randall has an adoptive mother that loves him unconditionally and someone who wants to get to know him—I wish I had something remotely close to that.

Kelly knocks on my door. "Bro, could I come in?"

"Yeah."

"I hate that you have to go through that. No one deserves to endure all of the shit that you've been through."

"Thanks man…that was it though. I don't see myself reaching out or taking anymore of her calls…have you ever met someone who is so broken at such a young age?"

"Bro." Kelly brings me into a hug. "Don't ever say that again."

"You don't get it."

"Fuck her. Fuck him. Their loss. They're missing out a dope ass dude." I break out of the hug. "They don't deserve to know you anymore. You gotta get up and choose to be happy, dude. You just have to. Fuck anyone that doesn't get it."

"Thanks for the pep talk."

"I'm serious Brandon…you're happy, stay that way. Who knows, the universe may convince your mom to go get some help."

"Yeah, I'm not going to hold my breath."

9:30am

English isn't so boring today.

Today, we are talking about book to movie or television adaptions. This is the one conversation I want to enjoy but I can't enjoy it without Randall. He's the one person that I know that loves talking about television. When I hear one kid talk about how *Pretty Little Liars* was the worst television adaptions from a book there was—I looked to Randall's desk, I just know he would have some kind of clapback. He would've found a way to find a positive into how horrible that show was.

Someone in class states that *You* should be cancelled. She claims the shows glorifies stalking—it does. She's going on about how Joe needs to be the one on the receiving end of all that he puts women through. I don't disagree but I would've so loved hearing Randall…yet again, justify this dudes' actions. He would wound up some elaborate gut-wrenching plot outside of the book and as a class we'd go along with it. Randall has a way of turning bad stories into a good one. *I need that skill.*

"…Randall. You are late…that is a shock." Mrs. Chambers says. She hands Randall a pink slip. "You know what that means…theater drills in rehearsal later today."

"Apologies, I had an appointment this morning." Mrs. Chambers corrects her posture. It's as if she gives in to Randall. "The last time I'll be late…promise."

"Oh…you should have led with appointment." Mrs. Chambers snatches the pink slip out of Randall's hand. "No drills. Just practice."

"It's fine." Randall recaptures the slip. "Plus, Rebecca saw that I was late…so you know. Don't worry, I'm literally okay with it…with everything."

Mrs. Chambers takes a moment. "Fine. Take your seat young man…Mr. Marciano looks like he's dying of boredom."

"…yeah, you're right." I take my bag out of Randall's seat and scoot my desk a little bit closer to his. "This is cool, right? Mrs. Chambers?"

"Oh, of course…young love…it's quite a sight to see."

"So, what did I miss?" Randall asks.

"We're talking about book to movie or television adaptions."

"Oh, cool. I have one." Randall raises his hand. "*Pretty Little Liars*…that was the worst of television adaptions. We legit wasted seven years of our adolescence…just for the ending to be lackluster. Don't get me wrong it's an awesome binge but it was a horrible show."

"Good one Randall…someone has already done that one." Mrs. Chambers says.

"*Gossip Girl?*"

"We've mentioned it…think the response to that was that it lacked enthusiasm." Mrs. Chambers sits on the edge of her desk.

"Oh, this is a good one…*The Fault in our Stars*."

Mrs. Chambers eyes widen. "What did you like about the book and or movie?"

"That it was honest. Gus and Hazel reminded me of actual people. I love how we knew about their challenges from the first page of the book and the first few minutes of the movie. They're two teens who are fighting this very nasty disease and somehow, they figured out a way to fall in love…even though they knew it wouldn't be that so called happy ending we hope for in our books and movies. But, somehow, when Gus died…I think Hazel got her happy ending though…"

"Really? How so?" Mrs. Chambers asks.

"At the end of the movie, it ends with Hazel laying on the grass in her backyard she's reading the note Gus wrote for her, he's pouring his heart out to her, but keep in mind we've spent close to two hours watching these two characters leap outside of their comfort zones—in short, I think Gus wanted Hazel to keep doing that with him gone…Gus wants Hazel to keep going long after he's gone…yeah…Gus wants Hazel to keep living and experiencing long after he's gone. The letter is her new starting point."

"Perfect explanation."

"Thank you." Randall sinks in his seat. "One last thing, can we all agree the book was still a hundred times better?"

"We agree." Mrs. Chambers says.

"Hey, you, okay?" I ask.

"Oh." Randall snaps back into reality. "Yeah, I'm fine. Just really loved that damn movie…and the book." Randall forces himself to smile.

"I never saw it."

"What! Why not?"

"Oh, I don't know…I thought the premise of the movie was a bit too morbid. Like, I don't even know how I would even react if I were ever in that predicament…being with someone and either of us has cancer…or even worse we both have it. I'd lose my mind. I wouldn't even know how to react."

"Yeah."

The class bells rings.

"Alright class. Take care." Mrs. Chambers is the first one of the doors as usual.

"Brandon, hold on a second." Randall pulls me back into my seat. "I want to ask you a question…and be straight up."

"Alright…shoot."

"Hypothetically say—"

"Nope. I don't want to do hypotheticals with life…my dad died from that shit. Short answer…I'd lose my shit if…if you…let's just get out of here."

"Yeah, I get it. That would so suck big time. Sorry for even brining that up."

"No. It's cool…you know something?"

"No. What?"

"If we weren't sitting in these desks, I'd so lean in and give you a kiss."

"Oh, then let's fix that mister." I lay a pleasant kiss on Randall and exchange energies. It is this moment where for just a second that I felt Randall truly wanted to tell me something that could possibly alter our entire friendship but more importantly our relationship.

I grab Randall's bookbag and help him up from the desk. "Wanna come watch me mess around in the band room during our free period?"

"Yeah." I can sense there's something Randall is just itching to tell me.

November 16th 2:10pm

"Randall. This is a new change." Rebecca says.

"What. Are. You. Talking. About." I'm so winded. "Are you about to give me a back handed compliment again?"

"Goodness, No." Rebecca attempts to give me a hug.

"Randall, dear…your timing has been impeccable today." Mrs. Chambers takes hold of my hands. "I can certainly tell you've been practicing." She turns to a grinning Brandon. "Is that because a certain someone has been pushing you further to greatness?"

I take a long look at Brandon. *That boy is so fucking fine.* "No…I mean…well…"

"Someone has you flustered." Rebecca chimes in. "Opening night is in two days…you all are super close to perfection like Mr. Randall."

"Go Randall!" Brandon shouts. "He's the fucking best!"

"Language. Young man." Mrs. Chambers says as she has Rebecca usher her to her director's chair. "Young love." I can hear her whisper.

"Everyone!" When Rebecca yells a single shot of pain shoots from the tip of my head all the way down to my toes within seconds. "Take five minutes." Rebecca leaps from her seat and almost slips. No one wants to be the first person to laugh. "You know what, I'll give you people ten minutes." She fixes her skirt then heads away with Abiyram.

"I have to go make a phone call." I say.

"Go find a corner. Do not leave this theater." Rebecca demands. "We have a lot of work to do."

Of course, I disobey. I make a quick break for the hallway. "Hi, Mom."

"Hi, Mijo. Que pasa!"

"Just wanted to let you know that Brandon and I may be hanging out for a little bit after rehearsals today."

"That's fine, mijo. Your abuela and I will probably just take it easy tonight."

"Well, alright, I see you later. Te amo."

"Randall. Have you thought about having your talk with Brandon?"

"Yeah, I have plans." As I'm stealthily wiping the sweat from underneath my wig, I see Brandon exiting the theater. "Mom, I have to go. See you later. Love you."

"Hey—" Brandon pulls me in for a giant hug. "They're summoning you all back onstage, we're going to do a run with music and everything."

"Oh, cool."

"Everything, alright?" Brandon caresses my shoulders.

"Yeah. Of course." I don't want to feel like a bad person but after spending basically everyday with Brandon over the past two months, I'm starting to feel really bad. Had Brandon been any other person I would not feel bad for them not knowing what's going on with me. "Just had to call my mom."

"Dope."

"Yeah…you do know we're gonna get in trouble, right? Rebecca is crazy. She is like the worst junior director ever. That girl needs a boyfriend."

"I thought she and Abiyram were…Oh wait, never mind…but Picture this…us in a dark movie or drive thru with some popcorn two sodas…or we could share a soda. Then, afterwards we could chill back at your place and if it's cool with your mom—I could crash there."

"Oh, that'd be so awesome…the movie. Maria will never let you spend the night…especially not in my bedroom."

"I'll work her up to it. But the movies after rehearsal. We're a go for that?"

"Yeah…no, Kelly and Jason though." He says.

"That's fine. I like you all to myself anyway." Brandon is not a good winker. Sometimes he looks good winking but most times it looks like he's having a hard time sneezing.

2:40pm

When Brandon and I walk back into the Theater, I immediately notice Rebecca searching through my backpack as if I stole her last good box of red hair dye. I kick my converse into high gear and speedily approach her.

"What are you doing?" I ask. Rebecca attempts to put all of my things back into my bag but halfway through she just gives up. "What are you looking for?"

"Randall. I asked you all back five minutes ago."

"Don't deflect. Why were you going through my things?" Rebecca swiftly shoves the bottle of pills Dr. Rickards prescribed me for my nausea after chemo in my face.

"What's this?" She shoves. Now, the rest of the theater club plus the band is paying attention. "What is *Aprepitant*?" I snatch the bottle before anyone else could see the bottle and the spelling of Aprepitant—which will cause their minds to wander and lead to them googling the word Aprepitant and discover that it is used to treat nausea specifically for chemotherapy.

"Nothing. It's pain medicine."

"I have never heard of this kind of pill."

"That's because you don't suffer from migraines."

"Nope. Still never heard of it." Rebecca folds her arms and gives me a blank stare. It's like she's wanting me to spill my entire truth in front of everyone. "Randall. As junior director and future class president, I must know what is going on with my crew at all times." Rebecca inches forward at the same time I notice Brandon looking down to see what the commotion is all about. "Randall—"

167

"Whatever! Get pass this. We have a play to put on in a few days. My pain pills are going to remain pain pills and I do not want you snooping through my things again. Is that alright?" I look up to give Brandon a thumbs up, sort of like a signal for him to retreat and not feel the need to attempt to fight this battle for me.

Rebecca retreats. "Sorry, my bad." I walk onto the stage, take my mark, and I get ready for the band to start playing the opening song for Fiddler on the Roof. "Places everyone, places." Me raising my voice to Rebecca leaves her scrambling to give further directions.

When Brandon and Kelly and the rest of the band players (*what are band players even called?*) start the first beats for 'Tradition' the opening to the play, I am fully my character Perchik. I do all of the moves correctly and I recite the lyrics word for word—I even have my best Yiddish accent down. I've been practicing for weeks on this accent in between classes and my chemo sessions. *I should yell at people more often.*

"Excellent young stars! Excellent! That is all for today." Mrs. Chambers pulls a cloth from her purse. "That was pure brilliance Randall."

"Thank you." I mumble.

"I must admit, I was nervous about you playing this part, but you have proven us all wrong. You are a dream and don't you forget it." Mrs. Chambers pulls me in for a hug. "You are so strong." She whispers. "Keep at it."

I am only able to give her an appreciative look. Mrs. Chambers throws her scarf around her neck and basically floats out of the theater.

"You were excellent, dude." Abiyram approaches giving me a pat on the back like I just hit the final homerun at a baseball game. "Like, I was so proud. You really did an amazing job. We're going to be the talk of the school come Tuesday. Great job today."

"Gee. Thanks a bunch...it really means a lot."

"We should..." Rebecca motions for Abiyram to join her side. He leaves our conversation to basically become Rebecca's kickstand. She does this possessive lean only insecure possessive girls do to their boyfriends. "I was just gonna say, we should have some sort of cast party."

"Oh, definitely. I'd be down for that." Abiyram chimes in. No one audibly speaks. Everyone currently in the room just nods their head just to acknowledge that Rebecca said words...again. "Well, I guess Rebecca and I should get out of here...we'll post details about the cast party soon." No one acknowledges verbally, so the two of them prance out of the theater hand and hand.

One by one everyone leaves rehearsals, leaving me all alone to listen to the band go over the music for the play over and over until the instructor and Kelly feels that they've finally mastered the closing song of the play.

When the clock reaches five, the janitors swarm into the theater like a swat team which cuts the bands perfectionistic tendencies short.

"Ready to get out of here?" Brandon hands me his phone. "There's a six o'clock and a seven o'clock showing...which one?"

"Oh, definitely the seven."

"Cool. Let's swing pass my place and get some blankets and stuff."

"This is going to be my first drive through experience."

"What!"

"Yeah, my mom and my dad used to wait for the movie to come out on DVD and then we'd make a huge ordeal about it."

"Wow. Mr. Price, I learn so much about you every single day."

"You're welcome." I grin.

"Let's get a move on...here, I'll grab your bag...my little actor had a long day today."

"Aww, my hero—" Mrs. Chambers catches us hand in hand as we're maneuvering through the crowded parking lot. "Hi!"

"Mr. Price, you were marvelous today." Mrs. Chambers is all grins. "I have never seen you so engaged or happy to be involved. It truly warmed my heart. I have no doubt, this is what you need to be doing." She pulls out her souvenir heavy keychain from her purse. "I want you make this a career."

"Really?"

"Yes. Randall, talent like that doesn't just come out of nowhere. You are a natural. "When you set your mind to something...I've just noticed that you crush it."

"Gee. Thanks so much."

"No. Thank you. You're the kind of actor that I like to train. You're the kind of actor that makes it…anyways, don't let me stop you. Have a great night."

"Maybe you'll end up at Julliard too with me." Brandon nudges me. "How perfect would that be? Us both at the same school."

I take a second to let my inner demons do their demon thing. "…Welp, our movie starts soon, and we don't wanna be late."

"Get some rest, young men…big day Monday." Mrs. Chambers says as she pulls out of the parking lot.

6:55pm

"So, here's the thing, *Crybaby* is one of my favorite movies." Brandon says as he begins to make the trunk of Kelly's truck comfortable. "I know almost all of the words and I definitely know all the songs by heart. Hand to God."

"Oh, we'll see. *Crybaby* is my number three pick when it comes to musicals."

"Number three? I gotta know your top five."

"Well, number five will forever be *Dear Evan Hansen*…at my old school, we took a trip to New York, and I lived. Number four would have to be *Footloose*; it was my dad's favorite movie— therefore, I love it. Number three…*Crybaby*. At number two, *The Greatest Showman*…I don't even need to elaborate."

"Everyone please tune your radios to AM 450…the movie is starting in five minutes." An older lady says from a loudspeaker. "Five minutes!"

"So, what's your top musical…my mouth is watering." Brandon inches a little bit closer to me. "What is it?"

"*High School Musical.*" I say.

"What!"

"Yeah. Picture a four-year-old me dancing and mumbling all of the words then by seven and three movies in, knowing every single word. That movie was everything in primary school."

"I was not expecting that."

"I know." I grin. "But there's a small sentimental story as to why I loved that movie…in short, I was sick and home from school and that movie made taking medicine much better." One day, I'm going to tell Brandon that when High School Musical 3 finally premiered in the movies, they did a special screening for all the kids at the hospital. Some of the cast like Ashley Tisdale, Corbin Bleu, and Vanessa Hudgens watched it with us. It was so much fun. Vanessa let me lay my head on her lap. That was the one and only day I didn't have to think about any of the *bad stuff* going into my body. "It was good time back then."

"Three minutes until showtime." The older announcer lady says. "Three minutes!"

"That's cute. I thought you were gonna say *Rent* or something."

"Nah. I only just saw it in movie form and wasn't really impressed, haven't seen it staged anywhere. I'd love to see it though."

"Randall!" I hear from behind me. "Is that Randall Price?"

"You know that girl?" Brandon points to someone. I don't even attempt to turn. "Oh, she's coming in hot."

"Randall?"

"Oh…hi…Bella!" Butterflies instantly fill my body. "What's up?"

"Oh, I'm here with a guy from the club" She winks "…my dad didn't even put up a fight when I asked if I could come here…he let the kid drive while he followed but he still let me come out the house…I mean given how stressful this club is he let that kid drive…like, Joseph was flying here…going like sixty in a fifty."

"Cool…didn't know Joseph was sixteen…oh, this is my boyfriend, Brandon."

"Hi, Boyfriend Brandon…yeah, just got his provisional like a week ago…you would know that but you're not on the same schedule as us anymore."

"How do you two know each other?" Brandon asks.

"From the doctors." Bella says.

"What kind of doctors?" Brandon asks.

"Remember, my birth mother is an oncologist. That's how we know one another. She gets treatment there. She's usually there when I help my doctor mother out with Shauna." I lie.

"In short, Randall does community service and I'm always there."

"Oh, dope." Brandon says. "Had no idea."

"Sixty seconds!" The old lady announces. "Sixty seconds then it's lights out." She finishes.

"Oh, well. Randall, I guess I'll see you at your school play on Monday. Get some rest okay. Take care." I am not able to get one last glimpse at Bella. I just look up to Brandon trying to examine his eyes. I'm looking for signs that he knows that I just lied to him. Then, my mind starts to race because my mother has just proven yet again that a mom always knows best.

I pull out my phone to get ready to text my mom and Dr. Rickards that I need their help in telling Brandon in shorter terms about my cancer. I get so deep into my paragraph long text when Brandon says: "She seems cool."

"She is."

"We should hang out with her. It's cool to see you have other friends than Shauna." The movie starts and I can't stop smiling up at Brandon. "Let's get comfortable." Brandon pulls out another blanket from his bag and we use that blanket to cover us from the chill of a Seattle evening. "How's that?" Brandon tucks one end of the cover underneath me and the other end underneath his side.

"Wait. You really don't mind that she has cancer?"

"Why would I?"

"I don't know…I just heard a bunch of stories around that place."

"Well, she don't gotta worry about me making her feel like she's in her last days or anything. She didn't do it to herself, so there's literally no judgement from me." I honestly feel my heart get warm. I plan to tell Brandon my truth after the play. I press send on my drafted text to my mom and Dr. Rickards and snuggle back under Brandon.

Twenty minutes into the movie and my head gets heavy and finds its way onto Brandon's shoulder.

Thirty minutes into the movie and I find my way onto Brandon's chest. His heart beats in a calm rhythm my heart only wishes to imitate.

An hour into the movie and I am no longer interested in my third favorite musical because all I can think about is coming clean to Brandon. Part of me thinks he already knows, and I always ignore that part of me.

"Hey! This is probably the best part of the entire movie." Brandon nudges me and I snap back into attention mode. "I used to know that entire line dancing number…Kelly and I were such stans for this movie."

"Oh, cool. I lack rhythm so I've always just admired anyone that can dance well." Brandon snaps back into movie watching mode, allowing me to continue resting on his chest.

When the movie is over, Brandon and I don't rush to leave. We are staring up at the stars not minding any of the drive-in workers cleaning around us.

"How long do you think they're gonna let us sit here?" I ask.

"Hopefully all night." He responds. "Let's find our star…oh there it is…hey, Estrella."

"Oh, you've been practicing. That double l was perfect. I'm gonna have you speaking it fluently by the end of the year…just you wait."

"I would love that." Brandon inches a little bit closer to me.

"Dude, you don't have to be nervous to kiss me." I say pressing my cold hands on his cheeks.

"Hey guys, we're getting ready to let the eleven o'clock folk in." A clean up person stops me from getting my kiss. "Sorry if I ruined a moment."

"No. It's cool." Brandon says to the guy while looking at me. "It's fine. We'll get out of here." Brandon jumps up from the ground. "Let's go." He helps me up and I just knew this would lead to a pull in kiss…not as passionate but I would still get a small taste of the boy I feel myself falling in love with.

10:00pm

We are one stop light and one right turn from my street. "Hey, tonight was a blast." Brandon turns the radio down before deciding to turn it completely off. "I swear I am falling more and more for you as the days go by." Our light has turned green, and Brandon still has not put the car in motion. "Hey, so…" Brandon goes for it. We both lean all the way in, and I can feel both of our butterflies or there's just so much electricity between us that I can feel his heat with my heat.

"What are you so nervous to say?"

"I don't think I've ever..." Brandon's lips are warm. They taste like the winter mint gum he's always chewing whenever he needs to focus on something. Compared to our last kiss, this time I can feel the texture of his pillowy lips. "Wow." He pulls away.

"One more time." I pull Brandon back onto my lips. His little bites on my bottom lip makes me feel things I have never felt before in my entire life. I wish kissing with your eyes closed wasn't so weird because I so want to see him, and I want him to see me. "I think—"

"I love you too." Brandon beats me to it. We spend a moment grinning back and forth. Ignoring the cars who honk at us because they need to make a turn from the right lane we're currently blocking. "Let me get you home before you mom rings our necks." When we make it to my street, I see my mom on the porch with my Abuela. "Wow. They even wait up until you get home."

"Yeah." I turn to my mom and Abuela and give them the biggest smile. "You'll have this kind of relationship with your mom too one day."

"Sadly, I don't believe that will happen." Brandon tightens the steering wheel. "It's alright though. I found my tribe. I'm starting to find myself. I'm happy I found you...or we found each other."

"I want you know that you matter and that whatever or whichever way life goes—you'll always have a family here with us. We're your Westlake peeps." I kiss Brandon on the cheek.

"Love you." Brandon says as I get out of the car.

"Love you too." That does it. Come Monday, Brandon is going to know my secret and we're going to reconfigure our love story from there.

RANDALL

November 18th 6:40pm

Here's the thing, I am hoping that I fall flat on my face tonight.
Twenty minutes until curtain and I have completely changed my
mind. I don't think I want everyone at school to know who I am.
Plus, we have to do this play for the next five days and the thought
of having to prance around a stage on purpose makes me want to
throw up.

6:47pm

Thirteen minutes until curtain and not even Brandon can convince
me to want to go out on that stage and pretend to be someone else
right now. I know I know all of my lines and I know I know the
choreography, but I think I invited too many people. My mom and
abuela are out in the audience. My doctor mother and Shauna are
out in the audience. Plus, Bella just texted me letting me know
she's sitting front row.

"Thirteen minutes everyone!" Mrs. Chambers announces. "There is a packed house."

Shit. My palms are sweating heavy as hell.

"Randall, dear, Brandon told me that you were a bit nervous...what's going on?"

"Oh, I...think...it's just first show jitters."

"Listen, after everything you've been through...this is a walk in the park." Mrs. Chambers leans into me. "I know you got this."

6:55pm

"Hey, I forgot I left my guitar pick in your bag." Brandon scrambles through my things. "Perfect! Hey, you got this! Just go out there and just stare into the lights."

"Why would I want to do that?"

Brandon shrugs. "I think I saw it television somewhere."

"Oh, cool...you know it's not too late for us to just got and just chill the rest of the night. Some place."

"Dude, it kind of is. They're about to play that creepy play music."

"Brandon!" Mrs. Chambers calls. "They're summoning you."

"Shit. I have to go. Hey, you got this. I believe in you and so does everyone else. You're gonna do amazing." Brandon takes off.

"Five minutes everyone!" Rebecca yells. "Hey, Randall, you're gonna kill it. Plus, they give you gifts at the end. Flowers, chocolates, and other good shit."

"Places everyone!" Mrs. Chambers pushes everyone in the directions that we're supposed to be going. "Randall, center stage...now."

7:00pm

When the curtains open and the first face that I see is my mother my nerves go away. Instantly. Maria Turía Garcia Price brings me peace me no matter the situation and no matter the moment. When I see her smile from that one corner of her face (the right) it brings ease to my body.

"Ladies and Gentlemen, welcome to Crestview High's performance of Fiddler on The Roof." Mrs Chambers announces. When the band starts to play the opening song Tradition, it's go time in my brain. Marching around the stage doesn't seem so crazy to me. I'm thoroughly enjoying myself. I even have time to catch Brandon give me a wink.

8:00pm

Once intermission hits, I am the first one backstage once the curtains close.

"Randall, great job." Abiyram says. "I legit cannot believe how well we're all doing out there, you look like a seasoned pro."

"Gee. Thanks." Abiyram sinks his head. "What's up?"

"Oh, nothing. Just Rebecca thinking she has some sort of control over me at all times…like she thinks I'm not allowed to chat with my friends." I turn to see that Rebecca is sulking.

"Five minutes folks!" Mrs. Chambers reminds. "Let's close this out correctly!"

"You can come over here." I say to Rebecca. "We were having a decent conversation about tonight."

Rebecca ignores me.

"Let me go check on her. We can chat after the play." Abiyram leaves our conversation with his head still down.

"Most definitely." I murmur.

8:50pm

The last half of the play is an entire blur. I snap back into reality once it's time for Abiyram and Rebecca to perform *Do you love me?* And we join in on the chorus, after that, I tune back out and all of a sudden, the play is over. When the curtains close, we all take a moment to do one giant group hug. It is one big sweat filled hug and for some reason that doesn't even matter to me.

We start to do our bows; Rebecca takes someone else's turn, and she walks out with me instead. I know Mrs. Chambers is somewhere fuming. "What are you doing?" I whisper.

"It makes much more sense this way." Rebecca says.

"What's your issue?" I ask.

"Randall…" Rebecca takes a moment to swallow. "There is nothing wrong with me. Promise. I just really want to take these clothes off…I have to pee, really bad." Talking to Rebecca causes me to miss our applause we give to our director Mrs. Chambers so now she is glaring at me. "You have to pay attention." Rebecca teases and she hops to Mrs. Chambers side.

"Thank you all so much for coming out tonight. From the bottom of all of our hearts we truly appreciate it, and we cannot wait—" Mrs. Chambers gets thrown off by Rebecca. The two of them are having an off-mic moment. I am the only one wondering what they could be discussing that has them both talking with their hands. "Alright everyone, our Theater president has a few words she'd like to say." Mrs. Chambers passes the mic onto Shauna, and she takes a step back.

"To add to what was just said, thank you all so much for your support." Rebecca does her nervous pause again. "We have a newbie who is totally new to acting." I immediately cover my face. "Randall Price. Would you come here, please?"

"Do I have to?" I ask.

"Oh, that's right…you may be a little tired." It then dawns on me that Rebecca's noisy ass doesn't know how to let things just be. She always has to go digging for answers. "Our boy Randall did amazing, right?" The audience gives me a round of applause

"Whatever you're gonna do, please don't do it." I say softly.

"No. Randall is currently going through way more than any of us could ever imagine—"

"Rebecca, please do not do what it is that you're about to do." I beg. "Brandon doesn't know. Please let me be the one to tell him." I plead again. She ignores me.

"For him to have given it his all tonight and help us succeed is a great thing." She takes another deep breath. "Even battling something so serious. I am in awe of his strength."

I look out into the audience, and I can see my mother is a puddle. She knows what's going on. I don't want to look at Brandon.

"Randall, cancer is something serious...let us give him a round of applause everyone..." Not a single person claps. "Battling cancer actively and being in a production of this magnitude" The room grows even quieter for a moment. Out the corner of my eye I see Brandon stand from the orchestra box. I don't make full eye contact with him. "You are a true hero. I hope you are around —" Someone does me a favor and cuts Rebecca's mic. The curtains close, and the last sight I see is that of Brandon.

It takes me a moment to realize what has just happened. Rebecca told the entire school that I have cancer. She took my moment from me.

The world is frozen. Everyone is wanting to fight this battle for me.

I snap back into reality when she's the one now in tears. "Rebecca! How could you?" I ask. "What you told the entire school isn't just some ass random secret. I have fucking cancer and could die. I'm not doing alright. Why would you do that?"

Rebecca doesn't even look up at me.

"You're a bitch! You know that! You just ruined my life. I was not ready to tell anyone about this. You took that moment from Brandon. How dare you?"

Abiyram ushers her away but I am so angry that I follow after them into the pouring rain. "Randall, dude! Let's do this tomorrow."

"Fuck no and fuck you Abiyram, I want to know why she just upended my life. Why? Why the fuck—Brandon…"

WINTER

RANDALL

November 18th 9:00pm

"Brandon." I try to inch closer to him, but he steps back.
"I'm sorry."

The rain seems to be getting harder now. "Why…"
Brandon wipes his face, and the sight of Rebecca instantly turns his
olive skin red. "What the fuck bro!" Brandon lunges at Abiyram.

"Dude. Don't attack me!" Abiyram pushes Rebecca out of
the way. "I wasn't the one that did it. I told her that was fucked up.
No one needed to ever know what he was going through."
Abiyram tries to continue walking in the direction of all of the cars
and the crowd of people beginning to form. "Your issue isn't with
me."

"No! Dude! My fucking issue is with you…you could've
stopped her from pulling that shit up there." Brandon's fists are
balled up, Abiyram notices. "I'm fucking livid."

"Hey, you don't want to fight me. You're angry dude. I get it. Let's not do this. Let the school and Randall handle this with her." Abiyram turns his back to Brandon and says: "I'm really sorry. It was messed up. I agree with you." Then he walks away.

"Don't walk away from me!" Brandon says. "Come back here!" Brandon then breaks down. "Come. Back. Here." I rush to console him. His emotion takes us both down to the wet ground. "Why didn't you tell me?" Brandon forces his head into my shoulder. "I could've been there for you. I could've helped you. I can't lose you—"

"Hey…hey…you're not going to lose me." I say. Brandon doesn't allow me to see his face. "I'm not going anywhere…look at me." My pocket starts to vibrate. I'm sure it was just my mom or Shauna. "Hey…look at me." Brandon takes a moment to gather himself. "I am not going anywhere. I've been fighting this, and I am going to win."

"What kind?" Brandon doesn't make eye contact with me. "Huh?"

"What kind of cancer do you have?" He asks. "I wanna know."

"Leukemia."

"What stage?" He follows up.

"Stage 2. I don't have that many treatments left. We're at the point of looking for a bone marrow donor. If I can get a donor, I'll be in the clear…hopefully."

"Are you in pain?" He asks. He finally locks eyes with me.

"No."

"Are you just saying that?" He questions.

"No. I promise. I only get tired after treatments. I've been taking pills and they've been helping tremendously. Especially with the nausea."

"Is that all?" Brandon takes a minute and examines me. I finally notice how hard the Seattle rain is coming down on the both of us. My wig has lost its volume and my clothes are basically glued to me. "Randall, did you tell me everything?" Brandon grabs my wrist and pulls me in to examine me further.

"I don't have a DNR bracelet if that's what you're looking for."

"Do I know everything?" Brandon swallows very loudly. "Is that all?"

"Yeah. You know all there is to know. I have leukemia. I get treatments every other week—that's down from every week I was doing just a few weeks ago. You know everything now." I'm hoping for Brandon to acknowledge the hopefulness in my voice so it in some way eases his mind, but his emotions aren't budging. His face is flushed, and his head still bowed.

"I…Um—"

"One second." I cut Brandon off. "I have been fighting cancer and life for years since I was almost nine to be exact. I swear you are not going to lose me. I will never give up. There's just so much life left for me to live. I apologize for not telling you…I swear I do. I just wanted to know what life was like without someone knowing I had cancer. Each time someone found out they treated me different or like I was contagious."

"Brandon." *That deep sigh is gut wrenching.*

"No. Wait, let me finish. When we first started getting to know each other, It made me forget all about the current happenings of my life. You made me somewhat whole again. One day of not telling you turned into a week which then turned into months. I really am sorry—"

"I get it." Brandon kneels down in front me. "I love you. Just sucks you weren't able to tell me this yourself. Just promise me there's no more secrets. I don't think my heart can stand another hit. I love you, Randall Price."

"I promise I don't have anything else to keep from you. You know everything." Brandon gives me a kiss and I can taste the salt from his tears. The pressure from his body causes me to fall backwards onto the wet ground. "Brandon Marciano. You're everything."

"Let's get you home and then we can sort things out from there." We interlock hands and Brandon tightens his grip not letting go until we meet up with my mom and abuela.

10:00pm

My mom and abuela get out of the car leaving Brandon and I alone. Brandon sits with of his hands tight around of the steering wheel. He doesn't make eye contact with me, and he also doesn't give in to me when I tug on his arm.

"My mom said you can come in and stay over if you want." Brandon bites his lip and glares right at me. "Hey, I apologized. I'll do it a million times if you want me to. Please don't shut me out." Brandon shuts his car off and gets out his car. "That's no way to handle this—"

"If you wanna fucking talk, let's go inside." When he storms inside my house, he doesn't even accept my mother's hug nor gives in to my abuela's encouragement. Brandon just storms into my room and slams the door shut once I cross the threshold. "Let's talk."

"First, you know everything—"

"Do I?" Brandon sits on my overcrowded bed.

"Yes. I have leukemia. I've been battling this round of it for about a year. I've had cancer a total of three times. I've stayed overnight in the hospital more times than I'd like to count right now. Last year was the toughest year because Dr. Rickards told me that this time may take me out and from that day, I've been fighting so hard ever since. I was doing chemo about once a week for four hours. Now I go once every other week still for four hours. When, I get a donor, they'll have to prepare my body and that basically means I'll be depleted of all my energy just to receive a bone marrow transplant—the last time I went through this process was a little more than a year ago, we got so close to this being all over, and we found out our donor lied about being a heavy drinker and their horrible sexual history, and a week later my dad died because some idiot didn't know how to not drink and drive."

Brandon doesn't say anything.

"Speak. Please don't leave me hanging or in flux."

Brandon gets up from my bed. "I just don't know. As he runs his hand through his hair, I am thinking of all the things he's going to continue saying to me. "You mean the world to me. I was honestly prepared to take a break on us. I can't say that you lied to me, but I can't say that you trusted me either. I can also admit that I have no idea what it's like to have cancer. You also know my dad died from cancer. I just…I don't know."

"Would we be this close if you knew about my cancer? If I would have told you back in August about my diagnosis, you would have wanted to be just friends. There wouldn't an *us*. I didn't want to risk that."

"I would have understood."

"But we would not exist in the same vein as we do now." I reach out for Brandon's hand, and he meets me—taking possession of my hand. "My original plan when the school year started was to be myself. I planned on walking into the school as a different person, a confident version of myself. I planned this out in my head the entire summer. I was going to take my wig off—"

"You're wearing a wig?"

"Yes. Let me finish…I changed my mind about taking my wig off cause I knew I wouldn't have been able to be myself. All I want is to feel normal. That's it. I need to feel normal. I haven't been myself in eight years. That day I walked into your AP English class was the first day I felt like myself again. We would not have a history had you met me as I physically am. Our story would be different. Very different. I didn't want that."

"Randall, you don't know that though. The connection was there before you opened your mouth. I was attracted to you the moment I saw you stand up to Sarah in the office days before you came into our class. Your heart is what drew me to you. Had you came as you are into that class, your heart is what I would have saw first."

I'm speechless.

"Randall Price, you are my dream. There could be an infinite amount of people around and you would still stick out to me. I don't want you to ever think you can't come to me. Let's make a promise that from tonight on you will keep me in the loop about everything. Nothing is too much for me. Promise."

"You have my word. From now on, I'll tell you everything. Speaking of which, I have a doctor's appointment coming up and you are more than welcome to come."

"You got it." When Brandon pulls me in for the tightest of squeezes, he is very warm that it makes my body tingle. "Hey, can I kiss you?" I nod. And his lips taste like a mix of tears and the Wintermint Chapstick this boy is loyal too. "I'm glad we got this off our chest. I'll call you tomorrow. Love you more than you love me."

"Not possible.

November 25th 10:00am

I forgave Randall because I understood.

I forgave my father for giving up during his last days. Randall has chosen to fight and that is all I can ask for. I get why he kept me out of the loop. After sleeping on it for a few days, I think I would do the same if I were in his shoes. He didn't want to feel like a burden. Who am I to judge him for that?

"So, you and Randall are good?" Kelly asks. We arrive to a little hole in the wall café. We decided to take the off from school to clear our heads and maybe get some writing done since this big winter showcase is coming up. "I'm really happy that y'all are good." When Kelly goes to take a seat—I swear I heard the chair let out a screech. "I'm shocked he came back to school so soon."

"That kid is resilient."

"Yeah. Braver than anyone I've met in the longest of time—"

"Fuck yeah, they have waffles." I motion for a waitress to come take our order. "I should get some bacon too, right?" I feel Kelly's facial expression change. "What? You want me to get something vegan?"

"No. I want you to stay in your emotions a bit longer. It's like we're always conversation hopping when the situation gets too deep."

"What do you want me to say Kelly? I'm not mad at him about anything. He's a strong ass boy." Our waitress approaches our table, holding a bedazzled notebook, and chewing more gum than her mouth can handle. "He literally told me everything. What else should I be doing?"

Kelly gives the waitress the one-minute finger. "I'm not expecting a big grandstand of sorts but Randall aside, you've been through a lot in just this last year alone and—"

"And what? Do you want me to be crying all the time?" Our waitress taps her note pad which sets me off. "I'll take the fucking waffles and bacon. He'll take just the waffles and make it as childish as you can…oh, and if you all have a can of emotions, I'll take two servings of that as well…and bring my friend some mind your business soup." The waitress takes in all of what I just said then leaves the table. "Dude, I'm going to need you to stop telling me how I need to be feeling at all times."

"That's not—"

"Yeah, it is. You expect me to be emotional about everything. Here's the thing, Randall and I spoke about every single thing, and I told him to never ever hide anything from me again. My mom and I will never be on good terms. I'm over my dad shit. Sure, I miss him every single day but I'm not going to cry over it. In life you can't sweat the small stuff."

"All I'm saying is voice your emotions more, you'll be able to exhale more. You give your all to everyone. It's time you start giving yourself your all too."

"I hear you bro, but I got it." I take long and loud gulp of my water. "I'm good."

"That's the thing…I know you got it. I'm not going to stop being your best friend though no matter how mad you get at me. I only asked about your feelings because it was an observation and I'm going to keep observing cause that's what bros do."

The waitress arrives with our tray of food. "Here's…" Her voice does not match her rocker girl persona. The high pitchiness of her voice throws Kelly and I for a loop. "Here's your food. Waffles and Bacon for the dirty blonde. And a kiddie waffles and side of m-y-o-b soup for the dark-haired guy."

"Wow, thanks." Kelly says.

"No worries. The soup is just clam chowder…and we don't have drinks for emotions, sweetie. At your age live in those emotions…or don't it's your life." The waitress leaves our bill on the table making sure we see that she stamped it as paid.

"How about this. I will try to stay in our conversations no matter how tough they get. And also, do know that I'm going to keep some things from you because some things just aren't your business."

Kelly and I spend the rest of our morning deciding on my vibe for the showcase and try to map out some other places I could perform at post show so I can be even more confident for my Julliard audition in a few months. I was actually able to get through the rest of our breakfast without thinking about Randall and his diagnosis or anything about him being sick—It must've been an hour without Randall and cancer now being in the same sentence. The positive to this—is that it was forty-five minutes longer than the day before. *Baby steps, right?*

RANDALL

November 28th 4:00pm

In my house we eat Thanksgiving Dinner before the big football game. The big football game is the one sporting event that my mom watches each year—unless it's a year when the Olympics are happening. My abuela buys endless amounts of snacks and drinks and they're glued to the television for the entire fifteen hours it seems like the game is on. This year Thanksgiving is going to be a bit different. I invited Brandon over. Since he's into sports, I may actually force myself to watch the game this year.

"Hey, you've been over there daydreaming for a moment now." Brandon says. "What up?" He drops a duffle bag onto my aging bedroom floor. "You thinking about me?"

"Always." I grin.

"Awe. That's so cute. I'm honored." Brandon joins me in sitting Indian style in the middle of the floor of my sterile room. "What's on your mind?"

"Well, I'm shocked my mom is letting you sleep in my room and that she's still not finished cooking." I force Brandon's hand onto my grumbly stomach. "I skipped lunch for today...my mom makes the best turkey."

"Wait." Brandon inches closer.

"Yeah." I inch forward too.

"Do you guys eat anything special on Thanksgiving...like is there special Mexican food you guys eat?" Brandon leans a little back. "Shit. Was that offensive?"

"What! No...well, I don't think so...hmm...yup, I don't think that was offensive. Crazy that you have to even ask that...but to answer your question, we eat what everyone probably eats on Thanksgiving. My mom does makes this random ass soup...I never saw that in black people or white people movies. We also have green bean casserole...oh, and Tres Leches Cake...it's a tradition in this household...everything else is not that different...just her food is so damn bomb!"

"Oh, cool. I'm excited to try everything. Love thanksgiving. It's a special day to me."

"Thanksgiving was my father's favorite holiday because to him it seemed like it was the only day no one called him."

"Weird. Thanksgiving was my dad's favorite holiday too. He'd invite my mother's family over and I used to love hearing my mom and dad's family bicker about who made the better potato salad…in my dad's words *black people make it best.*"

"…you wanna hear a story? This may actually help you when it comes to your own race struggles."

"I'm all ears."

"Okay. So, a few years ago we were at a market…my mom asked me to go find some Plantains, but she asked me in Spanish…some asshole cursed her out…that man looked just like me…my mom didn't argue with the man and nor did she make a scene…she just said to me *se una buena persona.* It means be a good person and anytime anyone would give her the same treatment she just say *se una buena persona*…that's when I realized—"

"Realized what?" Brandon places his hand on my thigh. "What'd you realize?"

"That race actually does exist…like, when I'm home my world is multicultural…but when I leave the house with my mom and she's speaking Spanish to me, we have to keep watch to make sure no one is annoyed that we're conversing in Spanish…but then when I look on the news all I see are men who look like me either being hounded by the police or we're hounding each other…crazy, right?" Brandon doesn't know what to say. "Yeah, I have a lot going on in my brain…race definitely wasn't on mind to talk about today."

"No. No worries. I'm glad we're talking about these things. I want to know more about my other half."

"We're going to get it wrong and that's completely fine. We're just confused teens. I just wish there was a way we could be thought of as humans and humans who didn't react to other humans because of the color of our skin."

"Totally agree." Every time Brandon wants to kiss me, he drops his smile and just stares longingly at me. I assume time has just stopped for him and he's waiting to catch me in a calm state before he plants one on me. "I want to kiss you so bad—"

"I'll come back then." My mother interrupts.

"Mom!" I yell.

"I'm sorry. Was just going to tell you two that dinner is ready." In my entire sixteen years of life, I have never seen my mother blush. She looks so pretty when she's flustered. "Finish up. Then come eat."

I look to Brandon. "This moment has been ruined, right?"

"Definitely ruined." Brandon stands. "Here, let me help you up."

4:20pm

"I'll pray." Brandon offers. My abuela gives him a disapproving look. "Sorry, you're right...I'm a guest."

"It's not that, mijo." My abuela says.

"What?" Brandon nervously smirks. "Did I miss something?"

"Nope. We're just not religious...long story...I'll explain on another day. We just sit and whoever is the first to dig in...that's basically our prayer...unless you truly want to pray?"

"No. Haven't been to church in years. I just wanted to be cute."

"Randall, you better not ever leave him." My abuela says. "I will disown you."

"Yes. Brandon. It's really nice having you involved with my son. His dad would have loved you...don't you think, Randall?"

"Yeah. He definitely would. He'd be obsessed." I spot my mother's marvelous Turkey staring right at me. "I'll dig in first." I grab a bunch of slices—ignoring the gravy. I hand my plate to my mom so she could add some mac and cheese, rice and beans, black eyes peas, potato salad, candied yams, and I was even in the mood for some collards. "I have been starving since breakfast."

"I can tell." Brandon fixes a smaller version of my fat man plate. "So, what was your dad like?" Brandon takes a sip of his water.

"He was the best husband. The best father. He and Randall were like two peas in a pod. Everywhere he went Randall wanted to go...even if it was just to his family's flower garden." My mom takes a pause. "Baxter...he was my life partner. When I brought Randall home—mind you, I didn't tell him we were adopting Randall originally..." My mother takes a little bite of her Turkey. "...he loved him from day one though. Randall gripped his finger and never let go." A tear rolls down my mom's face. "I miss him every single day."

"Oh, Mija. I'm sure he's proud of how you carried on with Randall." My abuela blow my mom a kiss.

"Thanks mom."

"el siempre esta mirando…he's always looking." My abuela smiles.

"I wish he was here some days to teach Randall how to move throughout this world."

"Mom. You're doing just fine. We're doing alright." I grip my mother's hand. "We're gonna be okay."

"Brandon. How's your relationship with your dad?" My abuela asks.

"My dad died…. it's okay. He died a few years ago. From cancer."

"Oh, my goodness this disease. I am so sorry." My mother says. "We had no idea."

"It's no worry…but we did have an amazing relationship…when he got his diagnosis though he became like a zombie…then, he died. But I got to enjoy him for close to fourteen years. I'm grateful for that."

"Let's talk about something happy." I demand. I've also finished eating. My plate is borderline glistening. "Like, what are your winter break plans?"

"Oh, probably going to be working on my music. I'm going to take Sarah up on that New Year's Day gig."

"Yay! Taverna will be opening back up soon, but hopefully Sarah gives me the night off and I can be your cheerleader."

"I'm going to hold you to that…there's also something else and I was hoping you guys would allow…I'll just say it. I'm going to California in December and would love for Randall to join me."

My mother wipes her mouth with her cloth napkin.

"...you want to take him all the way to California? What for?"

"Oh, my friend Kelly is going there to record a demo for some people. He wants me to play some instruments and probably sing some of my own stuff as well—"

"Say no more...I'm approve."

"Really, mom?"

"Just as long as you clear this with Rickards, she has to approve with no conditions...and you cannot miss taking your medicine while you're there...Brandon...promise me you're going to make sure he takes his medicine."

"Oh, I promise. I'll even take video and send to you...I'm definitely not joking."

"I have a request...or pregunta...question...will you be missing Christmas?" My abuela glares at Brandon. "He cannot miss Christmas."

"Oops. I forgot to say that it was a two-day trip."

"Oh. Well, you have my permission. Randall can go to California with you next month...if there isn't anything else, the big game is minutes from showtime." My mom takes her plate and the cake into the living room and the rest of us follow.

6:05pm

We settle into our seats on our extra-long sofa. My mom finishes her food and my abuela wastes no time wheeling in the snacks. I reach right for my slice of Tres Leches Cake and scoot under Brandon.

"It's kick-off time." My mom exclaims. She kicks back onto the couch and she becomes a complete Saints fan even though I bet she could not tell me what their current record was without looking at the screen.

"You having fun?" I ask Brandon.

"Yeah. I'm really enjoying myself."

"Well, I'm happy too. Brandon, you are permanently implanted in this family. No matter what happens, you are my boy too." My mom gets up to give him a kiss on the cheek.

"Thanks. It means a lot." Brandon says with his eyes welling up.

We spend the rest of the night watching the game and trading stories about whatever comes to mind. When the game is over Brandon, and I head straight for my and within minutes he's out like a light.

"Happy Thanksgiving, Dad." I hug a photo of them then cuddle up next to Brandon.

BRANDON

December 20th 8:00am

I've been crashing at Randall's place since Thanksgiving. His mom and abuela wince at the thought of me going back to Crestview. Spending the past three weeks with his family has made me realize how family is actually made up. I've always thought that family was blood deep. I now know that isn't always the case any longer.

Seeing how Maria and his Abuela have taken in Randall and the way they cherish him; it really makes me wish I could rush through life so I could make this permanent. For now, I'm going to soak up all of the love they're giving me.

"Something smells amazing." Randall saunters into the kitchen. "I had no idea you knew how to cook. It's a nice sight by the way."

"Yeah. It's one of my many talents."

"Cool. What are you making?"

"Some pork bacon…" Randall scrunches his face up. "What?"

"We don't eat pork." He says.

"Shit! I'm sorry—"

Randall bursts out into laughter. "I'm joking. My mom likes her bacon crispy as hell. Borderline burnt. You nailed it."

"*Phew*. My heart almost sank."

"I love this version of you. You're a lot calmer. I can tell you've been worrying less about all of the outside noise. It's been cool to bear witness to."

"Some of this calm if due to you…How do you guys like your eggs?"

"Umm, however—"

"It smells really…Brandon, sweetie, you didn't have to cook for us. I can take over if you like." Maria is the sweetest and she's the strongest women I've ever known. "Here, let me help—"

"He got it, mom. Wait, until you taste his cooking." Randall hypes me up, it causes me to blush. "He's really good…plus, he cooked the bacon the way you and abuela likes it."

"Oh, well I guess I'll go have a seat." Maria grabs herself a cup and pours herself some coffee. She takes a quick sip, smiles, and I know I've done a great job on the coffee as well. "Brandon, you can never go home. We'll find you more space around here. There's a room above the garage. We'll make some adjustments. Give me a day."

"Oh, I couldn't stay here permanently." I catch Randall's smile dissipate. "Unless you want me to stay a bit longer Randall."

"I guess we can see how California goes." Randall grabs a dish from the counter for me to place the mountain of scrambled eggs onto. "I'll put everything on the table."

"So, let's eat everyone." I take my seat next to Randall, abuela takes her seat next to Maria. When I offer to make Randall's plate, Maria swats at my hand and says that it's her job. We all take a moment to breathe in the smells of the bacon before digging in.

12:00pm

Taverna got a major makeover since the last time I was here. It went from small upscale hole in the wall to just upscale. It's no wonder why newer Seattle musicians would kill to perform here. The last time I visited Taverna I remembered there being rugs and small sitting pillows on the ground and the stage. Now, when I walked in it seems like Sarah's parents opted for concert garden.

The wood floors that made this place smell have been replaced with concrete, the wood paneling on the walls have been replaced with exposed brick and flower vines overtaking the place. The bar that used to be in the bookstore area remains unchanged and the ceiling of the entire place has been replaced with glass, it really makes this place stand out.

"This place would look so legit if you're performing and it rains." I take in this new version of the space. I can't stop smiling. "Man, this is awesome." I take a moment to just take in everything and imagine myself playing on this stage in a few weeks. My pocket begins to vibrate. "Hey, babe. What's up?"

"Just wanted to get your thoughts on the updates they made to Taverna."

"Oh, it beautiful. Randall, I have to go. Love you." I notice a guitar on the massive stage, and it instantly starts to pull me in. I inch closer and closer to it, and I notice the fucking guitar is signed by Kurt Cobain. "What! No fucking way!" My restraint allows me to just hover over the guitar. I'm impressed I'm keeping my drool in my mouth. Kurt Cobain is one of my guitar heroes. "This is legit as hell—"

"You can pick it up, you know." Sarah appears out of nowhere causing me to almost topple over. The guitar angels kept me propped up. "I'm serious. Give it a go."

"No. I Couldn't." I'm hesitant. "I don't want to get any of my sweat on it."

"Dude! Its Kurt. You have to. It's only right." I can feel Sarah move closer to the stage. "Go on. I'm serious." I do as I'm told. I pick the guitar up as gentle as my emotions would allow me to, placing the strap around my body. "How does it feel?"

"Like, heaven."

"Give it a strum…is that a music word?"

"Yeah." I do what she asks, and I let my hand gently brush against the strings. Each string makes a different angelic noise. I strum it once again and it's as if my hand takes over. I keep a slow and steady rhythm playing my version of one of my favorite Nirvana songs 'Big Cheese.' I get all the way to the last chorus, and I look up and notice Sarah gleaming at me and it makes me nervous. "Sorry. I didn't mean to get carried away."

"No. I love Nirvana. Bleach is quite possibly one of mine and my dad's favorite records to listen to while we clean this place." Sarah pulls her blonde hair into a ponytail. "That was a perfect instrumental by the way."

"Thanks."

"Why do you get so nervous?" She asks while hopping onto the edge of the stage. "Don't you sing for Randall or play any instruments for him?"

"Not lately. I've only since got the urge to push myself with my music and I'm just now getting comfortable talking about music with him. I'm auditioning for Julliard...February 20th to be exact! I gotta get out of my headspace."

"First. Congrats on the Julliard audition. Hope you get it. Next, you are a powerful singer. The guy in that YouTube video was not shy about anything...sure, he had a lot of baggage and shit behind that voice but the past few weeks seeing you walk the halls at school and how you are with Randall...I can tell that you've let some of what you're holding behind."

"I guess...I guess that boy makes me fucking happy." I smile. I always smile when I think about Randall. It could be just the thought of his name and I instantly smile. "Like, really happy."

"As he should. Now, treat your music that way." Sarah turns to face me. I'm still standing so she's looking up at me. "Can I ask you a serious question?"

"Yeah, of course."

"Randall's not...he's not—"

"No. He's good. Just fighting onward and going to beat this thing."

"Oh, then good! That alone should be your motivation to power through. He's fighting for his life and dreams and so should you. Don't fight his fight for him…just be there for him. Treat yourself well too. You deserve it."

"I get the point you're trying to make. That is why I want in the showcase. I want whatever spot you have left for me."

"Ok. But, first let's do something…here." Sarah hands me a piece of paper. "I want you to perform two songs…one of them I want it to be about your happiness today. I want to hear that song for the first time at the showcase."

"That'll be easy." I grin.

"No. I don't want it to be some basic I love you bullshit. I want this song to be honest, pure, and full of hope. I want you to sing like you know you belong in this space. Oh, and one last thing…I want you to perform last. Right before the clock strikes midnight."

"You have my word. While I'm in California for the next few days, I'll work on this."

"California? What's happening in Cali?"

"Oh, I'm helping Kelly record a demo…I may record some of own stuff too. It's not set in stone—"

"You're recording too. No maybe. We're done hearing about you helping other people. Help yourself too Brandon. Kelly is gonna be this huge emo singer…you're gonna be a Rockstar too. You're good. Like really freaking good."

"Not gonna lie, Sarah you've been so amazing."

Sarah leaps from the stage, dusts herself off, then forms a devilish grin on her face. "I have another challenge for you."

"What, record a song?"

"Nope. Perform for a crowd…I'm assuming you're gonna be staying in Los Angeles. Make your way to Sunset Boulevard and perform for a crowd of random people…and before you doubt yourself…yes, you can do it.

"I'll do it. I can work my way up to performing. It probably won't be Sunset Boulevard, but I can do a nice spot or something."

"I want to see a video of some sort of public performance. I mean it…don't make me get Randall and Kelly in on this bet. Brandon, this is your time. It's time you let yourself just *be*. You've earned it."

7:00pm

"I totally agree with Sarah." Randall tosses two t-shirts my way. I'm helping him pack. "We're telling two different stories that somehow intertwine." He hands me his toiletries bag but remembers to take his toothbrush and deodorant out. "I think you should focus on your music. After all you are about to end up at Julliard."

"So, you're not mad?"

"Why would I be mad?" Randall stops handing me things to stuff in his duffle. "I would never feel right if you missed out on any of your opportunities because you were worrying about me."

"Then, I guess. I'm making some of my own music while we're in Cali." I take the last bit of clothes from Randall and stuff them in his bag. "You're everything. I mean it."

"I know. Plus, I think I would be a bomb ass roadie in the future. Don't you think?"

"Yeah. You're gonna be the loudest one in the crowd." I grab hold of Randall pulling him onto me and we go crashing onto his bed. "We're gonna be alright."

"We sure are."

RANDALL

December 21st 12:00pm

The plane ride to California wasn't all that bad. Take off had me second guessing this entire thing. The plane felt like it was barely going to stay in the sky, then it leveled, and I was able to breathe a sigh of relief. It helped having Brandon an experienced flier sitting beside me.

The flight to California is a little over two and a half hours. Which confuses me because they're basically on the same coast. It's takes five or so hours to fly to New York from Seattle according to google. *So, like, someone please explain.*

"Palm Trees." I mumble. They're as green as they appear on television.

"What'd you say?" Brandon asks.

"This place really looks the same in real life like it does on television. It's so blue here and the trees…look at these things. California is a total vibe."

"Could you see yourself here?"

"Yeah. Totally...honestly, I don't even know. After college, I have no idea where I want to end up but thank goodness, I'm not a senior."

"Gee. Way to rub it in." Our uber arrives to our hotel. "No rush for you to figure it out though." For us to have chosen Uber Black, it does not come with any perks. The driver does not open our door, nor does her takes our bags out the back. "I'll grab our stuff." Brandon hops out of the car, helps me out, then gathers our two bags. "Let's get this adventure started." I take my bag from Brandon even though he didn't offer it to me.

When we make our way inside of the hotel, we are bombarded with a herd of people all dressed in pretty dresses, they smell of spray tan, and a lot of them look like they copied the same person's wig. "It must be pageant season." I say.

"Shit. Kelly did say that a pageant was gonna be hosted here." Brandon's excitement for these next 48 hours seems to have been thwarted.

"...and we're going to make the most of these next few hours." I say. The smile returns to Brandon's face.

"Yeah...I'm gonna get us checked in." Brandon heads over to the check-in desk and I turn my attention to a mother daughter duo who are both dressed in head-to-toe blue sequins, they have the same high ponytails, and their spray tans have colored them burnt orange. "Woah. That's freaking unfortunate." Brandon hands me a key to our room. "I think you're going to love this room. Shall we head to our kingdom...for two days?"

We arrive to our room on the seventeenth floor. I do a double take when I notice that our room has two doors while all the other hotel room doors have one. "Wait. How'd you pull this off? It must've cost a fortune."

"Groupon had a discount on all the rooms including suites, plus, your Abuela chipped in, and she basically made me upgrade...she wants you to have a good time." Brandon inserts the key and opens the door extending his arm for me to enter first.

"This room is beautiful." I'm greeted by the floor to ceiling windows. As I continue to observe this place, I notice there's a small kitchen tucked behind a corner. The showstopper of this place would have to be the bedroom. The bed can at least fit five people comfortably and my abuela and mom would love to watch their telenovelas on the massive television hanging from the wall. "Thank you for this."

"There's more." Brandon leads me through the closet which opens up to the bathroom that is equally as massive. "I know that tub can fit at least two people." Brandon winks.

"I bet." I smile. I walk out of the bathroom and finally place my bag onto the bed and begin to unpack it.

"Hey, can I ask you something?" Brandon stands in the doorway of the bathroom.

"Yeah. Go for it."

"Do you think we're ready..,for...you know?"

"I have no idea. Like, my parents never gave me the talk. I was just going to follow what they did on the movies."

"Which was?"

Brandon is stumped.

"How does someone know?" In all of my time of watching teen movies, they should have told you how to know when you're ready to have sex with either your boyfriend or girlfriend. Everyone just goes for it in those movies. "Like, shouldn't it just be a feeling and if it is a feeling…I definitely have that feeling. However, I don't want to plan anything…I just want it to happen." I turn away from Brandon briefly, so he doesn't see how flustered I am. "You know what I mean?"

"Yeah, of course. I totally agree." Brandon approaches the bed, and he unpacks his things too. "Happy we're on the same page about this."

"Whenever it happens…It'll be my first time so—"

"Mine too." Brandon interjects. "It'd be my first time as well." This leaves me speechless. "You alright?"

"Yeah. I definitely thought—"

"I know."

"That's awesome."

"Is it?"

"Yes. Brandon. I'm shocked I'm even at this point and I'm even thinking about possibly having sex with my boyfriend for the first time." Brandon smiles. "I feel special."

"You should." Branon hops onto the bed and places his hands behind his head. "I waited for you. My boy was like we're waiting for Randall Price and that is what we did." He laughs. He takes one glance at the clock and shoots back up. "Fuck. I told Kelly we'd be by the studio at 1:30. It's almost two."

"Well, let's get out of here...we always find a way to pass time when it's just you and I."

"Always." Brandon gives me a peck on the lips, then heads for the door. "Come, my King. Let us march on." His accent has improved in the hour since he tried it last.

"Sure. Your majesty...right?"

"Yeah."

2:30pm

When we arrive to the studio Kelly is in the middle of a session with Jason sitting on a bench on the other side of the soundproof glass in the room. Jason motions for me to join him on the bench while Brandon goes to inside of the booth with Kelly.

"It's really dope that you came out here to California." Jason says. "Like, I always think back to the end of the school year trip where you had a legit breakdown before getting on the bus." Jason has the weirdest memory, my breakdown to get on the bus last year had nothing to do with not wanting to spend ten hours at a lousy amusement park. "Everyone talked about that for like the longest time." I clench my jar and fold my arms. "Shoot. I'm sorry. I didn't mean to bring that up."

"No. It's cool...I mean it's not. I actually had just started some treatments at the end of last year. I was having a weird reaction to the chemo...plus, I wasn't supposed to be at school since I was doing radiation too."

Jason clears his throat. "Oh fuck. I'm sorry. I'll change topics and I won't make jokes about that day ever again. Very childish of me…how was your day?"

"Dude. It's alright. Like, I don't even worry about that kind of stuff…but my day has been amazing so far—"

"Hey Randall, can you come here for a second." Brandon calls out. "I want you to listen to something."

"Sure."

"Listen to this." Brandon sits upright at the grand piano in the studio, and he positions his fingers in the playing position. His fingers begin to move with grace, each finger knowing their place. The piece Brandon is playing seems like a sad song, but it could also be a happy song, like those songs that start off sad but somehow the artists find the happy ending for the song. I think for a moment that Brandon loses his playing train of thought because he and his fingers come to a hasty stop. He then starts tapping a single key and he looks at me then smiles. I am instantly put into a trance when Brandon continues playing. The sounds he's creating are both dramatic and airy at the same time. His beat has high and low points. The butterflies in my stomach has butterflies—we just don't want it to end. Then it does and it leaves me wanting more. "Did you like that?"

"Hell yeah!" I can see Kelly's face light up in the background. "That was outstanding! I can't wait to hear the finished piece Kelly…that song is gonna be amazing."

"Thanks…but, that song is for Brandon and him only." Kelly says. "I set all this up for Brandon. I already have my in when it comes to Julliard…now, we're gonna get Brandon ready for his audition in a few months and that performance in a few days."

"Wow. That's so nice of you." I know Brandon isn't going to shed a tear, but I want to shed one for him. "Brandon, this is huge for you."

"Yeah…just gotta add some words to this. I already found my inspiration, just gotta add some more words to this piece of paper." Brandon double blinks in my direction.

"You two are so cute…we're gonna crank this song out now." Kelly says.

"I'll go back out there and chat with Jason."

"I'll probably be another few hours…you can go exploring with Jason if you want." Brandon suggests.

"Nah. I'm good."

Brandon extends the smile that's already pasted on his face. "Perfect."

I join Jason back on the waiting bench and from this side of the glass, I once again am not able to hear anything that is going on in that booth with Kelly and the other music making people. For the next few hours, I watch Kelly and Brandon collaborate on making music. I'm in awe of their friendship and how true it is. They can bounce a million ideas off each other in thirty minutes flat.

"They should just be in a band together." Jason says. I can instantly envision it. I picture me front row in some big arena like Madison Square Garden yelling their names or their band's name. I picture me leading the charge for them to do at most four encores. I can see it so clearly us spending the rest of our time on this earth being happy with one another. "They're like the perfect duo...in music."

"Is this kind of stuff fun for you?" I ask Jason.

"What do you mean?"

"Like, do you like being in the studio for hours on end? Not being able to hear anything."

"Yeah. I love it...and usually it's not like this. Kelly said that Brandon wanted to work on a special song and that he wanted it to be a surprise for you. Isn't that cute? Kelly surprised him with all this."

I catch Brandon staring at me and he mouths five more minutes. "He's honestly the best thing that's happened to me."

"I think...I know he says the same about you. Like, I know we're teens and whatever, but we've found good guys. Gay teens like us who've had a tough upbringing...we deserve this."

"Yeah. But I wouldn't call my upbringing bad...sure having cancer three times sucks ass but, my parents' blood or not...they're the best."

"Yeah. My stepdad is pretty cool. My birth dad wants to play catch up, but my best friend Malcolm doesn't like that shit." I am thrown for a shock when Jason mentions that he has other friends.

"And here I thought you and Kelly were one of those couples who spend all of their time together."

"Yeah. I have other friends. Like, an entire friend group. We're just going through a rough patch right now." Jason nudges me. "I don't spend all my time with Kelly. We do have our separate worlds."

"Dope. Could I maybe hang out with you all?" Jason seems hesitant. Almost like he's regretting even speaking to me. "I promise not to be weird."

"Shit. It's not you...It's me. Like, they are bat shit. Maybe we can start with Malcolm and then work our way to rest of the group. Look, they're all dark. You are a happy person. I don't want them to bring you down. Rich people be cray...sometimes I wish I lived in Westlake so things would move slower there."

"The university is nice...from what I've seen. My mom doesn't like it when I go near that place. What are your ideas post High School, Jason?"

"Oh, when we graduate...I'm heading right to New York...maybe even Pennsylvania. My mom went to Penn State. Think I may try my luck at getting accepted there."

"Dope. NYU or Columbia for me." I say. "I have the GPA and grades for both."

"Dude! That's fucking dope...but will you be alright by the time we graduate next school year?"

"Yeah...well, I hope so. I'm getting better every day. Things are looking up...no cancer talk, please."

"You got it. Sorry."

"No. Don't apologize, just I'm feeling better, and I don't want to make it a thing anymore. We're growing as friends, and you'll be in line to know info if anything goes array with me. Promise."

"Yes! I'm on the list." Jason jokes.

"Hey, let's get out of here." Brandon approaches.

10:00pm

Brandon and I were going to explore the Hollywood walk of Fame and get a bite to eat but the thought of just sitting in our room and ordering room service seemed like a better idea to the both of us. The television in our room has like a thousand channels plus the television has Netflix—we opted for watching Netflix. We got settled into watching *La Casa De Papel*, we could've watched it the American way, but the show is way more intense when it's played in Spanish. Brandon didn't mind because he wants to practice his Spanish every chance he gets.

We're about four episodes into the show when Brandon decides that he wants to get ready for bed. So, I pause the show to give him some time in the bathroom and he's agreed to do the same for me. As soon has he steps into the bathroom my stomach begins to do a multitude of dances. The feels I'm feeling I have never felt them before. It's a mixture of nerves and angst.

"Hey, are you busy?" I call Shauna because she's had experience with this sort of stuff. "I really need to ask you something."

"What is it?" Shauna sounds like she's eating cake. Her voice sounds like it's full of some kind of wet food like macaroni or something. "...Randall!"

"I mean. I am very much so ready to have sex with Brandon, but I don't want to seem like a creep by just walking in the bathroom behind him. I mean he did walk in the bathroom and gave me a glance."

"Randall. Why are you on the phone with me?" Shauna stops chewing. "If you feel you are ready...go fucking tell him...then when you're done tell me all about it when you come home...I'm not joking."

"Well, how do I initiate?"

"Randall. I think you know how to get things started. You're supposed to be nervous your first time...but you're also supposed to just go with the flow...so get to getting. You don't need any more advice from me. You got this...don't overthink. If you're truly ready, just go for it. Holding nothing back." Shauna hangs up on me and I spend a few moments getting myself together and the rest of my body on the same page as my very eager mind.

Stepping foot inside of the bathroom my heart starts racing crazy. Each step I take towards the foggy shower doors my nerves intensify. It is when I am standing face to face with the front of the shower door that these nerves slow.

"Hey." I open the door. Brandon doesn't flinch. "Are you gonna come in?" He asks. I quickly undress. My pile of clothes now getting splashed with water.

"You sure?"

"Come on in." He holds out his hand.

We spend a moment letting the water run down our bodies. "I want you to see me as me first." I pull my wig off revealing a bald head. "Sorry, I didn't show you this sooner—"

"It doesn't matter. You're still perfect. No need to over explain." Brandon pulls me in for an embrace. When he kisses my neck this time, I feel things all over my body that I haven't felt in my entire life. "Do you want to continue this?" Brandon kisses my forehead.

Taking charge, I say: "A thousand times yes." I turn the water off, grab Brandon by the wrist and lead the way to the bedroom. Throwing him onto the bed, I forget that less than ten minutes ago I was a nervous wreck about this. "Promise to go slow at first."

"Promise." Brandon sits up to kiss me. He reaches into the nightstand and pulls out a condom, he slides it on as I watch briefly. "Ready." Before Brandon pushes himself inside of me. He looks me in the eyes and says, "You are my everything." Then, he is in.

I thought it would hurt, there's a slight pain but the more Brandon kisses me on my neck, chest, and lips the pressure gets better and better. We interlock our hands, and he lays back on the bed and I give him permission to increase in speed. That is when it feels the best it's ever felt. We roll over and I land on the remote causing the paused television to play. "Just keep going." I say. He does.

BRANDON

December 22nd 10:30am

"Hey, I ordered us some breakfast. I really don't want to eat alone." Randall tosses a robe at me. Last night is still at the top of my mind. "Brandon, come on…pretty please." I force my eyes permanently open and throw on the robe to head to our makeshift dining room the room service people set up for us.

"What is this?" Randall probably ordered every single breakfast item room service had. "I think our biggest bond is breakfast food." I joke.

"I thought I'd order the entire menu…since you kept asking for breakfast in your sleep last night." Randall bursts out into laughter. "Eggs, please. Eggs, please. That's what you kept saying last night." His impression of me is somewhat spot on. "I thought it was cute…are you tired from last night?"

"If I'm being honest…I'm still tired. Who knew first times made you hella tired?" Randall smirks. "What?"

"I'm actually not that tired." He smiles. "I feel fine…all things considered." Randall slides my plate towards me. "Last night was everything."

"Well, let me eat then catch up to you." I down my orange juice and Randall graciously pours me another one. "But can I ask you something?"

"Yeah, go for it!"

"Can you take your wig off? I think you're much better without it. It's your honest you. I love every ounce of you."

"I guess it's my armor. I've been putting this thing on for years. It's helped me look like the other kids at school."

"Who wants to look like those people? —you're no different than anyone else without the wig." Randall takes a moment and second guesses himself a few times before he slides his wig off and hands it to me. "What's this for?"

"Just keep it for safe keeping."

"You got it! So, what do you want to do today?"

"I thought we were gonna go to the studio with Kelly and Jason."

"We did. Yesterday was a Kelly and I day. Today, you and I have the entire day to do whatever…we could even stay in and finish watching *Money Heist*…I mean *La Case De Papel*…if you want?"

"No. Let's go find something to do." Randall pulls out his phone.

"Perfect. Kelly left us his rental before he and Jason went to go visit family in Northern California. Let's run the gas all the way out in that bad boy...where to first?"

"Santa Monica Pier and maybe the beach." Randall says. "I saw that place on television and have always wanted to visit in person."

"Let's get to it!" I scarf down the rest of my food and inhale my second glass of orange juice then head for our bedroom to get ready.

12:30pm

We arrive to the Santa Monica Pier in under thirty minutes. This is something that could never be done in Seattle—even with California being notoriously known for bad traffic. I've never gotten to Westlake in under an hour. There's always a delay on the Westlake pass bridge—it's either closed due to maintenance or backed up. Randall and I share in our excitement over the quick drive to Santa Monica.

"Don't you think it was hella cool of Kelly to leave us his rental?" I pull into the first parking spot I could find. I do some strategic maneuvering and am able to fit into a tiny spot. "Like, we'd be racking up a hefty Uber bill had he didn't."

"Yeah." I catch Randall looking at himself in the mirror. "I do have a question though...how did he—"

"Fake ID. Kelly looks fucking old to be eighteen. Nobody bats an eye when he pulls it out. I think the damn thing says he's twenty-five or something."

"Nice."

We get out the car and immediately I can tell Randall is nervous. I can see him playing with his fingers and his head is down. "Hey, come here…" I kiss him on the cheek. Hoping that it cheers him up. "You're perfect…perfecto!" He smiles. "…I'm serious, Randall. No one else matters when it's you and I…except for your mom and abuela…oh, can't forget Shauna…she's crazy and I'm scared of her." I hold out my hand. He takes it. "Let's have some fun today. No need for us to be hoping we were other people."

"I freaking love you." Randall scrunches his nose to me. "Literally the best…onto the pier we go then." We hold hands the entire walk to the pier. I had no idea that the Santa Monica Pier was an entire experience.

I was prepared to see multitudes of food carts, ice cream trucks, and even a random cotton candy stand. In addition to those boardwalk staples this California pier has full restaurants. Randall and I *ooh* and *ahh* at all of the many offerings. There's an ice cream place, a seafood place, a chicken place, a burger place, a random food court, and very weirdly there's a Starbucks. Out of all the places tourists can eat at, they've chosen to crowd inside the Starbucks for a coffee they can get in their small town.

"We should get a bunch of food from some place and have a picnic on the beach…what do you think?" Randall asks.

"Sounds amazing to me." I turn my head towards the burger spot we'd just passed. "You thinking what I'm thinking?"

"Rollercoasters?" Randall says.

"No. Burgers…I just saw some guy walking around with a big juicy burger in his hand…now I would like a burger…plus, besides, aren't you on your medicine? Doesn't it specifically tell you to stay away from things like rollercoasters?"

"Buzzkill."

"Hey, I'm just looking out for my number one guy."

Randall's eyes brighten. "…it doesn't say that you can't do any of the rollercoasters. I'd love to watch you get on one."

"Ha! Nice try. You know I would never do anything fun without you. Let's go win some teddy bears instead." Randall jets off ahead of me. He makes his way to the High Striker and cuts the line to whisper to the gamemaster who then points at me. "Hey, what are you doing?"

"Your boyfriend here says that you can beat the current high score." The gamemaster says. "I'll give you the pick of the litter if you can hit a 150…heard your guy say he'd like our last dragon teddy bear." The bystanders in the line are now staring at me.

"Randall." I mumble.

"You can do it…it's just fifty more than the person before you." I take the hammer from the gamemaster guy. The hammer almost pulls me down. I may have a slight muscular build, but I definitely do nothing to maintain this physique. I guess it's just genetics. "Just go for it." I am able to lift the hammer to a resting position on my shoulder. I inhale a bit. I grip the base of the hammer, tighten my grip, and then put all of my bodyweight into the swing. "Go. Go. Go. Go. Go!" Randall cheers.

"Young man. You did it." The gamemaster moves his high score marker to the two hundred mark. "You surpassed the high score. You are our current champ. Great job." The gamemaster hands Randall his dragon teddy bear. "You two have fun, now." I wave him goodbye, and Randall and I carry on our way.

"Was it as heavy than it looked?" Randall is caressing his teddy bear like it's his little baby. "I would have been down for the rest of the day had I done that."

"It was alright." I lie.

"Let's do one more activity before we go find some food…. I know! Let's find one of those water balloon gun shooting games."

I stop for a moment to spot one for us. "I think I found it."

"Cool. If I win, what kind of teddy bear would you like?" Randall asks. We make it to the game and the crowd of people that were waiting in line spot us and encourage us to go ahead of them. "It's cool. We could wait our turn." The people waiting in line scoot to one side to allow Randall and I to go straight to the game. "I guess. Thanks."

"You young men ready to win a prize?" The gamemaster of this water balloon shooting game looks at Randall. "Do you just want the teddy bear? "He kneels to Randall's level like he's fucking six-years old.

"No." Randall glares. "We'd like to play."

"We'd like to play now." I interject to keep the man from upsetting Randall further. "We got it. Let's get this game going."

"Well, alright...wait, let me fix your water gun young man." He takes Randall's water gun and I witness him alter the trigger. I guess this is something they do to help little kids squeeze the trigger a little easier or help them hit the target quicker. "Fixed."

"No. Fix it back." I say. "Fix it. Right now."

"Brandon. Don't worry about it." Randall starts the game without the man telling us to start. He aims then shoots the water from the gun directly into the target, not even three seconds go by, and the water balloon pops. "That's one." Randall is able to pop another balloon within seconds of boasting about his first one popping. "That's two." I'm still not able to get the water to aim correctly. "That's three." Randall is two away from a win.

"I got one!"

"I won!" Randall cheers. "We'll take the big brown bear." The gamemaster guy hands Randall the teddy bear and he immediately accepts the bear and gets up from the game.

"Sorry you had to witness that shit."

"Don't apologize for other people...sometimes you know I think people think they're helping...but nowadays people just go overboard when they see someone, they believe is different from them. They're always feeling bad for us...there's no need to feel bad for me. I'm fucking breathing just like they are...you don't need to stick up for me in those situations."

"I feel like it's my duty."

"I'm not decrepit. Your pep talk earlier was enough. Plus, I got a glimpse of how good I look bald."

"You're Right. My guy is so damn fine." I take the teddy bears off of Randall's hands and we take our time walking through the pier.

"Oh, look, a karaoke bar." Randall stops in place causing me to jolt a little bit forward.

"Don't even think about it—what about the picnic idea?"

"You gotta admit that the karaoke bar would probably be so cool."

"They're all drunk in there."

"Even better. Drunk people are always honest, plus, no one can judge anyone. I bet you're going to sound better than anyone in that place."

"Fine. After this though, the rest of the day is mine."

"Oh, of course." Randall grins.

2:20pm

After about twenty minutes Randall and I are finally given a table. It's right in the middle of all the action we can see every angle of this place. The lighting is not suitable for people with bad eyesight or anyone who hates gaudy red lighting and flashing lights.

"Hi! You two. Can I get you something to drink to start…and maybe add you to the lineup…you can sing any song you want?" The preppy waitress smells like peaches. "What can I get you to drink?" She stares me right in the eyes.

"Uh, we'll both take two waters. I'll do a hamburger and some fries…Randall?"

"Oh, I'll just have some French fries."

"Perfect! Can I also add you to the list? There's probably five people ahead you. You get one song of your selection. We'll record the entire thing and post to your socials, our socials, and wherever else you want...if it's good."

"Cool... I guess you can put me down."

"Excellent, sweetie pie. I'll go put your order in and can't wait to see you up there." She winks and then struts away.

"I think she was trying to flirt." Randall says.

"That's unfortunate." I say. Within minutes a waiter brings out our waters followed by our food. "This burger looks really good."

"My fries are so good."

"You sure you don't want anything else?"

"Yeah. Those chemo pills really has a way of suppressing my appetite. So, I have to force myself to eat...really random but a doctor once told me that eating actually makes the sickness disappear. I still believe her to this day."

"Well, eat up..." I take a huge bite of my hamburger. "Do you still talk to that doctor?"

"Yeah. Definitely...it was Dr. Rickards. My birth mom, I was like eight...back then I remember her being a superhero to me. I used to call her Superwoman Christina...a part of me still thinks she's a superhero. That woman has saved so many lives...including mine...twice. We're going on three times now."

I get a little misty. "Love that!"

"Hey! It's your turn. Just go up there, choose a song, and sing till you're blue in the face...still only one song though." The preppy waitress leaves some kind of card on the table. After a quick glance the card has a link, I can go to once I finish my song.

"You got this!" Randall kisses my greasy lips. I approach the stage and everyone in the bar is clapping and cheering for me without ever hearing me sing. These cheers make my nerves disappear completely.

"Hey everyone...I'm gonna be singing an original...it's a song about my dad." A random instrumental begins to play, and I take a moment to let the beat sink in. Once I know what I am going to sing I belt out a song I made for my dad. I sang about the day I lost him. I sang about all the little things my dad and I would do together and how they made me who I am. Everyone in this place has their phone out and each one is recording this moment. Randall is beaming the entirety of my time being on the stage. This song I wrote for date is still a work in progress, so I end it abruptly. "That's all I got." The audience stands to applaud me. "Thanks everyone." The applause continues all the way till I am back in my seat.

"That song was beautiful. Your dad would have loved that." Randall and I hug, and I am transported back to last night. We really lost ourselves in each other last night. I had never been that vulnerable with anyone. Last night I had butterflies for majority of the day, and then when Randall and I consented to be each other's first, I had no idea that it would intensify my love for him. "Wanna go find something else to do?"

"Yeah. Of course."

We decided to make our way to Griffith Observatory after spending a while googling places that might be of interest to the both of us. At one point we both settled on going to a museum but we both realized how boring that would become. I don't know how to properly do the museum. I don't get people who go there just to read about artwork and sculptures.

We pull into some random theater's parking lot and have to bus it all the way up to the observatory. The bus is packed with like-minded individuals. The bus driver has to cut people off from getting on the bus.

"This is quite the experience." Randall says.

"I know right. Seattle buses are never this packed."

"Westlake doesn't even have buses." Randall reaches for one of the hand holds on the bus. I grab his hand instead. "Thank you for being cautious about my health, but we're legit on a bus with a bunch of people in close proximity of one another. If I were going to get sick, I would have by now."

"Good point." I say.

"Griffith Park everyone!" The bus driver announces.

"What time does the light show start?" Randall asks.

"Eight on the dot. We're right on time. Let's go try to get a good spot."

We make our way through the crowd of people, and we find one of the few spots not bombarded by people.

"Let's use our jackets as blankets, so we better see the sky from above." Randall places his jacket on the ground, then gets down and places both of his hands behind his head. "Brandon, what are you waiting for?"

I get down on the ground alongside Randall. "We spend a lot of time on the ground looking up at the sky." I say.

"The last time we did something like this you didn't know my entire truth. Now you do. You're seeing me as I am. Thank you for the past two days."

"No, Randall, thank you. I have never felt this full of life until I met you. I'm starting to believe in those happy endings my dad used to talk about." The light show starts above us. I drown out the excitement of the crowd and only focus on this moment being spent between Randall and me. "You're a light Randall Price. You are a fucking light, Randall Price."

"So are you, Brandon. I want you to chase your dreams. All of them. Every single one of them." Randall lays on my chest. "You deserve everything you are receiving."

December 25th 7:00am

In my house, we wake up to open presents as soon as the sun starts to rise. My abuela heads down to the kitchen and starts the coffee, my mom likes to check in on me while I'm "sleep." At this point in my life, I'm pretty sure that she knows that I'm never sleep, but I love our Christmas traditions. When my mom would close my door, I'd jump into my Christmas pajamas, brush my teeth, force myself to use the restroom, and be ready to open presents as soon as those folks from the that morning show kick off the Christmas parade.

Brandon is here this morning and in my bed. This morning, when my mom came into my room, I felt her linger. I heard her whisper *oh my son is happy*. She stayed in the doorway for a little longer and then I heard her follow after my abuela.

Brandon jumps awake. "Shit. Did I startle you?" I ask. I had been watching him sleep. When Brandon is sleeping you barely know that he is there. His stomach barely rises up and down and he is the only person that I know that sleeps completely still— it's his sleep talking that gets me. I am probably the worst sleeping companion. My mom says it's like I'm fighting wars when I'm sleep, that's how active I am. "Sorry for being weird."

"No. You didn't scare me. Thought I overslept. Can't wait to show you what I got you." Brandon kisses me. "Oof. Morning breath. My bad."

"No. It's no big deal."

"If it's no big deal. Then, kiss me again." I lean down to reach his lips and he sits up to take charge over this kiss. "I better stop myself before your mom kicks me out."

"Yeah. We also better get moving before my mom forces us out of bed." Brandon heads for the bathroom, while I quickly make my bed then head downstairs. "Good morning, Mama." I don't get tired of giving my mother hugs. "Merry Christmas."

"Merry Christmas, Mijo. How'd you sleep?" She asks.

"Oh, fine." My abuela is holding two gift boxes.

"Where's Brandon?" My abuela asks. "I want you both to open your gifts at the same time." My abuela has two medium sized boxes in both her hands. In one hand there is a blue box and in the other hand there's a white box. "Brandon! Oh, Brandon—"

"Hi, good morning." Brandon walks into the kitchen. "Merry Christmas, everyone." He gives my mom and abuela a kiss on the cheek.

"Oh, great! Open your first presents." Brandon and I both accept our boxes. "I hope you love them." My abuela stands proud of her gift. I open my box to find a bracelet with all kinds of intricate beading interwoven together. There's also a charm with the letter B on it.

"Oh, I love it!" I say.

"The B on your bracelet is for Brandon...and the R is for Randall. My parents would make these bracelets for all of the new lovers we had join the family. I'm so happy to be finally sharing this tradition with you two." My abuela picks up her coffee cup and takes a sip. "...Brandon, I am so happy that you chose him."

"Oh...I think Randall chose me." Brandon grins. "Do you have one of these?" He asks my mother.

"Let's go into the living room." My mother says.

"Where's your tree?" Brandon asks.

"Who has time for that?" I say. "We tried having a tree but then it stayed up till Easter one year and we decided to never get another tree."

"I get it. My mom used to put the tree up the day before and take the tree down the day after Christmas...so much wasted labor." Brandon says.

"Alright you two, I found the bracelet your abuela made for me." My mom hands me an even better-looking bracelet than the one I had just received. Her bracelet is a mix of beads, charms, and a name plate with my dad's name on it.

"Wow...wait, when did you meet dad?" I ask.

"I was maybe nineteen. I met him on Christmas eve actually. Your abuela and papa were meeting me at the airport. My tire popped. I sat on the side of the road for maybe twenty minutes. Baxter was the only one to stop for me…the rest was history. I got thirty years with him." My mom hands me her bracelet. "Do you want it, mijo?"

"I couldn't. I have all of his other things." My mom sticks her bracelet into her pocket. "It's yours. Plus, I have my own now."

"Let's open these presents." My abuela says. "Brandon, did you want to start?"

"Yeah. Of course." Brandon gets up from the couch and picks up a box wrapped in red paper. "This is for you Randall…I saw it and I instantly thought of you." I take my time opening his present. "What do you think?" I pull the remaining paper off to see that it is a first edition of Jane Eyre. "I don't think it's an actual first edition…I saw it on eBay—"

"I love it." I inhale every inch of this book. I take in the red binding on the book, the smell, and I take a small moment to look at all of the old pages of the book. "How'd you know?"

"I figured that this book would make an excellent addition to your future bookstore or library." Brandon says. "I also saw you have a worn-out version on your nightstand. Plus, the quotes in your room. I just figured. And you're always walking around with a book. When do you read them?"

"Sometimes I just carry around a book. It's really weird. I know. It was something my abuelo and dad did."

"Nice. Way to honor them."

"In terms of Jane Eyre, I read this book for the first time four or five years ago when I in treatment. It was a great escape for me...the book is about an orphan, and it is very dramatic but It's my favorite book in the entire world. I feel like I can relate somewhat to Jane." I get up and hand Brandon his present. "I hope you like it."

I couldn't get my mind to focus long enough to sit and take the time to wrap his present, so I put it in a gift bag and wrapped in with a bunch of tissue paper. "Dude. Thank you." I got Brandon an actual songwriting book and some headphones. "I have been meaning to get myself one but have been too lazy to do so...thanks so much. These headphones will come in handy when practicing. Gonna go everywhere with both—just like you do with a book."

"Nice." I wink.

"Let me go get my camera." My mom says. "Don't move."

"This is my favorite Christmas." My abuela says. "Brandon, you have truly put a permanent smile on his face...thank you." My abuela tries so hard to be tough. "I'm happy you're here."

"No, thank you all so much." Brandon says.

"Alright. Randall and Brandon scoot close." My mom pulls out her polaroid. "1...2...3...Say cheese." She snaps the photo, pulls the film out and snaps another one. "Now, let me get my phone. "Ready, you two?"

"Mom."

"Randall. Just one more photo." Brandon pulls me into a hug. "Got it…I think this may be my new lock screen."

"Mom. Don't be weird…at least make it your screensaver." I joke.

"Parade is starting." My abuela says. "Everyone on the couch. I'll go get breakfast."

"I can help—" Brandon says.

"We don't do a big breakfast on Christmas…just cereal and juice…don't ask. We have some weird ass traditions." We all kick back onto the couch just as the first float makes it way down the street.

December 31ˢᵗ 7:40pm

Randall and I decided to go for a walk around his town. I wanted to actually see this place and understand why it is so cherished to most Washingtonians.

Westlake is a lot slower and serene. No matter where you walk on this island you can always find a spot to just look at the water. Randall lives within walking distance of the main streets of town. Restaurants and bars line the streets of Westlake, but the main draw during the evenings would have to be Taverna. That place stays packed during its peak concert season and with them opening back up tonight, the streets are lined with cars and people, and I can even hear ferries announcing their coming and their going.

"Why does the water look clearer in Westlake?" I ask. Randall and I settled for a spot right off of main street that leads us to the highest point in all of Westlake. "Everything looks so muddy in Crestview."

"I guess it's because...I actually do not know." Randall laughs. "I've actually never taken the time to study or even really look at the Washington water."

"Why not?" I ask.

"Because, then I'd have to pee...like I have to do now." He says.

"Honestly, don't even blame you." I say. "Shit. Now, I have to pee."

Randall laughs.

"Picture this...me on stage and I'm killing it and then afterwards we—"

"Chill someplace." Randall interjects.

"Yeah. I was thinking my place." I say.

"I'm down." He says.

"Well. Cool...to Taverna!" I exclaim.

11:15pm

"What are you thinking about?" Sarah asks. She catches me staring into the mirror. "You look like you're in serious deep thought." I don't have any performance rituals. I try to just go with the flow of the audience but tonight I am singing two songs that are very personal to me. I don't want to disappoint anyone. "Hey, talk to me."

"I guess I don't want to fuck this up."

"You're not going to mess this up."

"You don't know that."

"Who are you nervous about disappointing?" Sarah asks. That is a good question. I know I'll always have Randall, Jason, and Kelly in my corner but even though my mom nor dad are here I still feel like I have to be great. I at least owe them that. "Randall has been out there smiling for hours. Kelly, I'm sure he doesn't care how it goes down as long as you're having fun." Sarah removes the pin from her sweater and gives it to me.

Sarah hands me her very gaudy pin. "What's this for?"

"It's my good luck pin." She says while helping me add the pin to my shirt. "This pin has gotten me through so many nerve-wracking moments. Obviously, I came out on top…on a serious note, everyone is going to be so proud of you no matter what…just go out there and sing your truth."

"Yeah." I take one last look at the open page of my song book to internally remind myself that tonight is the first night I make tonight about me. This is the first night I get to show most of Seattle, that I am going to start living out my dreams. "I think I'm good."

"Great. I originally came backstage to tell you that you're up. They're out there waiting for you…just go out there and play to the audience." Sarah says. She pats me on the back and starts to walk away from me. "…and if you can't think of anything else…think about the love in your life, your friends, and all the things that makes you happy…I heard that's what Cobain did before a show." Sarah leaves out the room.

I inhale a few times, look myself in the mirror, and then exhale. "It's for all of us." I whisper. I get up from my seat and start to make my way to the stage. The closer I get to the stage the harder the vibrations become. I can feel the floor shaking. I can hear the heard cheering and when I listen closer, I hear that they are chanting my name. "All this for me." I murmur.

"Give it up one more time for my best friend, Brandon Marciano." I hear Kelly say. When he spots me at one end of the stage, he rushes to meet me and pulls directly onto the stage. "You're gonna kill it!" He says thinking he's off mic. "Everyone! Brandon!" Kelly hands me the mic and then he walks off stage joining a beaming Randall front and center.

"You're going to be great." Randall mouths.

"Hey everyone!" My guitar…Kurt Cobain's guitar gives off a screeching noise which causes my nerves to shoot through the roof. "Shit." I say out loud.

"You got this!" Randall yells. We lock eyes and I see him mouth *just you and me* and it snaps me back into the moment.

"Sorry about that everyone…who wants me to slow things down a bit?" People begin to cheer which mind boggles me because who wants to come to a concert that has been upbeat for three hours and the second my sappy ass hits the stage I slow things down, but this crowd seems to want to know what I'm gonna be singing about. Taste is an awesome thing. "Let's do this."

I don't intro my song because I don't want to tell the audience what this song is about. I want them to experience the song for themselves. In this song, I'm singing about hope and how I want to inspire myself to chase my dreams. This song was about the hope my dad had for me…the dreams my mom had for me before she met Sam. I talk about a moment that I never shared with Randall. I told this group of strangers how I had a dream that the love I had for a past friend was never reacquainted the way I had intended. This song was called *Loss of a lot of things*.

I end my first song to screams and people swooning. I look over the crowd and see all the couples have now bundled up. The lights in Taverna dim further down and somehow the only person I can still see clearly is Randall. "This next song…" I start to say but as soon as I open my mouth the audience starts to whistle and applaud. "This next song is about…" Kelly leads the crowd in applause. "Alright. Alright…this next song is for my guy…and it goes a little something like this…"

For this song about Randall, I sing about how the first time I met him how I knew he was going to shake my life up. I spoke about the first time I knew I wanted to kiss him—it was the moment at Jason's party when he and I played in the sprinklers. I'm telling the audience how I feel when we go hours without updating the other one. I then start to tell Randall how he makes my heart flutter and jump when he gently touches my wrist. I'm telling Randall how I've learned about life, love, and identity because of him.

I end the song by telling Randall that no matter where life takes us, he'll always be the first person I ever loved unconditionally and wouldn't mind an outcome that wasn't planned in my brain. This song was called *Happy endings aren't for suckers.*

"Everyone give it up for Brandon! You're going to be seeing more of him around here at Taverna." Sarah says.

"They are." I ask.

"Yes." She says. "He's going to be our go-to when we need a swooner in the mix." She says to the crowd. "Before we count it down…let's give it up one more time for Brandon Marciano." Sarah forces one of my arms up into the air as if I had just won a boxing match. "Great job." She whispers. "Now, go hug your guy."

Walking off the stage and Randall being the first person to greet me is everything. His hug warms me up immensely. The sight of him reminds me of how lucky I have become. His unconditional love of me and mine of him, has made me believe in so much more than love.

"You were amazing! I'm your number one fan." Randall says. "You freaking killed it." Randall presses his lips gently against mine. "Wanna get out of here?"

"I think you read my mind—" I say.

"HAPPY NEW YEAR!" Sarah yells into the mic. Instantly, I see fireworks going off above my head. The addition of the glass ceiling at Taverna was the perfect idea.

"This is gorgeous." Randall says looking up.

There are bursts of red, blue, orange, and green fireworks. "You all enjoy the rest of your night and be safe." Sarah finishes before leaving the stage.

"So, you wanna jet to my place?" I ask.

"Yeah." Randall stretches his hand out to me.

1:15am

When Randall and I make it back to my place, we go back to my room. I can tell Randall is thinking the same thing as I am, but he just wants me to initiate. I spend a moment taking in his fresh soap scent. I watch Randall as he starts to unbutton his shirt. He then starts to push my jacket off; I help him finish the job.

"Brandon...It's okay." Randall says. "I want to if you do." I start to kiss his neck and then his hand is on my belt buckle, and I unzip it for him. It's a team effort for us getting undressed. I help him take an article of clothing off and he helps me do the same. Soon, there's a pile of clothes all over my floor. "Start slow." He says.

"I promise." With me taking charge, I can feel my body fill with so much intensity, but I tame it by focusing on Randall. As Randall goes slow and steady, the intensity in both our eyes grow. I can feel all of him in this moment. "I love you so much." I say. When I finish there is no awkward disconnection. Randall clings to me for a moment and we both lay still until our heart rates have evened. "I love you." I state again.

"I love you too." Randall gets up and heads for the shower. I follow.

RANDALL

February 14ᵗʰ 10:00am

Brandon and I will not be celebrating Valentine's Day. That is not a holiday either of us subscribes to. We blame our distaste for not liking the idea of using one day to tell the person you're in love that you love them by showering them with gifts you can get literally any other day of the week.

This morning in Theology, we're talking about the laws of attraction…how very random. Our teacher Ms. Gelchin spends the entire first hour of the class talking about actual attraction to humans as opposed to the pseudoscience Law of Attraction— which is just the thought that thinking positive things will bring positive things into your life. Ms. Gelchin is going on and on about all of the ways we're ruining the holiday of Valentine's Day.

"Hey, are you even following what she's saying?" Abiyram asks. "She's been rambling for quite some time."

"I tuned her out about ten minutes ago…once she started talking about trees mating…that took me out of the conversation." I say. Abiyram bursts out into a loud obnoxious laugh. I'm embarrassed for him. The whole class turns to look at him in the back of the class and all I can do is feel secondhand embarrassment for him. "Dude, they're staring." I whisper.

"*Mmph*. Sorry class." He sounds dry. "It will not happen again."

"Your darn right, Randall…can you give us your example of law of attraction?" Ms. Gelchin asks.

"I actually wasn't the one laughing." I say.

"Ok. Example please." Ms. Gelchin folds her arms. "We're all waiting."

"Alright. Fine. Umm…My hair is going to grow back very soon…" I point to my very bald head. "…My cancer will be gone by my birthday." Everyone in the class has a blank expression on their face. "You all…I was telling a joke."

"Mr. Garcia—" Gelchin starts.

"Price." I interject.

"Mr. Price…I don't like that kind of humor. You did serve the point of the example but please no more dark humor."

"Si." I say. "I won't ever do it again. Promise."

3:00pm

When school let out, I asked Brandon to drop me pass Bella's house.

She sent me a very concerning text and in the short time that I've known her she's never spoken or typed with doubt. Bella has always been that person to get me through treatment. She has been my person that I vented to when I talked about my dislike for chemo and how the chemo pills taste like uncooked rice. She always helped me see the bigger picture about all of this treatment. Without her, I do not think I would be so close to finishing my treatments.

"Give Bella my best." Brandon says. "Let me know if you need a ride. I'll be around…gonna go meet Kelly at the library."

"Cool. I'll let you know." I get out of Brandon's car and start to walk towards Bella's house. Her house is twice the size of mine. It looks straight out of a magazine. Two big green bushes border her family's white farmhouse style home. My favorite part is the brick driveway. I don't typically see brick driveways in Crestview. When I approach the door, her dad opens it for me. "Hello, sir."

"Hey, Randall. Happy to see you…she's in her room."

"Excellent." I am greeted by a large grand entryway. There has to be a hundred photos lining the walls all the frames varying in size. "Sir, where's—"

"Oh, apologies. Her room is right upstairs." Her dad says.

"Thanks." I make my way up the large staircase. When I make it to the top of the stairs, I see Bella's door wide open, I invite myself in. "Hey, what's up?"

"Oh, nothing. Just stressing the fuck out." She says.

"Why? Your text had me nervous. I thought something had happened or you were thinking...never mind what I was thinking...you just scared me that's all."

"Well, I'm sorry to have scared you." Bella looks down breaking her eye contact with me. I sit in a chair across from her bed. "Randall, you can share the bed with me...we're cancer buddies. Sterile is our thing."

"I'll stay put...seriously, what's up?" I say.

"The treatments aren't working." She says. "Dr. Rickards told my dad and I today. They're trying to figure something out...but I told them..."

"What'd you tell them?" I ask. Bella doesn't look at me. She goes back to picking with her fingers. "Seriously, what'd you tell them?"

"That I don't want to do treatments anymore." She says.

"What?" I whine. I join her on her bed. "Why would you do that?" I ask.

"It's my choice now. In a few weeks I'll be eighteen...it's my decision. This isn't how I was meant to live my life...I'm ready for what's—"

"No. I don't think I want to hear that." I say.

"Well, Randall. It's my choice. I've already made up my mind. I cannot put my body through that again...look how much I weigh...look at that number." She shoves a paper from off her nightstand into my face. "See!"

"I don't know what to say. From our phone conversations I thought everything was alright. I just...I don't know."

"I weigh ninety pounds…ninety. Freaking. Pounds. That's it. In my old life, I was an entire soccer player. I got to live and play and cry because television was sad, I got to have a boyfriend. Now, look at me…I'm over it."

"Please don't give up. Think about the possibility of life though. You just have to think positive…do it with me…" I hold out my hand for her to grab it. "Bella, please."

"Randall. You fight. I don't have it in me to do this anymore." She says.

"You don't mean that." I say. Tears starting to stream down my face. "We can beat this together. Hear all the options." I realize the truth from looking her in her eyes. There is a look I know all too well within the cancer community. When the doctors have exhausted all options and we know when it's time to hang up the towel our eyes go numb, they don't move, there are no tears, our eyes just become calm, and our bodies remain calm.

"What options? Seriously, Randall…what options?" Bella holds my head up. "There's nothing they can do…it's all throughout my body."

"Oh. No." I calmly say.

"My dad has promised to invite you and Brandon to the funeral." She says. "Please don't think about this for too much…get out there and love on your boyfriend."

"Ok." I force any last remaining tears back into my face.

"Promise me one thing though." She says.

"Yeah. Anything." I say. My pocket starts to vibrate.

"Let's hang out once more before…you know."

"You got my word." I take a look at my phone and it's Doctor Rickards. Bella sees her name splash across my phone. She nudges me to answer it. "Hi. What's up?"

"Hi, Randall. I was hoping that you could swing pass my home. I have something I need to share with you, and it cannot wait." Doctor Rickards says.

"Yeah. Of course." I say. I disconnect before she can say anything else. "Sorry about that." I say to Bella.

"No worries. Take care of yourself." She says. We embrace for way longer than either of us had intended. "I'm sure I'm going to remind you of this…but Randall…please live your life. Don't be like me and let cancer become a part of your identity."

"I promise." Leaving Bella's room seemed so final. I can't help but want to breakdown. I hold it together just long enough to leave her house and cross over into public domain and I immediately leap right into Brandon's car.

"Hey, what's wrong?" Brandon asks.

"She's going to die." I say. "Bella's cancer has spread to her entire body. There's nothing the doctors can do for her anymore." Brandon pulls me into a hug. "I am tired of losing friends."

"I know." Brandon says.

"This fucking sucks. It sucks so fucking bad." I say.

"I know." Brandon continues to rubs my back. "Sorry, I don't have anything better to say."

"It's alright. I just want to be done with this cancer. I wish life hurry up and grant my wish to be healthy. I'm growing impatient."

Brandon shakes me. "Hey. You're going to beat this." He says. "I don't ever want you doubting again. I know I don't know what you're going through…but I don't ever want you to doubt your life ever again." Brandon smiles. "You're a superhero, don't you know?"

"Yeah. I'm a superhero." I say.

6:15pm

When I get to my doctor mothers house, I notice my mother pacing outside of her home. She walks from one end of Dr. Rickards porch to the other end and repeats the process. She seems to be on edge about the news we're about to receive.

"Hey, I don't have to go in." Brandon says. "Your mom is here." My mother spots his car and stops pacing. She gathers herself then motions for me to get out of the car.

"You have to come." I tug on Brandon's shirt collar. "I need your support. Whatever it is I want you to know."

"Alright." Brandon says. We both get out of the car the same time Shauna shows up to her house. She blocks her mother's car in and hops right out of the driver's seat.

"Hi! Randall and Brandon!" Shauna yells.

"Hey." Brandon says.

"Hi there!" We make it to the porch and Shauna lets us in. The door opens to a very nervous Dr. Rickards staring at her fireplace. "Hi, Dr. Rickards…I mean, Christina."

"Oh, Randall. How are you? Brandon and Maria, it's nice of you all to join him…I'll cut right to it…. I'm a match." I am in shock. I don't know how to react to the news. In all of the years I've battled my form of cancer. I have never heard someone tell me that they were a match. I waited for this day for years and to know that this entire time the woman that birthed me was my match almost sends me. "I found out today."

"What does this mean?" My mother asks. "You're his doctor. You can't simply operate on him. Don't get his hopes up."

"I won't be operating on him. My colleague will." Dr. Rickards says.

"Are they good?" My mother asks. Meanwhile, Brandon is overwhelmed and goes to take a seat on the couch next to Shauna. "Christina…is he the best like you?"

"Yes." Dr. Rickards says. "One of the best in Washington. He has a very high success rate almost all of his patients have entered into remission…Maria, this is a good thing. Randall will be just fine…the biggest issue is how tight the schedule is." Dr. Rickards makes her way into the kitchen.

"What do you mean?" I ask.

"The procedure is in a few weeks." Dr. Rickards says.

"How soon…wait, will I miss school?" I ask.

"Yes." She says. "The procedure needs to happen in the next couple of weeks."

"That means, I have to—"

"Yes, Randall. You'll need to check into the hospital tomorrow night."

"Tomorrow!" My mom screeches. "That's just not enough time…" The shock almost causes my mom to go into a full-on tailspin. "Thanks Christina, this is what we've been asking for. Will he be isolated?"

"From other patients, yes. From you all, no. That is why these next few days, you all need to keep yourselves healthy and away from germ infested situations. My team is going to check your temperatures every single day while he's doing the chemo and radiation treatments. After the procedure I'm going to get on all of your nerves for at least a month…if any of your temperatures are slightly high, I've instructed my team to keep you all away for two weeks. Watch what you do for the next few weeks."

"Cool. An entire month and some change of staring at four walls." I'm not really excited about the month plus I'll be in the hospital. It's the flip side of this hopefully being behind me that I look forward to. "Well, at least I'll be close to the end of all this."

"Yes, just think come April you'll be able to live a normal life…in 30 days you'll be able to have a future…even better envision a future for yourself." Dr. Rickards takes my mother's hand. "Maria, we are going to take good care of Randall and when I'm cleared to go back to work after my procedure, I'll step back in and take over."

"Well, alright. It's what has to happen." My mom says. "We're almost at the finish line."

"Yeah." I say.

"So, tomorrow, you're going to pack a bag enough for a month and we'll start the preparation." Dr. Rickards turns to face Shauna and Brandon both sitting on the couch. "You two...it's going to be very important that you're there as often as you can...Randall and Maria are going to need it."

"Of course...Ms. Rickards." Brandon says. "I'll be there."

"And you know I'm going to be there for my little brother." Shauna says.

"Anything else before we eat?" Dr. Rickards asks.

"Will I still get to ring the bell?" I ask. "That's all I want to do."

"Yes...I'm going to leave it at that." Dr. Rickards grins. "Now, let's all grab a dish and head to the table." We all pick up one of the dishes on the kitchen island and go into the dining room.

"Hey, how are you feeling about all this?" I ask Brandon.

"Oh, I'm feeling fine. This is your last stop and I just know this will be your happy ending." Brandon says. "You're going to be able to live the life you've missed out on." Brandon gives me a kiss and starts to walk ahead of me into the dining room. "Come on now...we gotta start planning our futures."

RANDALL

February 15ᵗʰ 9:00pm

I am not anxious as Brandon drives my family and I to the hospital where I'll be living for the next few weeks. All I can think about is how I am almost to the end of this journey. I keep telling myself just four more weeks of treatments, four more weeks of having my life disrupted by this disease. In just four short weeks, I'll finally get to sit and plan my future and it actually mean something.

When Brandon pulls into the valet section of the hospital Dr. Rickards and Shauna are standing outside to greet us. This makes me warm inside.

"Hi, are you ready?" Shauna wraps her long arms around me. Pulling me in tightly. Her puffy hair covering my eyesight momentarily. "That was a dumb question, I know you're ready for this be all over." She lets go giving way for Dr. Rickards.

"I'm so happy that we are at this point. Let's get you checked in." We follow Dr. Rickards through the main floor of the building, which resembles a very sterile Disney Land or a very basic Sesame Place. "This facility was originally built for kids a lot younger than you."

"No. It's alright…I love the drawings of bears and birds on the walls…and all of the coin operated machinery." I say. The walls are covered with paintings of rainbows, smiling bears, and birds that also seem to be smiling as well. "It's very Disney Junior." I joke.

Dr. Rickards leads us to the nurse's station. "This is nurse Tina. She'll be taking care of you for the majority of your time here." Nurse Tina has freckles covering her face and neck. Her hair is cut short and her ears poke through. "Once the treatments start, she'll be the only one of close proximity to you. So, be nice."

"Wait. I thought you they were going to allow us in the room." My mom says.

"And you will be. Just for treatment's sake, we don't want to take any chances. So, all visits will be done without touching and at a distance. After the procedure, the nurses and doctors will loosen the strings as his body reacts to the transplant." Dr. Rickards hands me a clipboard with pages of itineraries. The next few weeks have been planned all the way down to showering time. "I know it's a lot."

"No. It's alright. Just a few more weeks of this." I say. "In just a short time, this part will only be a memory." Nurse Tina takes the bags I'm carrying from out my hands.

"Let's take you to your room." Nurse Tina says. "I think you're going to like it."

"So, no touching you for over a month." Brandon takes possession of my hand. "Man, that's gonna be fucking hard."

"Only a short period of time." I say.

"Yeah, then, we're gonna spend all day touching…if you know what I mean." Brandon smirks. "I'm gonna be here every single day."

"Oh, you don't—"

"What do you think?" Nurse Tina welcomes us to my isolated room. This room is extremely white. The only places not covered in plastic are the drawers and the television. I notice a plexiglass wall by the window, and I go to stand behind it. "Yup, you guessed it…when your family visits they must be behind this wall."

"I get it." I shrug. "It's for my protection."

"Exactly." Nurse Tina motions for Shauna to help her unpack my things. "We promise this measure is just for the first weeks, while he's doing the chemo and radiation. His body is going to be very vulnerable. We're taking any and all precautions."

"Do I at least get to give my boy a hug before his stay commences?" My mom asks.

"Yes, Maria. As his mother…as his mom, you're entitled to staying the entire time but because of your work come as frequent as you want…just behind the glass" Dr. Rickards says.

"Amazing." My mom tosses her bag onto the couch. "What about his Abuela and Brandon?"

"We'll work on something." She winks. "Everyone don't worry. Nurse Tina is excellent at her job. Pass her your contacts and the minute he's able to have long term visitors other than Maria, she'll let you know." Dr. Rickards gives me a hug and she kisses my forehead.

"...and with that, Randall has a big day tomorrow." Nurse Tina says. "Say your last goodbyes for the night." She leaves the room followed by Dr. Rickards.

"I guess little bro, you better pull through this. Go in there and fight like hell." Shauna contemplates whether or not she wants to give me one a hug. I've never seen her so emotional. "You got this." Her voice cracks a little. "Fight like hell, bro." Shauna pats me on the back then rushes out the room.

"Mijo, I'll be saving all the good episodes for you when you get home." My abuela says. "Telenovelas won't be the same until you get yourself home. Te amo con todo mi corazón. Te amo mi pequeño rey. You are the best parts of all of us." My abuela kisses me on both cheeks a few times until she begins to cry. "I'll see you soon." She goes and stands in the doorway. Leaving just Brandon and my mother in the room.

"I guess it's my turn to give you some words of encouragement." Brandon says. His eyes are filling up. "I...I...umm." He releases his tears. "I love you so much. I'm not going to give you words of encouragement because I know you're going to kick cancer's ass. You're seriously a light. Picture this, six months from now we're on a beach somewhere or a Ferris wheel, having our Simon and Bram moment."

"I'm gonna hold you to that. That's August. I wanna be at a carnival. Just one month. I can do it."

"Like you keep saying this is going to just be a memory soon…a blip in your mind." I step up and kiss Brandon. His body warms me up even further and it eases my anxious mind a bit. "I'll let you and Maria have your moment." Brandon steps to the side.

"I'll be quick. Fight. Lucha como el infierno. Fight like hell. It's going to be a lot, but you got this. Your dad is right there with you in spirit. I'm going to shut up now." My mom holds her arms open. "Everyone! Get in here! Group hug…you too Tina." My mother pulls us all in for a group hug. "I just don't want to let go." "I love you with all of my heart. I'll see you tomorrow." One by one Shauna, Christina, Brandon, my mom, and abuela leave my room.

"Well, Randall, put on your pajamas and I'll be back in five." Nurse Tina jets out the room, leaving me all alone.

From the edge of my bed, I can hear kids' television shows, I can hear some laughter and I can faintly hear a child asking God to remove his sickness and to make him feel better. I am tempted to do the same. So, I get on my knees onto the cold ground, and I say: *God…or whoever is listening. I just want to live. My mom deserves to continue being a mom. Please reach with in my body and heal me. I want to live long enough to tell future little Randall's my story. God, let me be able to tell this story one day. I promise to make use of this second chance. You have my word. There's a boy I'm trying to love, and I want my mom to see be become someone in this world and find my place. I guess that's all…oh, and can you tell my dad that I miss him.*

"Just a few weeks." I whisper.

February 17th 3:00am

After a very excruciating day of being poked and filled with medicine. It took me five hours to finally fall into a deep sleep. My perfect dream of dreaming about my new life is ruined by the screams of a little boy in another white room like mine. His screams turn my dream into a nightmare, and I force myself awake.

"Noooo!" I hear coming from his room. I can clearly hear a struggle happening with the little boy's parents and nurses. "No more medicine." The little boy's cries get louder and louder outside of my door. "I don't wanna do this mommy." This time the little boy is closer to my room. "Please, stop it mommy."

"I'm sorry, Randall." A night nurse rushes into my room and closes the door. "Try to go back to sleep."

I'm too tired to get out of the bed. My arms are heavy and so are my legs. I lay in place trying to force the screams of that little boy out of my mind. "Randall, don't think about this." I tell myself repeatedly.

11:00am

When I go for my treatment this morning the nurses finally tell me that Dr. Rickards has finally started her leave to get herself prepared for the big transplant day. Today is going to be a chemo and radiation day. *Yay.* All I can think about is the lunch I ordered shortly before being wheeled in for treatments.

That poor sandwich is going to now go to waste because after chemo and radiation the last thing I want to do is eat. I can barely walk afterwards let alone think about eating.

At this facility we have to sit in the same chairs every single day. Each chair has a blanket with our names on them and to one side of the chair is a calendar counting down our last treatment day. I am also the oldest person in the room which makes me sad a little bit because I can remember being their age hoping for this to all be over. Just to have the rug pulled from under me years later.

"Hey, Mister…how old are you?" A little boy with red hair asks. He's also the first black boy that I've seen with red hair. "Are you like twenty?"

I laugh. "Nope. I'm like…sixteen." I say.

"Wow. How long have you been sick?" He asks.

"Not…" The nurse hooks me up and starts the treatment machine. "Not that long." The little boy knows that I'm lying.

"Are you being honest" He asks. His parents come to join him at his chair remembering to keep their distance. "My mom doesn't like it when I lie."

"I promise. I haven't been sick that long. Only like…a little bit. See, I'm almost done." I point to my calendar that's marked for the end of March. "Same as you."

"Oh! Cool! We're going to be superheroes after this." The little boy pulls his cape around. "Who's your favorite superhero? Mine is Black Panther."

"That's funny. Black Panther is my favorite as well…for obvious reasons…that guy was a fighter. He didn't let the bad guys win." I say.

"My daddy said that when this is all over if we fought hard enough, we'll become just like Black Panther. Do you think they're going to let us go to Wakanda?" The little boy's dad looks to me. "Do you mister?"

"Yeah…you wanna know something…my dad used to tell me the exact same thing. He would call the Avengers like every day to let them know I was almost ready to be a superhero…now, look, we're almost Avengers."

"Yup, we truly are." The little boy notices that I don't have anyone sitting with me. "Where are your parents?"

"You see, my powers are a little different than yours. My parents have to spend a little bit of time away from me for a little bit. But I see my mom every night."

"What about your dad?" The boy asks.

"Oh, he's on a mission. I talk to him as often as I can."

"That's it. Brady. I'm sure this young man has a lot to focus on." Brady's mom says. "Sorry, he loves talking to new people."

"Oh, it's no worry. I love chatting too." I say. Brady's nurse comes to help him out of the chair and into a wheelchair. "Take care."

"Thanks." His mom says. "If you don't mind me asking…how long have you been battling…you know."

"My earliest memory is seven or eight. It went away for a few, then came back when I was twelve, went away again, and then almost two years ago it came back, but I'm being hopeful this is the last and final time."

"It will be." Brady's mom says. "It will be. He's had it three times in his nine short years. I'm so happy his dad was a perfect match—"

"So was my birth mother. Dr. Rickards." I say.

"Oh, we just cherish her. She is truly the best in Washington. She's prolonged his life countless times. Please, hold her close even after the transplant. Keep her close to you." Brady's mom gets up and follows after her husband and son. "I don't know your relationship with her, but I'm sure she had her reasons. If at all possible, forgive her for yourself."

"I have."

"Awesome!" She says. "…Keep in touch."

"Oh, most definitely." I say.

February 19ᵗʰ 3:00pm

The full blast of chemicals pouring through my body is starting to feel a lot better all things considered. I still have the fatigue and a slight loss of appetite, but I'll take those symptoms if it means I am days closer to gaining a second chance at a future.

Nurse Tina stayed with me the entirety of today's radiation and chemo treatments. It was like sitting next to the world's fastest talker. Nurse Tina went on and on about how she's still finding the perfect medical school because she wants to be a pediatrics doctor.

"Hey, how about we go get some air?" Nurse Tina asks.

"Sure." I say.

"Well, hop in." Nurse Jackie wheels me to the elevator and before you know it, we are on the roof of the facility. It's more like a green roof. There are tons of seating areas, greenhouses, and even a rooftop garden. "Are you happy?"

"Yes. Thanks for this."

"Oh, you're welcome." Nurse Tina puts her phone on vibrate. "For the next few minutes, we're just going to spend it relaxing. We're not going to think about anything else but happy thoughts and moments."

"Sounds cool." I say.

"Perfect. Now, think about a happy moment." Nurse Tina says. The first thought that comes to mind is about my mom. Every thought that I have about her is a happy one. That lady has been my best friend and my confidant my entire life. The way she purely loves me without any stipulations or judgment is amazing. "You're thinking about your boyfriend. Aren't you?"

"Not this time. I'm thinking about my mother." I say.

"Which one Maria or Christina." Nurse Tina asks.

"My only mom, Maria. Dr. Rickards is like an aunt, that pays for things for me." I say.

"Wouldn't you want more from here?" She asks.

"I think I do. I just don't know how to go about doing that without hurting my mom. I love Shauna…but—"

"It's hard getting close with Shauna because it makes you wonder why she gave you up and kept Shauna."

"Well." She makes a great point. "Umm."

Nurse Tina covers her mouth. "Did I speak out of turn?"

"No. I guess you're right." I say. "I have to make things better between Dr. Rickards and I when this is all over with."

"I'm sure she'd like that too."

"You're clever...you planned this, didn't you?" I ask.

"What. Me? I do no such thing." She says. "In all seriousness, the way she talks about you and Shauna. I just know she would want a relationship with you if you wanted it."

"I do want. I want her to be a bigger part of my life, but my mom will have to come first." I say. "I gotta figure out how to say that exactly."

"Do it exactly like that. Just speak to her from the heart and the rest should be alright." Nurse Tina checks her watch. "...That's just my two sense though. Let me get you back so you can rest up...oh, your family can start visiting starting tomorrow. How amazing."

"Very." I do plan to make Dr. Rickards a part of my life. I want her to be there the same way my mom is there for me. I just have to have the conversation. *That shouldn't be hard, right?*

BRANDON

February 20th 9:00am

My audition to Julliard is in less than four hours and today my mom decided to reach out to me. I wanted today to be an amazing uplifting day. I was going to go to my audition then go check on Randall and maybe go have a jam session with Kelly and his guys until I somehow fell asleep.

My mother's call threw me off because the last time I saw her, it did not go how I had envisioned. I agreed to meet her for breakfast because she sounded somewhat different. The tone in her voice sounded as if she missed me or she genuinely wanted me back in her orbit. I gave myself a minor pep talk, basically reminding myself to not get my hopes up.

"Brandon! Over here!" My mom calls. Upon first glance, she looks amazing. Her hair is done. She looks like she's switched drinking alcohol for actual food, and that she's…happy.

I have no expression on my face. "Hi, mom."

My mom holds out her arms, but I just can't allow myself to hug her fully. I grip her hands instead. "I ordered you an avocado toast with bacon bits and eggs if that's alright." She takes multiple sips of her water. "So…how have you been?"

I slide into the booth not breaking my focus on my mother. "I've been alright. School and music. That's about it."

"I saw that you were dating a boy…sorry, I look at your Instagram from time to time. I feel close to you that way."

"No, it's fine. I get it. But his name is Randall. He's pretty amazing." I smile.

"I can tell he makes you happy." My mom pushes my toast towards me. "Do you love him?"

"Yeah. I love him very much." My smile widens. "Like, I don't think I've ever felt this way about anyone before. That guy makes me feel all of the emotions." My mom wipes her eyes with her napkin. "Shit, did I say something wrong?"

"No. I've just been missing out on so much with you. I'm sorry I put Sam before you…I'm leaving him for real this time. When you moved out and after our last blow up, I realized how much I lost because of him. You were the biggest part missing from all of that."

"Oh…I don't know what to say."

"It's me that owes you an apology. I've also restored our last names back to Marciano legally. You never went by Sam's last name anyway, but now you won't even have to write it on legal documents. I've erased him from our home."

"Oh, so this is serious. I'm happy for you mom." I say.

"I'm happier too. Oh! I gave up drinking...three months sober. I'm trying to be better for you. I want back in your life if you'll have me."

"I want that mom. Baby steps though."

"Brandon! Of course! Of course! Come back when you feel like it...no rush." A waitress finally brings our bougie toast to our table. "I would like to meet Randall, though."

"Of course. After his treatments and when he's better. He has leukemia." I say. The smile on my mother's face lowers. "Oh, don't worry...he's going to pull through it. Just a few more treatments. Then, it's—"

"I'm so proud of you. Most teens like you would not be able to do what you are doing. You are a much better person than I was at your age...even your dad. When I first met your dad, he was not the same person I married. In high school and college your dad was a nightmare to everyone. I don't know what it was that made him change."

"You." I say. "It was you. You made him grow up. With Sam you to made up for lost time. All the time you lost starting your family young, you made up for it when you got with Sam. I can't blame you for that. It was all the other stuff."

"One...how did I birth such a smart young man? Second, I am going to be better for you...for us. I promise. You have my word. No more screwing up." We simultaneously take a bite of our bougie toast. "Maybe you can give me some dating pointers." She jokes.

"I'd be happy to." I smile. We spend the next hour or so catching up and talking about any topic that came to mind. It was like I was chatting with an old friend. My mom reminded me of the mom I lost after my dad died. This version of Pearl was the version of my mom that I have be longing for her return. Our sync got disconnected the day she met and married Sam. After our lunch, I could feel the spark jump back into our relationship.

1:20pm

"It says here that you are a trained songwriter. But you want to study arrangement. Why is that?" The panel of counselors from Julliard all have amazing poker faces.

"Oh, I just feel like I'd be a better musician for not just myself but other artists I work with if I know how to make my own music. Songwriting comes easy to me. I want a challenge when I come to New York to study." I say.

"Well, then young man, let's get started." The counselor retakes his seat beside the two other Julliard counselors. "What have you prepared for us today?"

"I'm going to be doing a different arrangement of Big Cheese." I say.

"By Nirvana?" The counselor asks.

"Yup." I say.

"Well, let's get to it." The counselor starts the clock on his phone. "It's all you buddy." I do the same rendition that I did for Sarah at Taverna a few weeks ago. This time I soften up the strumming of the guitar in the beginning of Big Cheese.

When it's time for Kurt Cobain's solo about halfway through, I really go for it and show the counselors that I really know how to study music. I notice all of the counselors raise their eyebrows in surprise in unison. "Hold a second." The counselor pauses the clock for a moment. "Let's try something different."

"Go for it." I say.

"Play your version of Take me to heart." The counselor never looks up at me. "Take me to heart, was your back up. I want to see what you'll do with this song."

"Awesome. It's one of my favorite songs."

"A kid your age knows about Quarterflash?" The female counselor asks.

"Yeah. Pretty much anything from the sixties to nineties I know like the back of my hand." I switch from the guitar and walk over to the saxophone and begin to play Rindy Ross's iconic sax solo from that song. I'm not a pro on the sax but I give it my all. The solo in Take me to heart requires a lot of breath and thank goodness I do the solo without passing out. "How was that?" I ask. The counselors aren't reactive. "I hope that was great...it's one of my favorite songs...ask my boyfriend...or best friend."

"Young man, that was one of the best music auditions I have ever seen. I can tell you one thing: you're getting high marks from me. Just make sure your academics are on point and I'm sure we'll be seeing you this fall at Julliard."

"Wow! Thank you. That means so much to me. I'm going to get going before you all change your mind." I say.

"Oh, we won't be changing our minds. You are going to be an amazing composer and artist. This is only the beginning." The female counselor says. "Take care until August."

5:00pm

"So, basically you're going to Julliard in the fall." Randall says. He's hopped up on sugar so he's doing everything he can to stay up. I can tell by the rings around his eyes that the treatments are trying to win and make him feel horrible, but Randall keeps kicking their ass. "My man is going to be the next...who's an old school composer...I was so gonna say Billie Eilish."

"Oh, Johannes Brahms is a good one...but I think Billie Eilish's brother helps her produce her stuff. His music is pretty dope too."

"I wish I could like hug you; my mom has been having a hard time with all this. I'm happy they let her sleep here. This place is so weird at night."

"How so?" I ask.

"It's a hospital. The lights are always on, people won't stop checking on me. I could be sleeping solidly, and someone will come in and ask Randall, are you alright? Like, ma'am I'm freaking sleeping. You hear me snoring..." I can't help but to laugh. "Maybe, you can spend the night." Randall walks a little closer to the plexiglass wall that is keeping me away from him physically. "What do you think?"

"Not going to lie, as amazing as that sounds...I still have school tomorrow. Trying to save all my skip days"

"I get it." Randall says. "I keep forgetting the days still go by in this place…when you're stuck here it just seems like one long ass day. But, only a few more weeks of this. The procedure then monitoring. That's how I keep looking at things."

"Awesome way to think about it. Have you seen Dr. Rickards?"

"No. We've chatted on the phone but she's keeping herself healthy until her procedure next week. Then, she has to rest for a few days and then I'll get to see her."

"How does this all work?" I ask.

"Well…according to Google and YouTube, they extract the marrow and stem cells from Christina…she goes home. They harvest or study them. Then, they put them in me. Some people are able to go home a few days afterwards—I can't because this isn't my first rodeo."

"That sounds simple." I say.

"Yeah. And this time those new blood cells are going to work and then I'm going to be a happy camper and then my mom will be able to stop stressing as much."

"It's Maria we're talking about, she loves worrying about you. I think it makes her day seeing your face." I say.

"Yeah. I love that old lady too." Randall smiles. "Speaking of mothers, how was breakfast with your mom?"

"Perfect! She's doing much better. She's sober and she's divorcing her husband. Oh, and she wants to meet you."

"That's amazing! I'd so love to meet her that would be amazing." Randall practically jumps out of his chair. Nurse Tina comes into Randall's room motioning for him to get ready for bed. "Just five more minutes. I haven't seen him in days."

"Five minutes. Then, I really have to do your check up and give you your medicine." Nurse Tina leaves the room.

"Today has been a great day." I say.

"It really has. A lot of great things happened for you today. Sleep good tonight." Randall places his hand on the glass. "Where's your hand?"

I place my hand on the glass. My hand is slightly larger than Randall's. "I'll see you tomorrow. Have a good night. Love you."

"Love you, more." Randall says as he climbs into bed. "Text me, when you get home."

"Will do." The universe is really doing its thing lately. From my amazing audition to my mom finally realizing her worth, to Randall almost being done with treatments, I'm really starting to think my happy ending isn't that far out of reach.

RANDALL

February 27th 8:00am

In the past seven days a lot has happened. Sunday evening, Dr.
Rickards had a successful procedure. They were able harvest her
bone marrow and it call came back with flying colors. I however,
have been placed on a strict no breathing, no touching, and no
looking at anyone diet…or orders by the overly and amazing
doctors at Westlake General.

Today is the big day.

This is the day where we'll see if all of my wishes paid off.

Nurse Tina crashes into my room humming and singing. It
looks like she did her hair and even put on a little makeup for my
joyous occasion. She popped open the curtains, turned on some
children's program and forces me out of the bed and into the
bathroom to shower.

She literally waits until I am physically in the shower before she closes the door to leave me to myself. She became aware weeks ago that I've just been letting the water hit my chest. I have a bunch of wires attached to my body. I was too scared to get electrocuted or slip in the tub. That'd be so damn tragic if I accidentally fried myself days before getting my transplant. *There's a joke in there somewhere.*

When I come out of the bathroom, my mother, abuela, and Brandon are standing in my room. The barricade is gone. And they are dressed in hospital gowns with masks, gloves, and shoe coverings.

"Happy to see us?" Brandon asks. He pulls his mask down briefly. He's smile reaches both of his ears. "We've been waiting for you to come out of the bathroom for about half an hour." Brandon tries to approach me but is stopped by my mom.

"Hey there, my boy. How are you?" My mom tries to give me a hug but probably remembers the very strict hospital rule. The hospital acts like I can get sick in five minutes.

"Honestly, I'm nervous. But, after today…it'll be all over and done with." I say. "Right?"

"Yes. A year from now, you'll be preparing for college. No more hospitals." My abuela says. "This will all be put behind you and us."

281

"Yeah." I say. I look at the gown on my bed. "This is really happening." I slip into the gown and gently get back onto the bed. "Can we get this going?" I push the button that magically summons doctors and folks to my room. Nurse Tina immediately comes barreling into my room with a few other nurses and doctors who all look ready to pounce on anyone at any moment.

"Alright. Should we explain what's going on today?" The oncologist asks.

"Sure." I say.

"I think he'll take the information better coming from me." Nurse Tina says. She makes her way to the foot of my bed. "In short, the stem cells we gathered from Dr. Rickards' bone marrow and blood are going to be inserted into your body. Those new cells are going to multiply and produce healthy blood cells killing off any of the sick cells in your body that ever caused your cancer. In return, you'll get to live the life you were meant to have…how's that?"

"That sounds simple." My nerves calm. I turn to my mom, and I can see my mom finally exhale. "To think that eight years of this will all be over in a matter of weeks…that's amazing."

"Well, if you're ready, let's go help you start your new life." The doctor says. Nurse Tina pulls a wheelchair up to my bed and I slide right into it.

"Randall, you ready?" Nurse Tina asks.

"Yeah. But could I ask one thing?"

"Go for it." She says.

"Could my mom walk with us, and could I please hold her hand?" I ask. "Please."

"Of course. She has on gloves, and we checked her temperature. I don't see why not. Just no kisses."

"Now, let's go." Nurse Tina allows Brandon to push the chair. My mom is one side of me and my abuela is on the other. We arrive to Dr. Rickards' room first. She is up, dressed and is waiting in her room with Shauna sitting on the foot of her bed. "She didn't want to miss out on this."

"I hope that's alright." Dr. Rickards says.

"Yeah. Duh, I wouldn't be at this point in the process if it weren't for you." I smile. We then take our time getting to the procedure room. Greys Anatomy makes hospital rooms seem way more dramatic than what they actually are in real life. This room is painted bright ass yellow and has ample seating space. The chair where I'll be getting my new healthy cells is your basic reclining chair with no special bells and whistles. The doctor wheels in the same IV pump machine I've seen for eight years now.

"Ready, young man." He asks.

I take in one long breath before I say: "Yup!"

"Well let's…we don't typically do this but Rickards if you're up to it…would you like to turn the line on for him. After all, you two started this process eight years ago."

"That would be lovely." Dr. Rickards says. I can so tell that she wants to cry so bad, but she takes a second and the tears that were forming in her eyes disappear.

"I would love that that too." I say. "Go on. I almost called you mom, but we'll find a name for you soon." I motion for Dr. Rickards to do her last duty administering me my final dose of treatment.

"We have all the time in the world to come up with a name." She takes over for the doctor and turns the stem cell line on and the cells begin to trickle all the way down the line and into my body. "Now, it shouldn't hurt but if it does let me know and we can adjust." I don't feel any kind of pain. Relief is the only thing I feel entering my body.

"No. It's fine. I feel fine." I can describe the feeling of the medicine flowing into my body as elation. I am happy to know that this is my last step. I spent eight years hoping that this day would come. I had hoped for a day where Dr. Rickards didn't say that I was in remission just for a few years later for me to have a new lump and we spend weeks determining if its cancer or not just for Rickards to call and give us bad news. I can potentially start to plan my future tomorrow (really, in another month) and when tomorrow comes I won't have to dread it. "Now, it's time to heal."

BRANDON

March 4ᵗʰ 10:00am

I got my decision for my safety school. I never even told Randall that I even applied to NYU. I got accepted and they're offering a full ride. I toss the acceptance letter in my locker and head to Principal Pendergrass' office.

Although this man and I have a love hate relationship, he's the only real male figure I have in my life. I take his advice as bible even if it seems to him that I'm giving him way too much pushback.

"That's cool you just knew I was coming to your office, didn't you?" I throw my things in the empty chair and sit in the other. "How's it hanging?"

"You tell me." Pendergrass folds his newspaper close. "Mrs. Chambers has said that you have not been in class for weeks."

"I know. I'm still doing the assignments. She's still passing me and grading it."

"Brandon. What's going on?"

"I got accepted to NYU…full ride." I'm playing with the desk gadgets on Pendergrass' desk.

"Brandon. What's going on?" Principal Pendergrass motions for me to close his door. "You can talk to me. Is this about home or Randall?" I instantly sink my head.

"No. I don't think—"

Principal Pendergrass lifts my chin up. "Come on, man. What's going on? This is me you're talking to. What is it?"

"I guess. I miss Randall always being here. That English class was where I first had…you know…feelings."

"I completely understand that. But don't you think it would be better for you to be in class as if he were still there. You know who else he connected with?"

"Who?"

"Mrs. Chambers. And, you know who else Mrs. Chambers connected with…here's a hint, it was you. She loves having you in the class. Having you and Randall both in class is a bonus for her. You have all the support you need. Plus, I heard Randall's doing a lot better."

"He is. I guess I just miss him that's all." I say forcing my head back up. "I know I'm supposed to be focusing on myself and working on music things but that can wait for a moment."

"...and that's completely normal. But you also don't want to hinder your own growth. Look, when your dad and I were both students here, that guy was my best friend. I used to follow him around like I was his entire shadow. We got our classes switched to be in the same classes. We even lived right next door to one another...at one point we were even dating twins...that's beside the point. One day your dad got sick...come to find out it was...you know. I was for the first time alone in these halls. I had to break away from that sidekick title people known me as...In short, I'm saying. Brandon don't let your identity be known as Randall's boyfriend and don't put all of your eggs into Randall to the point it hinders your potential greatness. You are a great kid, and you can have an identity outside of Randall."

"I see your point."

"Yeah. It's alright to be in love but don't neglect the friends and people you had before you met Randall. I am pretty sure he'll forgive you if you missed a day from going up to the hospital. Hate to break it to you...he's going to be there for another few weeks."

I smile then hold out my hand. "You always give the best advice."

"...isn't that supposed to be my job?"

"Don't get a big head about it. You're right though." I start gathering my things. "I'll hit up Mrs. Chambers and let her know I'll be in class next week. Thanks for the chat."

"Anytime. And remember my place is still open if you ever need—"

"Nope. Mom and I are good. She's changed quite a bit. She's sober now. She's even cooking dinner tonight and told me to invite Kelly over and everything."

"See! That's what I'm talking about."

"Yeah." I throw my jacket on. "I better get out of here."

"Yeah. Tell Randall we all here at Crestview are all rooting for him to pull through and I'm really happy about your mom. Chat later."

5:00pm

Arriving back home after being away for all these months is a bit weird. I had every intention to stay away from this place for as long as I could.

Kelly and Jason are both coming to dinner at my house tonight. Kelly has his guard up when it comes to my mom, which is very understandable given that her former husband has been quite the homophobe towards Kelly. Jason is one of those hopeful people so he's just going to go with the flow of the room.

"Brandon! Everything is all set." My mother must've been sitting by the door waiting to hear the tires of my car crunching the gravel of our driveway. "Can I just say that this dirty blonde hair grows on me more and more."

"Awe thanks." I say. I spend a moment staring at her. Her marriage finger is still free of the cheap dollar store ring Sam got her. "Sorry, I'm being rude. This is Jason. He's Kelly's boyfriend." Jason stretches his hand out to her, and my mom pulls him in for a hug. "You know Kelly. It's been a minute."

"Hi Kelly." My mom says.

"Hi…I don't know how to address you now." Kelly says. My mom finally steps back into the house allowing room for us to get out of the cold Washington air. "Sorry."

"Oh, in a few days it will be back to Marciano. But just keep calling me Pearl…Brandon's mom also works."

"Cool." Kelly's dry tone causes the energy in the room to become a little bit stale. I shoot him a disapprovingly look. "So, what's for dinner?"

"Spaghetti." My mom says. "I tried to make it how I used to. With meatballs and everything. Oh, and fresh parmesan." My mother leads us to the kitchen. I take in all of the changes she's done to the house. All of the dark paint and the random photos that used to line the wall have been replaced with photos of me, my dad and I, and the three of us. Walking into the kitchen the biggest change are the cabinets. They have been restored back to their regular off-white color. "So, what do you think?"

"I love the changes." My mom is holding up her spaghetti for me to take a look. "I'm happy you did this."

"I told you I made these changes…I get it…trust. But what do you think about the spaghetti?" My mom places it back on the kitchen island.

"Oh, it looks delicious." I say. Jason helps my mother reach the dinner plates while Kelly grabs the silverware out the drawer. "I'm really happy to be back home."

"I'm happy you're here, son." My mom hands me a plate of food. I get right to eating. "Hey, wait. We're going to say prayer."

"We do that now?" I ask.

My mother lets out a laugh. "Just kidding." Hearing my mom laugh is so refreshing. The last time I saw or heard my mom laugh my dad was still alive. That's all they used to do. "So, tell me about your day."

"Oh, school was school. I chatted with Pendergrass about some stuff he gave me some great advice."

"That's nice. How's Randall?" My mom stops eating like she's prepared for me drop a different update then the one I gave her on him a few days ago. "How is he recovering?"

"He's doing alright. As far as we know his body is reacting well to the new blood cells. So, that's a great thing. He's going to pull through."

"He's gonna be fine. That kid is a trooper." Kelly chimes in.

"Agreed." Jason says.

"How are you doing, though?" My mom asks. "Being seventeen and the first boyfriend you ever have has this sickness."

"I mean. If you would've asked me in November my answer would be very different, but since I know everything. I'm doing pretty fine. I've been focusing on Julliard and music a lot more. Not as much as I should be though."

"What's stopping you from giving more attention to your music?" My mom asks.

"Umm—"

"Himself." Kelly says. "How many times have I been eavesdropping and heard Randall tell you to go work on your music and you brush it off?"

"Damn, blow my entire spot up why don't you."

"Look bro, that last performance at Taverna should have been a clear indication that you should be putting more attention on your music. The way the crowd reacted to you was insane."

"How did the crowd respond?" My mom asks.

"They were—"

"Ms. Marciano, they went crazy for him. Like literally crazy. People were yelling and demanding for more songs. He killed it."

"That's incredible." My mom says. She goes and puts her plate in the sink. "I want to be at your next performance."

"Of course." I say.

"I'm not forcing you. I just want to do more things with you." She says. "All this time I've missed with you…even before you moved out."

"It's fine, mom. Promise. All that matters is now." I wink her way. "Let's not get mushy or sentimental…Kelly wants some of that homemade ice cream you used to make and let's watch some old ass Disney Channel Movies…just like we used to do back in the day."

"Well, that's funny." My mom opens the freezer and pulls out a steel bucket of her famous homemade vanilla and strawberry ice cream. Kelly and I used to fight over who got the last spoonful of ice cream. "…so, who's ready for ice cream and Disney?" My mom pulls out four spoons and I lead the way to the living room.

"Can we watch *Zenon*?" Jason asks.

"Right after watch *Cadet Kelly*." I say.

RANDALL

March 11th 9:00am

Every single day since receiving my transplant I've felt like I've been living the same day over and over. It's basically been me waking up to the same breakfast, looking out the same window, having the same twenty minutes of fresh air, doing the same homework assignments, and listening to the same recycled news by same people. Doctors love to say: *Randall, your numbers are steadily increasing.* Or *you are a real fighter…we're still going to keep you for a few weeks.* My favorite is when Nurse Tina reminds me that I am lucky to have received my transplant. She reminds me of that at least twice a day. It's like she's trying to keep my humble.

"Randall. I am so shocked at how high your numbers climb each day. Your immune system is bouncing back pretty nicely." Doctor Mom says. "Isn't that exciting?"

"Yeah." I say. "Very much…I was reading though."

"Oh goodness." Nurse Tina groans.

"What were you reading?" Dr. Rickards asks.

"I was reading that not all patients who've had this transplant has to stay in the hospital for a month. Like, this one older person got to go home after two weeks."

"Did you happen to catch how long this person had cancer?" Doctor Mom asks. *Ok, I'm going to have to call her Christina.*

"No." Christina says.

"Well, the reason that you have to say is mostly because we were concerned about your immunity once you left the hospital. Look where you're at." Christina shows me a chart that's basically foreign language, it's a mix of lines, numbers, big words, circles, and other hospital paper things. "Compared to last week, your body is reacting well. Just two more weeks. You can do it. We don't want you to get home and get sick and your body not know how to respond to it."

"I know. I just miss outside." I say.

"That's all. You can ask or walk yourself up to the roof." She says. "Nurse Tina doesn't have to accompany you everywhere." It feels like Christina has just given me my golden ticket. "You do have freedom."

"Cool! I just had no idea." I wonder if they can see my brain working. "Vitamin D here I come!"

"Not too much of it though. I would say no more than thirty minutes of direct sunlight. Your skin may be too sensitive and will be for a few years or so."

"Welp. That's no fun." I say.

"Hey, you get to live. That's amazing, right?" Nurse Tina says. My eyes jump right to her giving her the deathliest of glares. "Someone has to keep you grounded here."

"Right." My eyes still locked on Nurse Tina. "Am I done?"

"Yes. I'll check on you later before I head home…oh, and Randall…eat everything on your plate and drink all of your water. Maria told me that you sneak it in the garbage when she's sleeping." Christina has been waiting for years to tag team parent me.

"Fine." I roll my eyes. "Oh, and I think since you basically saved my life for the third time, I can start calling you Christina."

"Randall. I'm just happy you're going to allow us to build a relationship. See you later." She smiles then snaps back into doctor mode my switching my folder for another one of her patients. "Head back to your room." I start the short walk back to my room and see that Bella is checking in at the nurse's station. One of the nurses is checking her temperature and handing her a pair of gloves.

"Bella! No way." I screech. "Oh, my goodness. More normalcy."

"Oh, Hi! Do you need some help?" Bella tries to reach for me but a nurse familiar with my situation makes her put on the gloves before extending her help to me. "They're strict at these places. Aren't they?"

"Very. I guess it's cool though. I definitely feel like an Obama." We make it back to my room and I immediately plop on my bed. "So, how have you been?"

"I've been alright...all things considering." She says. "I've been taking it slow. One day at a time. I guess that's all I can do...you know."

"Yeah." Guilt slowly creeps up my throat. My body forms goosebumps. I know I should not be feeling guilty about being so close to my finish line while Bella is extremely close to her ending point. "I feel you."

"Randall." Bella's head is down.

"Yeah." I say.

"Don't hold your excitement from me. I genuinely want to hear all about this whole process...trust me, my dad and I have come to terms with my prognosis. Don't dull your light for me. I'm fine. I wouldn't be here if I weren't." Bella sits on the foot of my bed. I don't make her move. "So, how was it? Did it hurt?"

"Actually...it didn't which was the most shocking part. I just knew I was going to have to beg my mom to hold my hand. I thought they were going to put me to sleep but none of that occurred. I was awoke the entire time...actually getting this transplant took way less time than getting chemo and radiation combined."

"That's awesome." Bella sees the photos of Brandon, My mom, and abuela on my nightstand. "How are your folks?"

"They're good. The hospital finally started letting my mom sleep her every single night. She still can't hug or kiss me though." I pick up my first hospital band and hand it to Bella. "You see how many people have squeezed their little signature on this little band?"

"That's cool." She says.

"It's like some tradition they do here. I had no idea about it. I saw it the other day and each day there are more and more signatures on it. I stopped wondering when they even have time to sign this thing. I am always in my room...but I just found out I could go up to the roof...so that's cool. I can't stay up there long though."

"Why not?" Bella asks, she hands me back the wristband.

"Something about my skin being too sensitive...hey, what's wrong?" Bella has tears rushing down her face. "Damn, I wish I could give you a hug."

"It's alright. I'm fine." She lies. "Truly, I am."

"No, you're not." I get up from my bed and close the door momentarily. "Hey, come here." I ignore the hospital rules for one moment. "Give me a hug." Bella is hesitant. "I'm serious...hurry before someone realizes my door is closed." I force hug Bella who doesn't accept it at first. "You're gonna be alright...I wish we both got to have this day but like you'd always say when I first started treatment...life sucks but at least we get to keep breathing for at least one more day. "Bella finally accepts my hug. "We just have to make this time count." We both leave the hug. "When I get out of here, what's the first thing you want to do?"

"I have no idea." She says.

"Yeah, you do." I say. I take my seat back on the bed. This time sitting as close to Bella as I possibly can. "A show...Prom...Maybe the beach on Memorial Day...what do you say?"

"I may not be here for prom...but that does sound amazing." Bella wipes her tears. "I only have a few more weeks. Doctors said I have three months at most about two weeks ago. Prom would be nice...seeing Brandon perform would be cool too...damn, I never even got to actually hang out with you two."

"I'll make it happen...don't worry...we have time...I'll make time." I say.

"How are you going to do that?" She asks.

"I have no idea but I'm going to do it...just you watch." Bella checks her smartwatch. "Do you have to leave?"

"Yeah. My dad is pulling up downstairs." Bella regathers herself by making herself smile a couple different funny ways. "I'll see you later. That's a promise." Bella gives me an air hug before she leaves my room. "Take care, Randall."

"Same."

10:00pm

My mother's favorite show to watch at night is *Don Lemon Tonight.* I think she mostly loves staring at Don Lemon. The hospital has one of those fancy televisions that lets you pause the television as often as you like. My mother has played and paused the television on the same corny joke. I should tell her he doesn't play on her team.

I go back to watching Brandon sleep in the chair beside me.

The hospital stopped making a deal about Brandon sleeping here after they realized that he wasn't going to stop doing it. Nurse Tina greeted him with a pillow and blanket one night and told him to prop his feet up on the extra chair for maximum comfort.

When my mother finally pushes play on the television the sound from the television startles Brandon causing him to jump up. I love how his first instinct is to protect me. He grabs my arm and before I can see what he's going to do next, he's sound asleep again.

"Mom. I think you scared Brandon."

"Sorry, Mijo. Just this Don Lemon is so funny."

"Is he though?" I sarcastically say. I toss something at Brandon, and he repeats the same action by protecting me...or he could be thinking that my arm is a weapon. "No, Brandon, I have to ask you something."

"Yeah." He groggily says. "What's up?"

"Bella only has ten weeks. That's what the doctors told her." I pull out my phone and show Brandon that Taverna has an open night in April. "Would you and Kelly want to put on a performance that night? Then, we could go get some pizza or something...no, Bella is vegan...we could go get some vegan food afterwards."

"I think that'd be awesome. Just gotta get Sarah on board." Brandon says.

"Already done. I texted her. She said that's fine."

"Well, let's do it. Maybe you could learn a solo or something and play for her." My mom bursts out into laughter. "What's up Maria?"

"Randall...is not musically inclined. His dad and I tried getting him lessons but that did not work."

"Yeah. I suck. I could introduce you...that's about it."

"I'm cool with that too." Brandon pulls his cover from underneath his butt and repositions his pillow.

"Awesome. I'll let you go back to sleep. Love you."

"Love you more, goodnight." Two minutes pass and Brandon is sound asleep. I spend the rest of the night thinking of other ways that I could make Bella's time here perfect. I want her to experience a few more happy moments and I'll do anything to help her get them.

BRANDON

March 13th 12:00pm

Julliard is trending today on Twitter today. My envelope isn't as big as all the other kids that have been posting their acceptance letters. When Kelly got his letter last night, he was so proud to show off his acceptance with a partial scholarship. We stayed up for hours talking about our plans for our apartment when we got to New York in the fall. When he asked me about mine, I dodged his question and told him I had that letter sent to my mom's house. He was too excited about his acceptance to question my lie.

In school all of the kids that got accepted to all of the big New York, Pennsylvania, and Massachusetts schools are basically yelling their excitement. Meanwhile, I keep digging my miniscule letter deeper and deeper into my pocket.

"Brandon. Are you alright?" Sarah asks. Her all-pink outfit on a Friday causes my stomach to turn. "What's going on? How's Randall?"

"He's fine…and yeah, I'm good. Just don't get why everyone is jumping for joy about being in debt for four years." I scoot pass her and arrive at my locker.

"Wait…didn't Julliard letters come out today?" She asks.

"Yeah. Who cares?" I put the wrong lock combination in and have to start again. "Didn't you apply to Columbia?"

"Yeah. Full scholarship." She says. "Shauna—she only got partial, and she got accepted to her safety school NYU…cool right?"

"Cool." I say. "I got accepted to NYU too…not gonna go though." I open my locker and shove my bag and skinny letter in and slam it shut.

"What! Why not? Are you crazy?" People are staring at Sarah. "Do you know how many people would kill to get accepted there."

"Look, why do you care?" I ask. "We're technically not really close friends."

"BRANDON MARCIANO PLEASE REPORT TO THE PRINCIPAL'S OFFICE." The loudspeaker startles Sarah for a moment. "BRANDON MARCIANO PLEASE REPORT IMMEDIATELY."

"Immediately. Shit. What'd you do? Sarah nudges me. "Julliard. What happened with that?"

"Oh, I didn't get my letter yet." I lie.

"I'm sure you got it." She says. "In New York, I plan to get closer to you as a friend. Afterall we're going to know like three people. We might as well get close now."

"Sure thing." We arrive to Pendergrass's office. Sarah stays behind and I walk in without knocking. "Hello, sir."

"Brandon. Have a seat." Pendergrass says. "I called your mom to see if she'd come pick this package up for you, but we thought it be best for you to open it here."

"Open what?" I ask. Pendergrass lifts a heavy box onto his desk. I notice the lettering immediately. It's from Julliard. I examine the box further and the first words I see are Congrats. I don't need to see anymore before I lose it. "I have to call Randall." I pull out my phone hoping to video him but remember today he has a day filled with tests. "I'll show him later." I use the pair of scissors on Pendergrass's desk and open up the box.

"Hey, what are you thinking?" He asks.

"I don't even know." Julliard really decked this box out. It is filled with all kinds of Julliard gear. There's a sweatshirt that's about a size too big for me but I'm going rock it the first day of class. They've also given me a water bottle, a bunch of Julliard stickers, and even gave me one of those small Julliard flags. "I so can't wait to post this stuff on social media...after I tell Kelly and Randall of course." Pendergrass hands me a letter.

"You should read this. I think you'll be pretty ecstatic about it." I grab the letter from him and begin to read: Brandon, we were blown away by your audition. You've shown that you are moldable and that you will be an excellent student...we would love to offer you a full scholarship to Julliard...we hope you accept this offer...we'd be honored to have you join our community as part of the class of 2023. "What do you think? Awesome, right?"

"That's beyond awesome. I got into my dream school…side bar, do you know how many kids here got scholarships to schools on the East Coast…sketch…but I'm super excited for me. I am really going to the only school I saw myself at."

"…and when you get there, you better show everyone what you have. You're going to be a star, Brandon. I want tickets to your first sold-out show."

"You got it…let me get to class." I grab my box of good news and head to class. "On second thought, can I leave this here till after class?"

"Of course, and congrats." Pendergrass gently takes my box of good news from me and places in on nicely on one of the side tables in his office. "Have great day in class, sir."

7:00pm

I take Randall on a little dinner date in the hospital cafeteria. His diet is limited to pretty much fruits and vegetables so I make the best of it by getting anything that I knew I would enjoy myself. When I presented Randall our healthy feast, he didn't frown his face at all.

At this hospital, things become dead around six and stays that way until the morning when all of the kids are up and moving with their families and nurses. At this time, it's mostly just the nurses catching up with one another on the day and doctors who appear to be hiding from their patients.

"So, you actually like the food?" I ask.

"Yeah." Randall takes another forkful out of his fruit bowl. "This is probably the latest I've ate since I've been here."

"Shit. Am I going to ruin something?"

"No. At least I don't think so. I think Tina would have said something before we came down here." Randall takes a sip of his sugar free juice which tastes like water with food coloring. "I think we're good. No stressing. You're Mr. Julliard now." He smiles.

"Yeah. Full scholarship. Don't forget to add that in." I say.

"So, did you tell Kelly?"

"Yeah. He's excited too. He keeps texting me apartments we could rent. Says his mom is going to look at a few of them for us on her next trip to New York in a few weeks."

"That's amazing because I don't know if I would have shared a little twin bed with you at Julliard when I visited." Randall pushes his food away from him. "Yeah. This shit starting to taste weird."

"So, you plan on visiting me often." I say.

"Yeah. I have savings and stuff. I'll visit as often as I can." Randall pulls out his phone. "See. We could utilize this thing called a calendar and add our busy days to the calendar so there are no surprises."

"Oh, look at you! This place turned you into a calendar person...who knew?" I say. I hand him my phone so we can sync our calendars. "Are we those people now?"

"We don't have to be." Randall quickly pulls his phone off the table.

"No! I like this. We can then have our own things going on and it not be a huge thing if we inadvertently miss a day…we're so fucking mature."

"We sure are!"

"You know…if you do miss an important date of mine now or in the future, you're going to owe me a bunch of massages." I say. I lean a little bit forward and remember I am still not able to kiss Randall. So, I take his hand instead. "You better get them hands ready."

"You're going to be Mr. big shot soon…I think I'd like foot massages instead." Randall leans forward a little too close to me. Our tension is fucking undeniable. "I cannot wait until I'm able to you know—"

"I know. Me too. I'm aching over here. "Can I just—"

"Nope. It'd be more special when we're finally able to safely." Randall gets up from the table. "Now, my older famous boyfriend…will you please escort me back to my room?"

"It would be my honor." Randall allows me to put my arm around him. When the elevator arrives, Nurse Tina is the first one out and she doesn't even acknowledge my arm on Randall. Randall and I are the only two people on the elevator and the ride is quiet as hell. "I just want you to know that I am never letting you go. You're stuck with me kid."

"That's not a bad thing." Randall says. The elevator opens on onto Randall's floor and I continue escorting him to his room and help him onto his bed.

"Goodnight my king." I blow Randall a kiss and head out for the night.

"You're not going to stay the night?" Randall pulls his covers over his legs. Meanwhile, Maria and his Abuela are channel surfing.

"Nah. Gonna give sleeping in my old bedroom a try tonight."

"Awesome!" Randall pulls out his copy of Jane Eyre. "Text me when you get home. No! Call me. I'll more than likely be up."

"Will do. And awesome book choice."

"Yeah, this guy I know bought me a collector's edition of probably one of my favorite books in life. If you really sit and look at the parallels and similarities of our life—we have a lot in common. In terms of going through a lot of turmoil in life but in the end we both got happy endings."

"I thought you didn't believe in those."

"I don't. But it's nice to reflect on how far I've come."

"I get it. Get some rest Randall Price. Love you."

March 30th 10:00am

I think I tricked my body into feeling like it can sprint a bunch of miles. Today, I woke feeling like I could conquer anything. In fact, for the past few days I have been feeling more and more like myself from before I got sick again during my sophomore year.

I'm still not able to eat the kinds of food that I want so this morning I am suffering eating my unseasoned eggs and Canadian bacon and sipping my orange juice that has a shit load of pulp. The oatmeal also tastes like chalk and looks like cement. I scarf it down anyways.

Nurse Tina typically gets me going in the morning by reminding me that taking showers less than five minutes is not good for me as a growing teen.

I get myself together and when I come out of the shower Nurse Tina has still not made her presence known in my room. I throw on my clothes and step into the hallway. Back in room, I go to text my mom and out the corner of my eye I see Brandon.

"Hi!" I screech. It's been an entire forty-eight hours since I last saw Brandon. "What are you doing here so early?" I give him a hug. I milk our hugs now. Christina gave me the clear to resume regular activities (no sex though) since my immune system and other body things have been rising by the day. "Seriously, what are you doing here?"

"I thought I'd take you up to the roof before it gets too sunny." He says pressing his lips gently onto mine.

"It's already sunny though." I say.

"Oh, I know. I guess I meant before it gets too much to handle…just come on. I have something up there to show you." I take Brandon's hand and begin to follow him. The first nurse I pass stops what she is doing and smiles at me. We inch a little bit further and the nurse begins clapping and cheering.

"What did you do?"

"You'll see." Brandon winks. We pass two kids and they along with their parents start cheering and clapping.

"Way to go." A woman says.

"Brandon. What are you up to?"

"Let's keep going. We're going to take the long way to the roof." Brandon continues leading the way. When we pass the nurses station all of the nurses stand simultaneously and hold up a sign that reads: *Way to go Randall!*

"This is too much…people aren't going to break out in dance, right?"

Brandon laughs. "We're almost there." Brandon continues to lead the way and each person we pass continues the same routine of seeing me and cheering and or clapping. It's a real pick me up. I've spent weeks in this hospital doing the same routine that included waking, showering, eating, and staring at the walls. I still have no idea why people are clapping for me, and I don't need to.

We pass Brady and his mom, and they are gleaming. Brady has a cape and poster in hand. "You finally get to be a superhero now. How cool?" He says. He hands me the poster of Black Panther as well as a cape. "Congrats, Randall!" Brady gives me a hug and I think this is the first time I've felt my actual body warm up and it wasn't a figure of speech.

"Congrats, Randall." His mom says. "Really proud of you." Brandon and I walk pass them and I finally see Nurse Tina. She has a shirt with my face on it and she's literally jumping for joy. This is when I see the bell and it all clicks together for me.

"Wow." I say. I'm at a total loss for words and the tears will not stop streaming down my face. There's a heard of people coming from all sides of me. Everyone is clapping, whistling, there's so many signs of encouragement from everyone. "I'm at a loss for words."

"There's your mom." Brandon says. "…and your Abuela." My mom looks beautiful (she looks fucking gorgeous every other day) she has on a floral dress and her hair is up. I don't think I've ever seen my mom with her hair pinned up. I basically sprint towards her.

"You didn't have to do all of this." I tell my mom. I am now inches away from the bell. Christina and Nurse Tina keep wiping their tears. Shauna has appeared out of the sea of people as well. She is a literal puddle.

"This was all Brandon." My mom says. "He got this all together...he's been planning this for weeks." I turn to Brandon who is blushing.

"What?" I say.

"Yeah. When Ms. Rickards said that your time here is almost up, I figured this would be the perfect send off. I got everyone on board."

"You're sneaky...I like that...wait...where is Bella?"

"I don't—"

"Right here." Bella is holding herself up with a walking stick. She's still all smiles and positive energy. "Congrats. Randall."

"Thanks." I say. Christina walks over to the bell and motions for me to join her. "Oh, it's getting real."

"It's very real." Christina says. "Everyone this is a tradition within the cancer community. Ringing the bell signifies the patients last day of treatment. Randall had his transplant a month ago and his body has been responding very well to the new cells and such. I've been his doctor since..." Christina gets a little choked up. My mom and abuela prop her up. This makes me smile because they love unconditionally even knowing our very strange dynamic. I've been his doctor since her was eight years old. I'm so proud to be a part of this moment." Christina places my hand on the bell string. "Ring away."

"Here goes." Ringing this bell means so much to me. I see flashes of the first time I had to get poked with a needle. I can still sometimes hear me beg my mom to please not let me continue through with this. I can even remember a time last year when I did not want to continue. I felt my body was done. Now, a year later, I am so happy I fought and now I get to just live. I no longer have the worry that my cancer will come back and because life is so fucked up if it does comes back...I will fight like hell again. "I am a survivor."

SPRING

RANDALL

April 1ˢᵗ 11:00am

I now cherish my humble twin bed.

Waking up in my own bedroom after a month and some change is refreshing. In the hospital people are always messing with you. There's a nurse that comes in to make sure you're breathing, a nurse that comes in to change your tubing, a nurse that comes back in to make sure that you've bathed, and a nurse that makes sure that you ate. After a few days, I wondered what Nurse Tina's job even was.

I had to force my mom to sleep in her own room. It took some convincing, but she finally left my room; our compromise was me allowing her to check on me at least once during the night. My abuela didn't care for my pleads. She slept in the reading nook on my window.

"Randall! Breakfast." Brandon calls. He slept in our living room overnight. I hop out of my bed and throw on some joggers.

"Good morning—I mean…Buenos días mis amores." I stroll into the kitchen and see that Christina and Shauna are also joining us for breakfast. "Hey! This is an amazing surprise." I give Christina a hug. "Is this awkward?" I ask Christina.

"No! I'm happy…your mom invited us over this morning." She says.

"Oh, cool!" I walk over to Brandon who's assisting my mom in the kitchen. "I see my mom showed you how to make the empanadas." Brandon hides the failures.

"Don't judge those. How do these looks?" I take the first one off the top and bite into it. "So, what do you think?"

"They're perfect!" I finish the empanada and go take a seat on the other side of the island next to Shauna. Our kitchen table was only meant to seat four, I don't think I've seen six people fit comfortably in our kitchen since my dad has been gone. This is great to see. "Here try one, Shauna."

Shauna takes a bite. She takes a moment to fully let the flavors hit her. "Damn, these are actually good. Great job, Brandon."

"Awe, thanks guys." Brandon says.

"Wait a second. Today is Monday, shouldn't you two be in school?" Christina wants me to stay home from school for at least another week. I overheard her talking to my mom and she had Principal Pendergrass install a bunch of hand sanitizer stations and is requiring all of the teachers to have disinfectant wipes in their classes to make sure the class and school remains somewhat sterile while my immune system bounces back. "Is today an off day?"

"No. We just decided not to go." Shauna says.

"I'd rather be here this morning." Brandon winks.

"Alright, shall we say grace?" Christina asks. My abuela shakes her head.

"That's not something we do." I say. "But if it makes you feel better, we can." My mom shoots me a smile, then reaches across the island and pats my hand.

"No, no. It's alright." Christina says. My mom walks Christina plate over to her, then slides one over to Shauna and me. Brandon takes a seat on the other side of Shauna.

"Umm. I am not about to sit in between two love birds." Shauna says. "Brandon, take my seat. I know you want it." She grins. "Damn, you two are cute."

"Thanks."

"I know we're about to eat…Randall, can I give you one compliment."

"Sure."

"I don't miss the wig. I love you like this." She reaches for my hand. "I've been meaning to tell you that."

"Thanks, Shauna." I run my hand across my head. The hair is a long way from growing back. "I think I like it too." We all start to eat and for a moment it is dead silent. All I hear are the forks touching the plates and people chewing and gulping.

"What do you think your dad would say, right now?" Brandon asks.

"He'd be proud. This is all we would talk about when I was younger and even up until last year."

"Do you still talk to his side of the family?" Shauna asks. From the corner of my eye, I see my mom put her fork down. "What are those people like?"

"No." I say. "They stopped calling me after my dad died. Brandon and I went to their flower garden a few months ago and I was shocked I didn't see any of my aunts or uncles working that day…pretty much deserted." Shauna looks down at her plate. I catch her catching a glance at Christina.

"That's so messed up." Shauna says.

"I guess they're grieving." I say. "It's their loss anyway."

"Yeah…or…I have a better idea."

"Nope. I don't want to do that." I stand to place my plate in the sink. "Whatever you're thinking I don't want to do it."

"…wouldn't it be nice to just check up on them?" Shauna asks.

"Yeah. I agree with Shauna." Brandon chimes in. "Maybe you gotta make the first step."

"Cool. I doubt I'm going to take the advice but trust me I am thinking about it."

"As long as you're thinking about it." Shauna says.

April 10th 1:30pm

My first day allowed to go back to school and it is closed due to staff development. I thought I was going to have at least eight hours before I had to break the news to Sarah that I was quitting. I feel like it only makes sense—given that I only worked two maybe three shifts since the school year started.

It makes no sense for me to be working when I have to worry so much about my immune system. I felt it would be smart to quit before my mom or Christina asked me to.

Brandon and I decided to walk from my house to Taverna (alright, my mom suggested it) and on this walk I forget how beautiful Westlake is. It is like the most gorgeous island in all of Washington. The trees are in full bloom and showing off their beautiful colors. Meanwhile, across the lake, Seattle is struggling to get its act together nature wise.

"Westlake is gorgeous this time of year." Brandon says. We take a different way getting to the main street and walk through a park that overlooks the water. "I'm jealous you get to experience this every single day."

"We're only a ferry or pass bridge away." I say. "That's what the people on television say." The park is the size of a city block and before you know it, you're thrusted onto the main street. "Damn. I just got nervous."

"All you gotta do is just rip the band aide off. Sarah should get it…she will get it." Brandon pulls open the door to Taverna and I walk in before him. "Shit. Rebecca is here."

"Oh, well. I guess I'll tell her tomorrow." I try to make a break for the door, but Brandon grabs me just as I'm in the starting position.

"Nope. We're bigger than that. Take care of Rebecca then chat with Sarah." I force my feet toward Rebecca, and I do not have plan.

I'm gonna let Rebecca greet me first and then maybe my ass will sack up and tell her how I'm feeling. *Shit, I got spotted.*

"Randall!" Rebecca greets. Her arms are outstretched towards me. "Oh, we're not there yet. Definitely get it."

"Hi." I give Rebecca a half wave. "How have you been?"

"Great. I guess I should be asking you that." Rebecca takes a seat on the ground. "You joining me?"

"No. I'm gonna stay up here…you'll be picking me up from the ground."

"No worries." She jumps back up and I immediately think to myself, *I'll be jumping up and down soon* once my immune system and body recovers. "I'm sure you wanna skip small talk."

"Yup. I just basically want to know why you did it."

"I still do not know. I thought I was doing you a favor…" I scrunch my face up and shake my head in disapproval of her statement. "…I was being selfish. I didn't know how people received your performance or our performances. I thought by letting the audience know about your condition that we would get some much-needed sympathy applause."

"Everyone in the crowd were cheering their asses off." I take a step backward. "That wasn't needed. What you did was hella selfish. I felt so naked up there. All those people were looking at me like I was days from dying or something…that's how you made it out to be."

"I'm sorry, Randall."

"Thanks. Had you really been a friend to me. I would have eventually opened up."

"I do apologize from the bottom of my heart."

"It's alright, it was months ago...just I wish you would have been a friend to me...cause even through all of the annoying shit that you kept doing during practice I still considered you a friend."

"We were...are still friends...only if you want to."

"I do want to Rebecca, but you have to be nicer to people. Life is too short to be competing with people or wanting the approval from others. We get to be teenagers once in our life, why would you want to spend this time being mean and competing with other people? That's no way to live, right?" Rebecca looks away from me. "Right!"

"Yeah, I will try to be better. I want a friendship with you, hell, I want a friendship with anyone now that I'm single."

"What happened to Abiyram?" I know the answer to this question

"Come on, anyone could tell that home boy was gay. He needs me as a friend more especially with what's going on in his life right now."

"What's going on?" I ask.

"His family...nope...I will not spread anyone else's business." Rebecca places her hands on her hips. She's proud that she finally kept one person's secret in. "See. I'm changing."

"Cool. I guess I'll just ask him myself." Sarah walks into the back office and I take this moment as my time to chat with her. "I need to catch Sarah."

"Oh, go ahead. We'll talk soon. See you in school."
Rebecca heads for the door and I head to the back. "Hey, can I talk to you?"

"Yeah, of course." Sarah says. "I am so happy to see that you're alright…you are alright, right?" Sarah takes a seat leaving me to stand.

"Yeah. I'm fine. I'm getting there at least."

"That's amazing. Also, there is no rush to get you into work."

"See. About that." My palms are sweating. "…I think I have to quit. I haven't been here but a few times in the past seven months. It's pretty much like I don't actually work here. I'd rather just show up for shows and sit backstage. Also, for my immune recovery, I don't think being in a germ packed with sweaty dirty people is the best place for me. One bad cold and it's check out time for Randall Price."

"I get it. You don't have to overexplain with me. It's fine."

"Really? You're that fine with it?"

"Yes!" Sarah smiles. "It is totally fine. Your health is more important, plus, Shauna already gave me a heads up. She wants me to get you a more sterile job at the bookstore this summer…the job is yours by the way. You wouldn't have to do anything but check out the books, read them if you want, keep some of them, it'll be sterile as sterile gets."

"Gee. Thanks. I'll let my mom know about the new job opportunity. I guess I gotta thank Shauna… she really is something."

"She sure is." Sarah's face beams.

"Uh, I didn't know you—"

"Don't tell Shauna." Sarah stands.

"I won't. Your secret is safe with me…you two will be at Columbia together in the fall…sharing a room."

"I'll deal with these feelings then." Sarah and I walk back out onto the floor, and I spot Brandon sitting on the stage writing in his pocket notebook. "Are you writing your next hit?" Sarah approaches him.

"I hope it's a good one." I say.

"Oh, just you wait." Brandon stuffs his notebook back into his pocket. "You wanna get out of here. We got places to see and life to live and air to breathe."

"Where are you two off to?" Sarah asks. "Can I join?"

"Sure. We're just going to probably chill back at his place and watch some television or play some boardgames." Brandon says. "We're simple like that."

"I like simple…I should say, I'm starting to like simple." Sarah wraps her arms around herself. "Can you invite Shauna? Let's see what she's up to."

"Cool. I think she was coming over anyway." I say.

"Well, let me grab my keys and we can get going—"

"Sarah, we walked." I say.

Sarah rolls her eyes. "Fine. I'll be practical. The air is probably good for me anyway."

"Yes! I like this version of you." The three of us head out of Taverna and we make the short walk back to my house.

April 14th 2:00pm

I chose today to introduce Randall to my mom. She's been itching to meet him ever since she and I reconnected. I guess I've been anxious to introduce him to her because I wanted to know where I stood with her. But, after two months of constant behavior from my mom I felt that today was the right time to make this happen. I just forgot that my mom invited her mom and family to Washington for a little family get together.

When my mom made amends with me, she also made up with her side of the family. A side I have never known. I've seen my grandma a handful of times but today was the first time I ever heard that my mom had any siblings. Everyone got in late last night and they crashed at our place. I was happy that I didn't have to give up my room or share it with anyone. There was just enough space for my new family members to lay their heads.

Randall gets out of my car as if he's known these people for years. He's not as nervous as I am right now. He walks to the front door, and I take a second to slow my heart down.

"You do know we could do this another time." Randall says. "I don't have to meet your mom today; this is very different…me meeting your family at the same time as me meeting your mom."

"No, let's get this over with." I get out of my car, grab Randall's hand and head inside. When we walk inside my home it instantly becomes quiet. Everyone is staring at Randall and I. "Hi, this is Randall…my boyfriend."

"Hello, everyone." Randall says. My mom gets up from the couch and approaches Randall. "Hi, Ms. Marciano."

"Hi sweetie. Call me Pearl. I'm so happy you're here and doing well." My mom gives Randall a hug and then kisses him on the cheek. "Oh, goodness, I am not supposed to do that. I was doing a lot of reading and I read that in a news article. I am so sorry. I haven't been sick in ages. I apologize sweetie."

"No, it's fine. I am out the clear with that kind of stuff."

"Oh, excellent." My mom motions for some of my cousins to get up from the couch. "Here, have a seat. Are you hungry?"

"Yes." Randall says. My grandma has been staring at Randall since he walked in. He catches her staring. "Hi, how are you?"

"Hi there, young man." My grandma says. "Pearl said that you had cancer three times."

"Yes, ma'am." He says.

"How old were you when you first got it?" From the few times that I've seen my grandma in my entire life, she's always been quite blunt and straight to the point. She's not like my mom who lets things marinate before she's ready to explode.

"Eight years old." The entire room groan in unison. "I'm good now. Got a transplant and it's working perfectly."

"That's amazing." My grandma says. She gets up from the couch and gives Randall a hug. "You have to be one strong young man to have been fighting this for eight years."

"Yeah. I wanted to live." Randall says. I smile because I am in awe of his pure strength. It makes me proud to be his boyfriend every time he talks about all that he's been through in his short sixteen years of life. My grandma gives Randall another hug before taking her seat back on the couch.

"Here you two go. Randall, does your mom cook like this for you and are you allowed to have all this grease?" On both of our plates are gargantuan pieces of fried chicken, some collards with bacon bits, mac and cheese, potato salad, and my mom follows it up with a cup of sugary juice. "I won't be offended if you don't finish it."

Randall takes a bite of the fried chicken. "My mom rarely cooks fried chicken—"

"What!" My grandma exclaims. "You're going to have to explain this one. That's a black staple." Last night, I overheard my mom and grandma going back and forth on whether or not the chicken should be fried or baked. They even argued about the mayo and mustard ratio for the potato salad. "Is she a great cook?"

"I was adopted. My mom is Mexican and Bolivian. So, we mostly eat her childhood staples. I enjoy this though...It's a lot of food...but it's good. Brandon is learning how to cook tons of traditional Mexican dishes."

"You are?" My mom asks.

"Yeah. His mom is an excellent teacher." I finish chewing my food. "I'd love to cook for you one day."

"I would love that. So, Brandon did you tell Randall your race make up? He can probably guess it."

"Yeah. I was pretty much like, my mom is...black and my dad was white."

"We lost touch for quite some time." My grandma chimes in. "We're happy things are looking up for everyone." My grandma wraps her arm around my mom.

"I was going through my own thing. I got married had a kid and I was caught up in my new life. One year had passed with my mom and siblings, then another, and before you know it, I completely cut them out. I wanted to be all about my family. Plus, I was going through some inner things...Sam didn't make things better...clearly...I'm just so happy I got some help."

"Me too." I smile. "I'm happy to be back here."

"So, Brandon, you're going all the way to New York in the fall." My grandma rubs her hand on my back. "Full scholarship I hear."

"Yeah. Gonna be studying composition and stuff. I want to be a music producer." I say.

"And you can do it." My mom adds. "New York is going to love you." She winks.

"Randall, what school are you going to in the fall?" My grandma asks.

"Oh, I'm a junior. I'll be doing summer school and then going right into senior year. I'm hoping to go to NYU to study either creative writing or become an English teacher. And possibly drama."

"Tremendous, young man."

"I want you to love New York and stay there Brandon. I want you to learn about yourself there. The lessons I couldn't teach you about being mixed race, I want you to discover all of you." My mom keeps it together for me.

"Randall, how did your mom teach you about being black?" My grandma asks.

"Uh, she didn't. I think my biological sister talks to me more about my blackness than anything. My adopted dad who was European and Mexican he didn't really teach me either. He just didn't know how to. He kept those kinds of conversations very short."

"Your life is interesting." My mom is taking Randall in. "Truly, inspirational."

"Is it?" Randall asks.

"Yeah." My mom says.

"In short, my mom worked for my biological mother's family. Bio-mom got pregnant with my sister and then a few months later she got pregnant with me just as she got into her dream medical school. My mom was my nanny at the time and my biological mother allowed her and my dad to adopt me. Eight years later she became my doctor, and I discovered it myself a few years ago. My bio mom was also my donor."

"Wow. I can see how you and Brandon ended up together."

"Yeah?"

"Brandon's dad was a lot like you. He was so strong. He was determined to do anything his mind told him that he couldn't. That man was a hero. He was seriously one of my most true loves. Not a day that goes by where I don't think about him."

"Same here." I say. My other family members that have just been listening at this point all get up and leave my mom, grandma, Randall, and I to continue talking. "That's another thing Randall and I have in common. We both lost our dads."

"Oh, I'm sorry, Randall." My mom says.

"Thanks. It's been more than a year." Randall comes from around the kitchen island and gives Randall a hug.

"You two are meant for one another." My grandma grabs my hand. "I don't traditionally like to see teenagers fall so hard in love, but I'll make an exception for you two. I can sense the love between you. It is so raw and pure. I've been in front of you two for all of thirty minutes and I can feel it. The love you both have for each other radiates heavy."

"Thank you." I say.

"Brandon, can I talk to you in the kitchen?" My mom asks. "Is that alright Randall?"

"Oh, yes." He says.

I follow my mom into the kitchen.

"Brandon, I am so proud of you. Your dad would be so proud of you. I know he is happy with the person that you're becoming. I sincerely apologize for the time that I missed with you—

"Mom. Don't apologize for that. It's in the past."

"No, I have to." My mom exhales loudly. "I've been holding my breath for majority of the afternoon. It's been itching at me all day."

"I get it." I can hear Randall laughing with my grandma. "Grandma must be really out there telling some good jokes."

"Hold on to it." My mom says.

"I will. I most certainly will."

5:00pm

Randall spent the entire car ride back to his house encouraging me to stay the night. I have never seen him so adamant about something. I stand my ground and jokingly tell him that I think my grandma will burst if I didn't come back home tonight. She and I are really building a nice relationship. I've been enjoying getting to know my mom's side of the family. Albeit it was short, and we have a long way until we can say we're close but I still enjoyed the day with them.

"Your grandma thinks I should reach out to my father's side of the family. I slightly agree. I have to do it on my own time though. I'm still the kid in this situation." Randall unlocks my door. His mom is sweeping the porch.

"I'll go with you if you want. Even if it's a year from now, I'll make that trip with you." I say. I kiss Randall very slowly on the lips. This is the only way I'm able to keep my urges down. Plus, his mom is staring. "I mean it, I'll go with you."

"You're sweet. That's why we keep you around." Randall jokes. "Take care, drive safe, and I love you." I watch Randall walk towards his house. "Oh, young man, text me when you get home…better yet, call me…no, video me!"

"You got it! Love you!" I drive off. I smile all the way until I get back into Crestview. I have so much to be smiling for. I pull down my sun visor to reveal a photo of my dad and I "Dad, seriously, thanks for sending me, Randall." I kiss the photo and head inside my house.

RANDALL

May 1st 11:30am

People have been doing cheesy promposal's all day. I call them cheesy because I'm super jealous. I have been secretly hinting at Brandon to do one for me, but it hasn't clicked yet. The entire car ride to school today. I was basically telling Brandon I wanted him to be as extra as he was with my hospital release. He is not that great of an actor, so I settled for him saying *hey, why don't you go to prom with me?* I of course said yes, but my jealousy shot into overdrive when I saw Rebecca get asked by some random boy. This guy was able to get the entire marching band to back him. I'm dating a singer—a damn good one, he could put on a show all by himself.

Arriving to my Physical Education class, all of the girls and gays in the class keep talking about how their boyfriends or girlfriends have been asking them to prom in the most extravagant ways.

One guy asked his girlfriend in the middle of a restaurant he booked completely out. A girl asked her girlfriend out by getting her cheerleading friends to do some cheesy but cute cheer and this one guy got asked by his boyfriend with the help of his soccer friends.

"Garcia-Price!" Coach Williams yells. "Why are you not sitting on the bleachers?" Ever since returning back to school all of my teachers have been very anal when it comes to keeping me healthy. My physics teacher put a plastic barrier around my desk just in case someone in class comes to school sick. "Randall. Butt on the bleachers. Thanks."

"Fine. Can I at least play catch by myself?" I ask.

"We don't have any clean balls…I mean, none of the balls have been disinfected." Coach Williams hands me a piece of paper. "Here. Draw."

"Sir, you do know that I can actually do the activities …well, try to do them—"

"No. Pendergrass sent out a very detailed email explaining you are to stay away from germs. That's what I'm doing. Plus, were you actually going to play dodge ball with these kids with anger issues?"

"Probably not. The option would have been lovely, though." Abiyram appears out of nowhere and hands Coach Williams a late slip. "Hey, Abiyram…how's it hanging?"

"Good. Abiyram keep Mr. Garcia-Price here company …keep your distance and don't breathe on him." Coach Williams goes back to watching the class.

"Everyone has you on lockdown." Abiyram smirks.

"Unfortunately. And you don't have to keep your distance. I'm good. Just don't cough or sneeze on me…just kidding. I think my mom and doctors are just being overly cautious.

"So, how are you?"

"Pretty good. I mean, I would love it if my hair would grow back. But I feel better every single day. Each day I wake up I feel like I get an old piece of the old Randall back."

"That's so perfect. It's really great to hear."

"Thanks. You want to know what's crazy…I don't actually know what better feels like, honestly. The past eight years have been spent dealing with cancer then my body trying to bounce back only to find out that the cancer is back…so, compared to three months ago, I feel like I can run a marathon. I probably shouldn't but that's how I'm feeling, right now."

"And for some folks, that's all they want. So, it sounds and looks like to me that you're much better than the Randall from seven months ago."

"Yeah, most definitely."

"See. That's all we can ask for from this life…is to wake up and feel better than we did yesterday."

"Ok. Mr. Good Advice." Abiyram and I awkwardly bump our fists. "So, how are you?" Abiyram sits on his hands and looks off to the dodge ball game currently happening. "Hey." I tap his leg. "What's up?"

"Nothing." Abiyram exhales. "I just thought coming out would make my life so much easier."

"Coming out is supposed to be a relief."

"Well, it's just been a shit show from the minute I came out. I kinda wish I could go back in the closet."

"Damn, I'm sorry. Is your family treating you some kind of way?"

"Shockingly, no. My dad took the news well and has been encouraging me to put myself out there. My mom and siblings don't care...they claim they knew. It's my dad's congregation. They saw my dad like a post of me coming out on Facebook and all of them are threatening to leave his church and go someplace else." Abiyram joins me on my row of the bleachers.

"That's very housewives like behavior...but what does that have to do with you?" Part of the reason why my mom and dad weren't very religious has to do with judgement. My abuela raised my mom to love all kinds of people and to allow people to love themselves. Something a lot of Christian churches haven't quite realized. "Like, I don't get why you're taking on your father's church congregation's issues...that's their thing."

"I just hate seeing my dad stress."

"I get it. Is your dad telling you about these issues? Or is he making it seem like it's your issue that his congregation suck?"

Abiyram takes a moment to think. "No. He's never said anything directly to me. I just hear the disappointment in his voice whenever he tells us another one of his members left the church and joined somewhere else." Abiyram sinks his shoulders.

"Dude. Your dad loves you. He doesn't care about losing those members because true believers from what I have seen on television are supposed to love unconditionally...besides, the gays love keeping good people in business. Let them flock to his church and make it a thing. Our LGBT+ brothers and sisters and non-conformers need safe places to practice."

"Do you ever have a negative thought?" Abiyram smiles.

"I mean, I'm a literal saint, dude." The bell for next period rings. I have lunch next so I'm in no hurry to gather my things. "Look, just put the message out there and the people will come flocking. The people that are meant to be there will show up."

"Would you ever come to a service?" Abiyram asks.

"Sure. Don't hold me to it though. I am not very religious...I know, I'm black and have never been inside of a Baptist church. "

"Why aren't you religious?" He asks.

"Honestly, my parents never liked the idea of a book dictating their life and actions. Also, said book was written by man...who is flawed. My mom is more spiritual...a let life do its thing kind of person."

"I get that. I'm still going to ask you and Brandon to come to church though. I think you might enjoy it. My dad isn't one of those preachers that preach down to his people. He's very encouraging. We're always doing little retreats and things. I think you'd like it." Abiyram throws his backpack on. "I'm serious. Think about it."

"I definitely will. Promise." We both simultaneously stand from the bleachers; the gym is now empty. "Wanna pinky promise?"

"Yeah." Abiyram and I intertwine our pinky's.

"Dude, I'll see you there…soon." I leave the gym before Abiyram. Brandon pops his head inside and he's all smiles. "There goes my guy."

"No, there goes my guy. Want me to walk with you to lunch?" Brandon opens his arm and I hook my arm in his. "Come on, king!"

12:30pm

During lunch, Shauna and Sarah are discussing their summer travel plans. I keep myself out of the conversation because I know that isn't something I can just freely discuss. The kids at Crestview plan and execute some of the most luxe vacations I have ever seen. June until August are the best months to catch Crestview students out posting each other on social media.

My mom would have to work double time cleaning houses just to be able to afford to send me on a nice summer vacation. I have a passport with no stamps in it. One day I will though.

"Catalina Island!" Sarah yells out. "No…we went there three years ago. I got sick from drinking the water.

"Greece—wait, you were just there last summer." Shauna says. Before I knew Shauna was my sister, she used to gloat about all the places that she'd travel to.

"Randall, where do you wanna go for break?" Sarah asks.

"Oh, Disneyland."

"Out of all places, you'd choose Disneyland." Sarah shows me a photo of a on the water hotel someone in Asia. "You're telling me you would not want to go to Thailand? We could go to Disneyland any other random weekend."

"Maybe you can." They've both seen my house multiple times. There's no way we have spare money for rich kid trips. "My mom would never pay for that."

"Your other mom would, though." Shauna pokes me in the side. "She'd totally pay for our trip to Thailand."

"Cool. But I don't think I'd want to do that to her…also, I'll be in summer school until July." Out of nowhere someone throws a rose onto the table. "Wait. Shauna is your boy toy being extra?" Another rose gets tossed onto the table and I again do not catch the person who threw it. Before you know it, there are roses being tossed all over the table. Person after person takes turn decorating my lunch table in roses. "What's going on?" This is kind of cute."

"Right." Shauna manually turns my head. "Your man is so cute." I turn to find Brandon standing in a black tuxedo, Kelly has a guitar and he's sitting on another lunch table. Everyone in the cafeteria has focused their attention on us. "Get up and get your dude." Shauna pushes me from the table.

"I'll have Kelly sing if you tell me no to my question." Brandon says.

"Ask me…I'm all ears."

"Randall Price, would you go to Prom with me?" He grabs a poster from Jason who has sat himself next to Sarah. "See, I even made you a poster. That means this proposal is real."

"You're cute…and yes, I'll go to prom with you." Brandon pulls himself into me and plants a very wet but loving kiss on me. He smells like lavender and green tea. "This was cute."

"Right. It took me an entire two days to come up with this."

"You did good, Brandon."

BRANDON

May 10th 8:00pm

Today is my eighteenth birthday.

Kelly and Jason have been planning my birthday party for weeks now. Jason pretty much likes any reason to throw a party. I started hearing people start the set-up process at six in the morning. I've been itching to take a peak, but Randall is pretty good at distracting me.

My mom bought me a pretty cool navy-blue blazer which causes Randall and I to become one of those color coordinated couples I've always dreamed about being. Randall has on an all-black outfit with accents of navy.

"There's a Bella downstairs waiting for you." My mom knocks. Randall invited Bella to the party tonight because we both thought it would be nice for her to get out the house. Randall has been checking on her almost every single day. Those two cannot go two hours without a check-in. "Is she?" My mom looks to Randall who nods his head to her question. "So sad."

"Yeah." Randall heads out of my room to go greet Bella. I spray one more spritz of my cologne then head out my room.

"Hey, Bella."

"Hey. I had no idea I lived so close to Brandon." Bella is wearing a black dress and her nails have been painted blue. She has on a black head scarf. "Oh, Happy Birthday Brandon." Bella hands me a card.

"Thank you." I say.

"We both got him the same card." Randall points to the identical decorative and very boisterous in color eighteenth birthday card that's sitting on our foyer table. "We truly are the same."

"Yes, we are." Bella says. "Oh, Brandon. Thanks for letting me tag along."

"It's no problem. Shall we get going?" I open the door and immediately I can see the strobe lights and hear the loud music blasting from Kelly's house next door. "We have a very, very, very, short walk ahead of us." Bella takes a moment. I hadn't noticed that she was carrying a walking stick. "Are you good, Bella?"

"Yeah. Just takes my brain a moment to do its brain thing...all good." Bella leads and Randall and I are trailing behind as we walk from my house to Kelly's. It doesn't take long for us to cross property lines.

"Hey, enjoy your party. Don't worry about us." We reach Kelly's doorway, and someone graciously opens the door for us. "Seriously, hang and chill with Kelly. I'll come find you if I need to."

"Alright." Randall kisses me on the cheek and then takes Bella's hand and walks with her into the party while I take in the scene of this party. There are people everywhere but somehow it doesn't seem crowded. There are snack tables in every corner I look in. There's a DJ in the middle of what used to be Kelly's living room. People are dancing and grinding. I can smell the vodka laced juice in every room I enter.

"Birthday boy!" Kelly yells. "Come take a shot with us." The crowd behind him cheers and they take their shot while some guy pours another round for the room. Kelly is still holding onto his shot.

"No. I'll watch you take a shot, though." I say.

Kelly tosses the liquid onto the ground. "…I am so glad you're here. All these people just came to drink some good shit. Also, I didn't even invite half these people, dude. Jason sent out one email to like twenty people and then all these people showed up."

"It's fine." I say.

"Hold up, where's Randall?"

"Oh, he's chilling with his friend Bella." Out the corner of my eye, I see Randall rushing after Bella. "Where's Jason?"

"Oh, he's somewhere dealing with his friends' drama. They're like too much" Kelly gets us both some water. "Pour it in a cup and they'll think you're drinking what they're drinking." I pour my water into a red solo cup then Kelly and I look to find a somewhat quieter room.

"They look like they're having some fun." I say. We pass people in the study on the ground when I get closer, I notice they are seriously playing Spin the bottle. "I really thought that game was played only in the movies or in middle schools."

"Let's play." Kelly says.

"Nope. I'm taken." I say.

"Dude, we're not fucking up our relationships. I just want to witness these drunk kids make fools out of themselves." Kelly doesn't wait for my response. He takes a seat in the first one he sees. I inch into the room and Kelly asks a guy if I can have his seat.

"So, we're just going to watch people kiss?" I ask.

"We're not doing this game like that." Rebecca chimes in out of nowhere. I don't notice her because her red hair is now a tint of yellow. "This is seven minutes in heaven." Two people rejoin the circle, and they look disgusted with one another.

"Nope. I'm out." I hop up from my chair and leave the room. I leave the room to find people outside by a fire chatting. In the months that I've been living with Kelly we never sat outside at this fireplace. "Can I join?"

"Yeah." Abiyram is the leader of the circle. Sarah and Shauna are both in attendance. "You're the birthday boy."

"Why aren't you inside dancing or drinking your life away?" Shauna asks.

"Oh, I'm not a drinker. I only came to be nice." I say.

"Where's my brother?" Shauna asks.

"He's with his friend Bella."

"Oh, cute." Sarah says.

"Well, we were just outside talking about life after high school." Abiyram says.

"Wait, you're a junior." I add.

"I know, I just wanted to know what everyone's plans were after high school. Shauna was telling us about her goals for Columbia. You're going to Julliard, right?"

"Sure am. I'm going to mostly just be doing my music and stuff." I say.

"Not hanging with me?" Shauna says.

"Of course, Randall would hurt me if I didn't hang with you."

"Nice." Shauna says.

"We're all going to be alright after high school. We all have bright futures and shit waiting for us. We just have to be ready to accept everything that's going to come our way. Make a plan and stick to it. Hang on to your friend groups. Most importantly, take care of yourselves." I see Randall walk back into my line of view and he is alone. I can't keep focus. "Yeah, I'm gonna go find my dude."

"Thanks for stopping to chat with us." Abiyram says. When I return back to the party it's like the music got louder. I pass two couples kissing side by side of each other. They are on full display of everyone at the party.

"There you are!" Kelly says.

"Here I am." I say.

"Come here." Kelly tugs on my wrist. "I want to show you something. I think you're going to like it." I follow Kelly all through the party. We push ourselves through the crowd of people dancing like the music the DJ is actually good. We pass some people taking body shots off some thick dude. These Crestview students are going to have a hard time waking up Monday morning. Kelly arrives to his room and on the bed is a sound board. "Do you like it?"

"Dude, how much did you spend on the sound board?"

"Does it really matter? My mom told me to get you a nice birthday present and she sent me her credit card. I saw you looking at this on your phone and I had Randall get into your phone and send me the link. He gave me half of his savings to go half with me on this." Kelly pulls an envelope from his drawer. "Speaking of which give your boy back his money."

"Wow. I don't even know what to say."

"Say, we're going to get a three-bedroom place and turn one of the rooms into a studio and we make some dope ass music on it for ourselves and other people." Kelly tries to lift the sound board up. "Say, you're going to accept this gift for all it's worth and we're going to chase our music dreams in New York."

I am at a loss for words.

"Bro, you are gifted as fuck. We wanted to invest in you the artist. Say that you're going to become a bad ass super genius on this thing—"

I pull Kelly in for a hug. "New York is going to be where our lives change. Thanks dude. Seriously, I would have never gotten this for myself. I would have kept hovering over this and got something way cheaper."

"No worries. I believe in everything that you are. Now, it's time that you do the same."

"You got it!" Kelly and I do our handshake—where we interlock our hands, snap over them with our freehand, clap, then interlock our pinkies, and hug. "I'm gonna head out a bit early."

10:30pm

I find Randall outside of Kelly's house sitting on the curb. He looks extremely cold and like he's in deep contemplation.

"Why are you sitting outside?" I join him on the curb. "Where's Bella?"

"She left. She got drunk and snapped on me." I say. Randall checks his phone and then he shoves it back into his pocket. "Her dad texted me. She got home alright." Randall grips my hand. "Bella is going through it. I don't even know how to help her. I've been so busy with my own stuff that I haven't even done any of the things that I wanted to do for her."

"Hey, we still have time…right?"

"I don't know. The more I ask about her and how she's doing the more she pulls away from me. I am seriously about to lose my first ever closest friend. I don't know how I'm even going to handle that."

"I'm here for you." Randall lays his head on my shoulder.

"I know."

"Hey! Why don't we go to prom with her and make the entire thing bigger than what she'd expect?" Randall lifts his head from my shoulder. "What do you think about that?"

"Yeah. We could make an entire day of it...wait, do you really want to give up your prom for this?"

"Yes! We have to do this for her. We just have to. I know she would do the same thing for you. We have to give her this one perfect night."

"Yeah. So, it's a plan." Randall says.

"It's a plan." I say. I pull the envelope with Randall's savings in it out my pocket, and I hand it to him. "Thank you for my gift."

"Kelly doesn't know what secret means. "I wanted you to have something for your birthday that you've always wanted."

"...and thank you for that. I also got something else that I've always wanted."

"Yeah, what's that? ...me."

"Randall, I wanted to be cute."

"Well, be cute and dance with me." I can hear a slow song playing. We both get up from the curb. Randall places his hands on my shoulder, and I grip his waist. "Sway with me." Randall and I keep swaying back and forth on the curb. We stay this way for the entirety of the song and when the song is over, we head back to my house, get ready for bed, and I spend the rest of the night holding onto Randall. "Thank you for these moments." I kiss the back of Randall's neck and within minutes he's sleep.

RANDALL

May 18ᵗʰ 8:30pm

I was able to convince Bella's dad to allow her to go to prom with Brandon and me. It didn't take much convincing. He agreed that it would be great for her spirit. To totally surprise Bella, my mom and abuela decided to go dress shopping for Bella.

Brandon and I had decided that date night was very much so needed because of how stressful finals have been for him. I have also been trying to play catch up in the few classes that I do have, and it has been quite annoying to say the least.

We stumble into one of my favorite bookstores called The Bookstore on Highland. It's a staple in Westlake. I used to come here often and sit and read with my dad. My dad would get his favorite green tea and some cookies, while I got my favorite drink at that moment, and we'd read for hours. "My mom keeps sending me photos of dresses for Bella." I hand Brandon my phone so he can make the executive decision on Bella's dress. "They're all so pretty. I can't choose."

"I like this white one…oh wait, this red one would seriously go with her eyes." Brandon sends my mom a reply in my voice. "Wait. This red dress has hella lace on it…will her dad…fuck it, we're getting it for her." Brandon is quite pleased with himself.

"That was so easy for you. It would've taken me all day to come up with a decision." I take a seat at an open table in the café.

"Yeah. I'm good with decisions I guess." Brandon smirks. "I'm gonna go get us some drinks. What do you want?"

"Uh, surprise me." I say.

"Alright. One surprise drink coming right up." Brandon goes to join the line of people where I notice they all have on t-shirts with white writing on it.

"Hey, is someone sitting in this chair?" A girl with long dreadlocks asks.

"Yeah. My boyfriend. He just went to get us some drinks." I say.

"No, worries." She says.

"Alright. One iced surprise drink…and I got myself a matcha. I saw this girl order it and thought I'd love to try that green drink…it's not that bad." Brandon sips his drink. The girl with dreads hasn't moved away from us yet. I catch her staring at Brandon. "Hi, is everything alright?" Brandon asks the girl with dreads as he takes his seat.

"Yeah. You two know about this meeting?"

"What meeting?" Brandon asks.

"The black union meeting." The girls says.

"Oh, we didn't know about the meeting, but we'd love to stay. We're both black and love unions." The girl with dreads takes one last look at Brandon before she goes to find another table to judge. "We can go if you want."

"Why? It could be a great meeting. Besides, I belong here too."

"Who's ready for an excellent discussion tonight?" A dark-skinned guy steps up to the podium. "It's going to be a good one. I can feel it." The guy scans the room and stops on Brandon and me. "My name is Elijah for anyone that is new here." Elijah nods his head to Brandon and me. "Who'd like to get something off their chest tonight?"

"Let's start with the new guys." The girl with dreads says.

"What are we saying?" Brandon drinks some of his drink. "I don't want to say the wrong thing. How should I do this?"

"There are no wrong answers Mr. Julliard…Oh, yeah. I saw your stuff online a while back…you're a dope musician." Elijah half grins. "Also, your friend Jason is my cousin."

"Oh, cool." Brandon says. "Well, I guess I've been having quite a bit of an identity crisis. Like, I saw on the news the other day about those officers killing that unarmed black kid. I wanted to post about it, but I remembered about a year ago, I tried speaking up on my social media and I got major backlash because people didn't like when I said that I sympathize and that it makes me scared as well."

I finally take a sip of my drink, then I place both of hands between my thighs.

"Maybe it was that sympathize word. White people feel like they know what we're going through and love throwing that word around...y'all don't know what us as black people are truly going through." The girl with dreads says. "Bianca, by the way."

"That's the thing. I'm not white. I'm both. Am I not allowed to still use that word? I know I may not look black, but I still want to acknowledge that it is a part of me." Bianca folds her arms and doesn't have a comeback for Brandon.

"Mr. Julliard's boyfriend, what have you been telling him."

I am very nervous. Being put on display is not my favorite thing in the world.

"My name is Randall...and that's Brandon. I haven't said anything. It wasn't because I didn't want to or didn't have the words for him. Just, I have always felt that as long as it's pure and from the heart why should it matter what version of black, he is."

"Technically, he's not black." Bianca exclaims. She hits her fist on the table. "If he gets stopped by the police, the chances of him being mistaken as aggressive...you know what, fuck it... If he get pulled over the chances of him being shot are slim." Bianca goes back to crossing her arms and playing with her dreads.

"I get your point." I say. "But he's aware of that. Does this mean he's still not able to sympathize with other black people? Does this mean he can no longer acknowledge part of his blackness? Is he now required to keep that part of himself a secret? Why isn't Brandon allowed to be proud of both parts of himself." Bianca attempts to speak but doesn't have much to say.

"He makes a great point. Continue." Elijah chimes in.

"This is a huge reason why white passing mixed race people have a hard time identifying with one or the other because they're dammed either way. We should be happy to have allies like Brandon and others who sympathize and try to feel our pain. You can't always be quick to judge. It's not right…life's too short for that." Brandon places his hand on my thigh and winks at me.

"Randall, excellent point. At a time like this we shouldn't be judging…in fact we shouldn't be judging at all. I say this all the time that everyone's experience is different but the one thing that we have in common is that we all ascend from the same continent. Black people come in all shades and all of them are equal. No one shade is indifferent and no one shade is superior." Elijah keeps his attention on Brandon and me. "Don't be afraid to show your support. Keep speaking up."

"Thanks for that, dude." Brandon nods in Elijah's direction.

"No problem. And with that, thank you all for coming out." Elijah immediately steps down from the podium. "Get home safe, folks."

When the meeting ends Brandon and I spend our time browsing the bookstore. In all of my time of coming here, I never realized how massive this place is. When my dad and I would come here, I'd stick to my one section and that was literary fiction. I have never been a huge fan of branching out when it comes to my reading options. It's all fiction or nothing. "How many versions of Jane Eyre are you gonna have?" Brandon asks.

"Not enough. I have the one we were given from school, my dad's copy he got when he was my age, there's the lovely present of the original run copy that you gifted me with and soon, when I've made space, I'm going to come back and get this copy."

"It's so old and has that old paper smell and looks very worn out. I'm pretty sure there's pages missing."

"I'm pretty sure there are pages missing too but I just love this story so much. Plus, I basically know this book word for word, so it won't be hard for me to recite the missing words on the missing pages." I place the Jane Eyre book in the wrong location with hopes that in a few weeks when I come back, I'll be able to come back to my spot and buy it. There's so many books in this place, I'm sure no one actually places the books back where they got them.

"Hey, you two." Elijah pops out from out of nowhere. "I enjoyed you two being at the meeting tonight."

"Thanks. I think we both enjoyed it too." Brandon says.

"Yeah, it was really great." I say.

"Come back again, alright?" Elijah grabs Glass Town by Charlotte Brontë off the shelf. "A freaking classic."

"It truly is." I say. "I've read almost all of her books."

"Oh, nice." Someone calls out for Elijah. "Look, I gotta get out of here. We'll be here once a month through the summer…then it's off to the big apple for me…gonna be attending NYU for English in the fall…so, hopefully I'll be seeing you two around."

"Yeah, most definitely…you already know, Julliard in the fall." Brandon says.

"What about you, Randall?"

"Oh, senior year…then hopefully NYU next fall…English too."

"Dope. it was nice meeting you both. Take care." Elijah rushes off.

"That's cool. Brandon, you're going to have another friend in New York. I think it's great. The universe is sending everyone to the east coast."

"Yeah. The more people from home that I know I won't be so homesick." Brandon places the book he's been holding on the shelf. "You wanna get out of here? I discovered this place and I just have to show you before we head back to your place."

"That's fine. One second though." I notice an opening on the bookcase where I've placed my future new copy of Jane Eyre. I take my future book out of its hiding place and place it gently into the opening. "I'll be back for you soon."

"You're something else." Brandon says.

"I know, right." I smile.

Brandon holds his hand out to me. "You're going to love this place. Trust me."

BRANDON

May 18ᵗʰ 11:00pm

Right next door to the Bookstore on Highland is an acoustic bar.
They mostly play jazz, and the place is always packed with students
that go to Crestview or locals from Westlake. "Have you ever been
to The Hightower?" Randall just goes with the flow; he hands the
man at the door his student ID and enters when it's our turn to do
so. "Isn't this place spectacular?" The Hightower looks very luxe.
The walls are painted black, and the white and black tables in the
space complement the hints of red décor nicely.

"I love this place." Randall says. A person gives us their
table, we take our seats, and I am focused on the older man
playing guitar on the stage. "Hey, look at what that person is
drinking." Randall is mesmerized by the woman drinking a
glowing red drink from a really fancy martini glass. "Ma'am, what
are you drinking?" The woman looks at Randall, smiles, and says
oh, darling, it's a virgin glowing cosmopolitan…it's delightful. "Cool, I want
that, I'll go get that…do you want something?"

"No, I'm cool. I don't think I can take any more liquid. My bladder may explode." Randall jets off to the bar to get his drink. I focus my attention to the guy playing guitar. He is playing a version of a David Bowie song I know but his arrangement of it is a bit strange but somehow it works. "Suffragette City" I whisper. My mom and dad used to sing that song all the time. I close my eyes and I can see my mom with her whisk to her mouth and she's mouthing all of the words to the song, while my dad is belting out the lyrics from the top of his lungs using the serving spoon as his microphone.

"Hey, I'm back. I decided to get fries instead." Randall cuts my dream short. "Wanna share these?"

"Yeah. Of course." I say.

"Are you alright, looks like you've seen a ghost." Randall places his hand on the back of my neck. "What's up?"

"Oh, this was my dad's song. He sang this song like once a week."

Randall listens to the arrangement for a moment. "Suffragette City? Is that right?"

"How do you know this song?" I'm a bit shocked and somewhat turned on that Randall knows this song. "You gotta tell me how you know it."

Randall finishes swallowing his French fry. "...at my first school on Prince Island, my roommate was a total music buff...he didn't sing or anything. He just played all kinds of music, and he always had all kinds of music references."

"Dopeeee. That guy and I would be total besties." The man on stage finishes the song. He places the guitar on the stage and then walks off. I want to fangirl so much, but I fight my urges and remain seated. "Damn, I wonder who's next."

"Your hand is itching, isn't it?" Randall tugs on my jacket sleeve. "Get up there." He motions to the empty stage. "Look, the lights are flickering for you."

"...or they could just be loose." I say.

"Brandon, what do you have to lose. I see you gaining more fans than anything." Randall turns and scans the room. "Look at all these people just having conversations...they need a master at music up on that stage right now."

"What if I'm taking someone else's turn?"

"...that's an excuse. You have nothing to be nervous about. Just look at me. The light is probably going to be bouncing off my head, so you probably won't see anyone." Randall urges me one last time.

"Alright, alright...and I'm not nervous. I just don't know this crowd or what they like." I take my jacket off lay it on the back of my chair. "Also, I think all musicians are a bit nervous before going up on stage." I make my way to the stage. I take a moment to decide which instrument I am going to play. There's a sax, a grand piano, a few different bass guitars, a trumpet, and a set of drums. I know how to play all of these instruments comfortably, but I settle for my favorite and most trusted the guitar. I place the strap on my shoulder and begin strumming. "Hey, I'm Brandon. I'm gonna play a classic for you all. Enjoy and tip your waiters."

My nerves calm a bit once I hear the people in the audience laugh. Kelly tells that tip your waiters joke because it loosen up the crowd.

"You got this!" Randall mouths.

"If you are a Washington native, you better know this song…" I have studied 'In Bloom' by Nirvana. I know all of the chords. I taught myself how to play it both acoustic and the way Kurt Cobain does on the guitar (I'll never be as good). I even know David Grohl's drum technique (still, not as good as him). When I start to play it the acoustic way, the audience doesn't respond how I thought they would. "I'll switch it up for you." I plug the guitar into the amp on the stage and I start from the beginning. It's as if someone turned a light switch on. Everyone in the room starts cheering along to the beat of 'In bloom.' The guy playing the guitar from earlier approaches the stage. He places a microphone on the stage.

"Sing!" He encourages.

"Sing!" I can hear Randall yell.

I start to sing the song word for word. I feel like a total Rockstar. The remaining people sitting in their seats stand up and continue to cheer and clap for me. Kurt Cobain and David Grohl have a moment about a quarter of the way in the song. The guy playing guitar from earlier makes his way to the drums and he begins playing the drum solo while I'm doing my best to play the Mr. Cobain's part. I start to hear people whistling and the cheers get even louder. When the song ends people start chanting one more song!

"Do you have another one in you...Chad, by the way"
Chad stands from the drums.

"Nah. I gotta get out here." I place the guitar back on the stand. "Just the crowd got my adrenaline pumping so hard right now, I'd never stop singing if I get back up there. I'd love to come back and perform some time though."

"Will you?" Chad asks.

"Yeah, most definitely." I write my number down on a piece of paper. "Here, I'd love to play here during the summer. I'm going to New York in the fall."

"Dope! I'll give it to my brother—he runs this place for me, while I'm back home in Nantucket. Maybe for the summer, we could do like a rock and roll night, what do you think?" I turn to see Randall standing by the stage.

"That'd be so cool."

"Then, when you're settled in New York connect with me and maybe we could set something up at one of my friends' bars in the city. I know a lot of people who'd love to hear you play and sing...you got talent dude...I saw your..." Chad points to Randall.

"He's, my boyfriend." I say.

"...I saw your boyfriend pushing you towards the stage. You got raw and natural talent. That crowd loved you. Also, you gotta start playing your own stuff."

"I here you. Next time I'm back you have my word. I'll play my own stuff." I offer Chad a handshake, but he pulls me in for a hug.

"I'm gonna hold you to it."

"Please do." I don't think my smile has broken since I've stopped playing.

"We'll talk soon…and I'm serious, when you get out east hit me up, so we can start getting you gigs more often…that pays too."

"Dope. I love things that pay."

"Have a good night…you two get home safe."

"…you were amazing." Randall kisses me then hangs on to me. "I told you that they'd love you."

"Yeah, you did." I give Randall another kiss. "I gotta start listening more. And taking more leaps of faith."

"You got it…I so can't wait to see you playing somewhere fancy one day. You're going to be big…just don't forget me when you do."

"Never. That would never happen…I'm holding onto you until the end of time…did you forget?" I take Randall's hand and he hands me my jacket and we head out of Hightower.

We take our time walking back to his place. When we get back to his house, Maria and his abuela are sitting on the porch; his abuela is doing some reading, while his mom rocks back and forth in her chair. We greet them and head right up to Randall's room and get ready for bed. I try my best to tire myself out, but my mind is wide awoke. "I'll stay up with you, wanna watch some random show?"

"No, it's alright. Get some sleep." I spend the rest of the night thinking about how proud my dad would be of me right now. That man would be trying to out cheer everyone. "Love you, dad." I whisper.

BRANDON

May 29th 5:30pm

I have been waiting for prom to happen since the start of the
school year.

I got up extremely early like they do in the movies and
started preparing. I redyed my hair. I died my hair back to its
original light brown color—the dirty blonde look wasn't doing it
for me anymore. My mom took me to get a facial and I did not like
the experience. There were Crestview girls all through the facial
place getting full body waxes, steams, and massages, I couldn't
enjoy the moment. All I kept hearing was them talk about how
special after prom was going to be and if they thought first times
hurt.

After all of our running errands we get back home, and I
have just realized that I left the shirt to my tuxedo at the suit shop.
"I'll just go without a shirt and tie." My mom frowns her face to
that thought. "All the rockers are doing it." My mom goes into my
closet and finds a shirt with the tag still on it.

"How's this?" My mom holds up a black short sleeve shirt I got a gift maybe two years ago.

"I think that'll work...plus it's short sleeve...even better." I throw on the black button down and my mom starts to tie my necktie but then stops midway.

"Oh, let me go get my camera."

"Mom, Kelly has a camera, we can take the pictures on his camera." I can't watch my mom learn how to get me in focus on our very old DSLR.

"Well, how will I get them?" She asks.

"Technology. We'll figure out a way to get you the photos." I go back to messing with my necktie. My mom laughs before she takes over with fixing my horrible necktie job. "...Brandon...you look just like your dad." She then helps me put my jacket on. "So handsome."

My mom starts to cry. "Hey, mom. It's alright." I try to give her a hug, but she stops me.

"No, I don't want to ruin your suit. You and Kelly go downstairs so I can get a photo." I hand my mom Kelly's very complicated camera and I head out of my room. "Kelly! Jason! Photo time." My mom goes before me while I wait at the top of the steps for Kelly and Jason to get ready. Kelly's parents and Jason's parents are all gathered at the bottom of the stairs watching as we all make our way down the steps. My mom is standing at the bottom of the stairs snapping away.

"Look at us. We look good." Kelly says. "Brandon, you didn't have to outdo us though. The all-black look. It's sick."

"Oh, come on, we all look pretty smooth…I'd think we were all straight."

"Yeah…okay." Jason says. We laugh in unison. "It's gonna be a good night."

"It's almost six. I told Randall we'd be there by six." I say.

"Well, let's get a move on. I'll drive so we can kill some time." Kelly says.

"I'll be following behind. I want to get some photos of you and Randall." My mom says. Jason's mom and Kelly's mom offer to tagalong. I see my mom warm up a little.

"Let's go everyone!" Kelly exclaims.

6:15pm

Kelly gets us into Westlake in record time. He dodged in and out of traffic and we arrive to Randall's house just as Bella showed up with her dad. I hop out of the car and go to greet her dad. "How's it going?" I race to the other side of the car and open Bella's door.

"Hi, Brandon. It's so nice seeing you." Bella looks so perfect in the red dress that was picked out for her. She smells like fresh lavender. "Thank you for this."

"Awe, you're welcome but this was all Randall." I help Bella get out of the car and I usher her to Randall's front door. Maria doesn't wait for a knock she opens and instantly bursts into tears…she could have also already been crying.

"Brandon…Bella…you both look so beautiful." Maria kisses us both on the cheek and she steps aside so we both can come inside.

"Mom. You keep crying like this, you won't have any tears for when I do this all over again with Brandon next year." Randall says. He appears at the top of the steps. He has on a burgundy suit. He looks like a fucking movie star. His smile causes my heart to skip a beat. For a quick second, everyone has disappeared, and it is just Randall and me. I watch him as his foots reaches every single step. Then, I grow impatient, and I rush halfway up the stairs and I take his hand. "You just couldn't help yourself, could you?"

"You know I couldn't." I kiss Randall and I let my lips linger onto his for a moment. "Sorry, I just couldn't help myself."

"Alright, you two…kiss again, so I can get a picture." His abuela says.

"I want one, too." My mom is beaming.

"Same here. Kiss you two." Maria says.

I'll kiss Randall anywhere and at any time, no place is off limits for me, and no setting is off limits. I love this boy with everything in me. I kiss Randall with all the passion in me and then lean him back. I cut it short this time because I felt some things fumbling upwards. "Damn." I whisper.

"Can we come down the steps now?" Randall asks.

"Not until I get a photo" Christina says. She takes her photo of Randall and I and then we both continue down the stairs.

"You both clean up nice." Shauna says.

Randall approaches Bella and the two of them embrace. "Bella, you look perfect. That dress fits you amazingly."

"Thanks. I'm so happy to be going to prom with you and Brandon." Bella wipes away a tear. "Thanks for this, seriously." Bella inhales and to me, it seems like she is struggling to exhale. She catches my glance, and she quickly straightens herself up. "Anymore photos?" Bella turns to the room.

"I ran out of space on this memory card." My mom says. "I'll use my phone."

"Guys, the limo is here." Jason announces. "Randall, buddy, you look good."

"Thanks." Randall says.

"...and Bella." Randall kisses her hand. "You look flawless."

"Yes, you do Bella." Maria says. "An absolute dream."

"Let's pile in." Kelly leads. "We don't want to get to prom when it's over."

Randall takes my hand and Bella grips Randall's hand, and we all make our way to the limo. "Ready for a great night, everyone?"

"Let's get it." Randall says.

8:30pm

We make it to prom just as people are making their entrances. Prom is being held at some fancy hotel in the city. The dress code and theme for prom is Oscar's red carpet. All of the students are dressed in their designers clothing but somehow everyone still manages to stop and stare at Randall and Bella as we make our procession into prom.

"Do every student here look this good every single day?" Bella asks.

"Pretty much." Randall says. I hand the ticket taker our tickets and he hands us a ballot for prom king and queen. I write Kelly and Jason's name down. "I'm putting Kelly and Jason down." I show Randall my ballot. "...and we think alike...he's a keeper folks." We hand the ticket takers our ballots and we enter prom.

Crestview spared no expense for this prom. There's gold pretty much everywhere in this ballroom. It's as if our prom committee found every single gold decorative item, ordered it, and tossed it everywhere. The dance floor is the only thing not gold, it is a burgundy and black checkboard. The lights in this place have been turned a shade of red and gold. Randall and Bella still shine through it all.

"Damn, do they still have money for graduation?" Kelly jokes. "This place is sick."

The DJ in charge of the music starts to play a slow song and all of the people that came with a partner head to the dance floor. I grab Randall's hand and we are center stage. Randall pulls himself into me and stays there as we move back and forth with the song. "I'm legit going to miss you next year."

"Brandon, we have a schedule. I'm going to keep up with it. Plus, we're going to call each other every single day."

"Yeah, that's not the same...I do have the option to—"

"No. Don't you even dare. You are going to New York, and we are going to make this work. We both want this. We're just going to have to wait nine months…there's breaks. Thanksgiving, Winter, Spring. That's how we have to look at it…if you think about it, we'll be together all the time." Randall looks up at me. "We're going to make this work."

"Yeah. Just gonna take some work on both our ends."

"…and remember we have our Estrella." Randall stops swaying for a second and looks at me. "All you have to do is find it, Brandon."

"How did I get some lucky?" I ask.

"You spoke to me in English…then fell for me at Jason's party."

"When did you fall for me?" I ask.

"Oh, when we were laying in the sprinklers. I knew then that we'd be here now. I knew that you and I were going to become friends. I had no idea that I'd be planning things with you at sixteen. Brandon Marciano…you really changed my life. You know that?"

"…and Randall Price. You've changed mine." The song ends and a fast one begins. Randall tries to keep up with the flow of the movements, but he gets a little winded and stops. I walk with him back to our table.

"Trust me, in a few weeks, I'm going to be killing all of the dances. I'm almost there." Randall does one final dance move before taking his seat. "Just you watch Brandon, we're going to be dancing too not just slow songs."

I turn to Bella who is tapping her feet to the beat of the song. "Hey, do you want to dance?" I have to basically yell through the music playing. "Are you up for it?"

"No, I'm good. Just going to take a moment to chill." Bella says. "Like, Randall, I don't think my body will let me do all of those spins...I'll dance to the next slow song."

"Cool." I say. I notice Kelly having a conversation with Sarah and then head towards me. "Next, slow song. It's you and me."

"Yo, Brandon." Kelly turns me towards the stage. "Let's get up there and liven up this place. One last performance together."

"I'm down." I say.

"Really, I thought I would have to pull teeth with you." Kelly approaches the stage.

"No. I'm learning to embrace my gifts." Kelly and I do our incredibly obnoxious handshake. "Hey, I'm about to go perform with Kelly really quick." I say to Randall.

"Yes! Bella, do you want to just stand at the stage." I notice Bella checking her pacing on her wrist. She stops when I catch her.

"Yeah." She gets up from the table and she and Randall make their way to the stage.

"Alright everyone, we're minutes away from announcing Prom King and Queen...or Queen and Queen, or King and King...or whatever you want to call it." Sarah announces.

Kelly and I take our place on the stage. I'm singing lead and he's chosen to play the drums. Kelly convinces one of his friends to hop on the keyboard. "Before we announce fellow seniors Kelsau...I mean, Kelly and Brandon are going to perform for you...so, give it up!" Sarah walks off stage and she joins Randall, Bella, Jason, and Shauna at the foot of the stage.

"Alright guys, we got two weeks left in this place. Let's do this." Kelly says from the drums. He kicks things off by playing a very upbeat song. All of Kelly's songs are upbeat and that's one of the things that I love about him as a writer. I know this song very well because I arranged it for him.

This song is about moving on but never forgetting where you came from. In the lyrics Kelly talks about how it's going to be hard to move on but he's hopeful for his future. I love singing this song because it was the one song that got me over my writing slump. When things were so bad with my mom and I, I would play this song, so it gave me hope that things between us would get better. As I sing this song, I see people wiping at their face. When you graduate high school and move on, it's so surreal. I've spent four years in this place growing. People don't realize how much you change as a person in high school. You experience your first heartbreak in high school. You learn about this so-called real world. High school is where you find your tribe. I became an adult here.

Sarah rushes to the stage. "Wow. I've always loved that song." Sarah motions for us to get off the stage. "Brandon and Kelly, you're going to do great things in New York."

I join Randall and Bella. I console Bella and the entire time I can feel her heart racing. "Hey, do you want to go sit down?"

"No, I'm good." Bella looks me in the eye. "Trust me."

"...and your next Prom Royalty is..." My mind ignores the rest of what Sarah is saying.

"Hey, you good?" I ask Bella.

"Yeah, seriously." Bella says. "Go on stage...you won."

"Brandon and Randall...get up here." Sarah motions with the envelope in hand. "You're the winner. Come get your crown boys." Kelly pushes me back on stage. Sarah crowns me first. Randall has invited Bella onto the stage with us. He asks Sarah if he could have the mic. She hands it to him.

"Hey, everyone...thanks for this." Randall doesn't notice that Bella is trying her hardest to remain upright. She is forcing her smile, but I can tell something is wrong. I know it is. "Thank you for tonight, Bella—" Bella collapses on the stage...

RANDALL

May 29ᵗʰ 6:00pm

I have to admit that I am nervous as hell for prom tonight. Then,
on the plus side, if anything goes wrong—like, I trip walking in, or
do anything embarrassing to myself like spilling on my rented
tuxedo…I at least have next year to do it all over again.

I tend to overserve sometimes. I am going to make tonight
all about Bella. When I surprised her with the text that we're going
to prom together she called me right away and we stayed on the
phone for hours. My mom made me go to sleep just as the
conversation was getting good.

As I put the finishing touches on my suit, I realize that I
have three more months of seeing Brandon every day. I have never
been in this kind of love. I never saw myself planning a future at
sixteen. Then I beat my cancer and that's all I keep thinking about.

"Oh, mijo." I can hear tears in my mother's voice. "You're
all grown up." My mom places a handkerchief in my top pocket.
"This was your dads."

"Mom don't cry. You're going to make me cry." My mom turns me to the mirror in my room. "We did good. You did good."

"I wish the accident never happened. I want your dad to witness this…he would be so proud of you." My mom takes the final lint from off my suit jacket. "I love you so much, my boy. You are my entire heart."

"…and you are mine too."

"Randall! Brandon and Bella are here!" My abuela calls.

"Oh! Let me go first…give me twenty seconds to get downstairs and get my camera." My mom rushes out of the room. I don't wait the twenty seconds. I am so anxious, so I have to see Brandon he has a way of calming my nerves.

As I make my way to the stairs, I can hear my mom crying once again. "Mom don't waste all of your tears. You keep crying like this, you won't have any tears for when I do this all over again with Brandon next year." Brandon and I lock eyes and the world completely stops. He becomes the only person in the room. I take my time going down the stairs, partly because my feet are killing me in these unbroken-in shoes, and I love savoring every moment with Brandon. When he rushes up the stairs to me, I hold my breath to prepare for his kiss.

"Wow." I whisper. "You look so good." I whisper in his ear.

"You look even better." He whispers back. My mom and Brandon's mom take a bunch of photos of us on the stairs. I get tired of standing in the same spot on the stairs.

"Bella! You look amazing." I give Bella a hug and her heart is racing so fast. "Are you doing, okay?" I whisper in Bella's ear.

"Yeah. Don't spend the night worrying about me." Bella says.

"Ok...but, you know I will—"

"Randall, you really pulled this off. I love this suit on you." Shauna slaps me on the butt. "Plus, look at your butt. It looks so good."

"Umm...eww...I think...you're my sister."

"I'm not allowed to talk about your butt?" Shauna asks. "You have a nice ass in this suit. Brandon...your butt looks nice too."

"Awe, thanks." Brandon smiles.

"Shauna, you look nice too...I'm not going to be weird any further, so I'll leave it at you look nice in your dress...oh, Bella, this is my sister Shauna."

"We met." Bella says. "In the elevator of the hospital and I think we attended a dance class together back in the day."

"Oh my! We did!" Shauna snatches Bella in for a hug. "I was a such a bad dancer."

"No, you were alright." Bella winks at Shauna.

"Should we follow Kelly and Jason to the limo?" I ask Bella.

"Yeah, let's go make this a great night." We head out the door and Bella takes her hand in mine as Kelly leads us both to the limo.

"No, we should let Bella get in first." Jason says.

"Agreed." Kelly says.

"No arguments here." Shauna says. Bella takes her time getting into the limo. "Randall, your turn."

I go in and immediately take my seat next to Bella. "Hey, this is going to be a great night."

"Randall, thanks again for inviting me. I feel like a total star." Bella kisses me on the cheek. "You are a really great friend."

"Thanks." Everyone else piles into the limo. Kelly sits right beside me, and I hook my arm in his. "Let's have the best night tonight, everyone."

"Yeah. Randall, you're lucky. You get to have this moment twice." Shauna says. I shoot her a look. She takes observation of both Brandon and Bella. "Shit. I'm sorry." She mouths.

"Hey, are you alright?" I ask Bella.

"Yeah. I just did not think I would be able to have this night." Bella and our conversation is not private anymore. Everyone in the limo takes notice and pays attention to us. "I am so lucky that I even got eighteen years of life. In this lifetime, I have lived multiple lives. Each time I was given the clear, I started a new life. I got to try to be a different version of Bella. I've used my ninth life. I've made peace with that."

"That's why I admire you both." Brandon says. "When my dad died…look, my dad didn't fight. He didn't try to overcome this. He let his cancer overtake him. You two are fucking fighters and don't forget that." Brandon reaches for both our hands.

"Thanks Brandon." Bella says.

"Hey, you remember that ice cream spot we went to after treatment sometimes?" I ask Bella. "We're going to pass it on the way into Crestview. It's right before the pass bridge."

"That'd be nice to go to tonight after Prom."

"No, Bella. I was thinking we could go there right now."

"Are you serious?" Bella asks.

"Hey, can we stop for ice cream?" I ask the group.

"Yeah." Kelly says. He taps on the window and chats with the driver briefly. "Let's go get some ice cream. I'll pay."

7:40pm

I chose two scoops of pistachio. Bella gets the same.

"Hey, how are you, seriously?" I ask her.

"I'm good, trust me. I do wish I had met you years ago. I wish we had met when we were both happy little kids. I would have so loved being your friend back then. I would have gotten so much strength from you. You are the definition of a fighter. I don't think I would have wanted to go through this this as many times as you have. I never had to hear that I was remission…you heard that twice before and you still kept fighting. I only got to stop treatment; I was never in the clear. The real fighter is you. Truth is, I gave up." This crushes me.

"Wait. What! I don't believe you." I say. Everyone goes to get in back in the limo. I motion for Brandon to go before me. "You said that it spread all over."

"No. Dr. Rickards gave me an option, it was surgery, then treatment, and a few months later another surgery. That still wouldn't ensure that my cancer would be gone."

"Woah." I literally feel like the wind has been knocked out of me.

"So, I told my dad and her that I did not want to continue with treatments. I knew the risks and I was fine with that. I had to make the best decision for me. I wanted to enjoy the air. I wanted to sleep with my window open and just listen to the Seattle rain hit the ground. I wanted to go to a party and most importantly…I wanted to spend my last days with friends. Randall, you have given me so much. I watch the love that you have for life. I wish I had your spirit. I want to thank you for loving me and caring for me. You have given me so much in the past few months than I've given myself the past two years of dealing with this. I believe God's path for me was help my dad learn that he'll be fine after I'm gone. I did the right thing for me. Thank you, Randall, for being my friend."

"Oh, you're welcome." I can see Brandon stick his head out of the limo. I immediately turn away from him. "I am going to miss you so much."

"I know and you are going to live…you're going to have to live the rest of your life and live it for you. Do you hear me? You got your happy ending."

"I'll never forget you." Bella and I hug, and I take in all of her. I will be losing a friend soon.

"Now, let's go have some fun, friend." Bella heads toward the limo.

9:10pm

"Hey, what are you thinking about?" Brandon asks. We have been slowly moving to a couple of the slow songs for quite some time now. "You look like—Oh, it's Bella."

"Yeah. I never thought we wouldn't finish our journey together. That's all." Bella smiles and waves to me from the table. "It just sucks. How come she doesn't get her happy ending, either?" I stop myself from crying.

"Because there are so thing." Brandon says. "Remember? One of the things I love about you is that you believe in letting life do its thing. Letting life run its course. Maybe this is how it was supposed to end up. Maybe she was placed in your life to teach you a lesson…or she was placed here to serve a purpose and her time is done." Brandon looks at Bella. "Bella looks content with whatever is next."

"Yeah. She said the same thing."

"You get to live."

"I guess it survivors' remorse." I say. "I want the universe to grant me more time with her. Just a few more months. I have like so much more stuff to show her." Brandon just lets me go on and on about the future plans I'm going to make with Bella. He lays my head on his chest and lets me make these plans. "I'm going to write this stuff down and show her later."

"I think that's a good idea." Brandon tries to sound optimistic for me but deep down I know he knows that I won't be getting to see these plans through with Bella.

When the slow music stop the DJ puts on a fast song. I do my best to keep up, but my healing body decides it is time to take a breath to allow me to recover and I head back to our table.

"I was just chatting with Rebecca…she told me she apologized to you." Bella has her hand on her chest.

"Hey, Randall." Rebecca says.

"Hi. You look really nice." Rebecca's hair is red again and she looks like a dream in her red dress. "I hope we can look this good next year for our official turn."

"Wait, are you saying you're going to be speaking to me next year?" Rebecca asks.

"…yes. And I'll even give theater one more try."

"Randall, I promise to be better." Rebecca says.

"I believe you." I say.

"Well, I guess I should go back to my date. He's looking very bored." Rebecca walks back over to her date.

"Hey, Brandon and I are about to perform for everyone." Brandon takes off for the stage. It isn't long before Brandon and Kelly are performing one of Kelly's songs. This song happens to be one of my favorite songs. I never told Brandon this but when I first heard Kelly's song about hope last year it got me through the few rounds of radiation, I had last year.

"What are you thinking?" I ask Bella.

"Oh, nothing, I feel absolutely free, right now. It's like Brandon is singing to me." Bella remains still. All she does is smile and continues letting the words speak to her.

"Hey, Randall." Abiyram says.

"Abiyram…is this your—"

"Yeah. I have a boyfriend." Abiyram grabs his boyfriend's hand. "We met after we had that conversation in the gym a few weeks ago."

"Cool." I smirk.

"He said that you two take physics together…did you set this up?" I shrug my shoulders to Abiyram completely acting clueless.

"I have no idea what you're talking about."

"Well, I'll be sure to thank this mystery person for setting us up…oh! It's good to hear you're going to keep doing theater next school year. See you around. Who knows, we can maybe all hang out this summer."

"Yeah, of course." I say. Abiyram and his boyfriend walks away.

"Randall, the matchmaker…how cute." Bella chimes. She places her hand on her chest. "I'm fine before you ask."

"Sure, you are." I say. Brandon and Kelly finish their song. The crowd spends a little bit of time cheering them on. Sarah cuts that short.

"You're about to win." Shauna says.

"Not going to hold my breath." Branson stands next to me. He keeps checking on Bella who keeps assuring that she's fine.

"Randall and Brandon, get up here." Sarah says. Brandon gets pushed onto stage first. Bella grips my hand just as I start to walk towards the stage. "Randall, come on. Come get your crown. You won."

"Hey, come up here with me." I say to Bella.

"Alright." Bella's breathing has gotten increasingly heavy. She is forcing herself to smile even though I can see that that she is having trouble breathing.

"Hey, could I say something to Bella?" I ask Sarah.

"Yeah, of course." Sarah hands me the mic.

"Hi everyone, I want to thank my friend Bella for being one of the many people who has been there for me. I love you so much. You don't even know how much you mean to me." Bella forces herself to smile. "Bella—catch her!" I yell. I rush to Bella's side. "Bella!" I cry. "Bella, wake up!"

"Someone call the ambulance." Sarah yells.

"She's not breathing." I yell. Principal Pendergrass rushes to the stage just as all the medics arrive. Brandon tries his best to pull me away from Bella. "No! I have to go with her. I have to be with her." I tell Brandon. "Let me go with her please." The medics start to wheel Bella to the ambulance. "Can I go with her, please."

"Only if you are family." The EMT says. "Are you family? …You can only go if you are family. So, are you?" She asks one more time.

"Yes. I'm family." I say.

"I'll meet you at the hospital." Brandon says. We sprint out of the hotel within seconds.

RANDALL

June 7th 11:00am

Bella died the night of prom.

She had a DNR, which meant her dad had to force himself to let her go. I was the one that discovered that she had a DNR when I checked her purse in the ambulance looking for her phone. So, all that arrived at the hospital was her body.

Bella got to do one final good deed. She was an organ donor which means that upon her death all of her organs that hadn't been ruined by the cancer were given to people who needed them. That made her dad smile. The hospital gave her an amazing send off before they took her body to the back to begin seeing what parts of her body could be donated. We heard five families got to keep their loved ones for a little bit longer because she was a donor.

Saying goodbye was the hardest thing I ever had to do. There was no final chat and no final cry with each other…she was just gone. Her dad stayed at the hospital through each of the five transplant surgeries, he gave each family a note Bella wrote months before her end. Her dad thanked me for being her friend.

Bella's funeral was so packed. I had no idea she touched so many people's lives while she was on this earth. People of every age is in attendance. Her dad did not want the service to be long, so he chose for no one to give a speech and he also didn't invite a bunch of people to the burial. Brandon, Kelly, Shauna, Jason and I were the only ones with him.

He didn't want to do say his final good alone. He wanted the people that was there her last day on this earth be with him in the end.

"Randall, can you close this out?" Her dad asks.

"Sure." I stand and face everyone. "When I first met Bella, it was at a time when I was feeling down about myself. She picked up instantly. We didn't bond because we had cancer. We bonded because we survived. Before I met Bella my thoughts on happy endings wavered. She helped me see that you don't need a happy ending in order feel accomplished or like you've won." I take a moment.

A butterfly lands onto Bella's picture. I study it for a moment.

"We win when we get up. Bella has helped me see that my life has purpose and that each day I get to open my eyes. I should do so like it is my last day. Bella was quick to say that she served her purpose and for that she is thankful. In her eighteen years, she touched hundreds of lives. I will never forget you, Bella. You will live in my heart for as long as I get to live." I had pages left to say but I felt myself about to break. I end my speech early. I hand it to Bella's dad, and we embrace. "Thank you for being so nice to me."

"Thank you for loving my daughter." Her dad says. "You were the best thing that ever happened to her. Promise to keep in touch. You're all that's left."

"I promise. You have my word."

"Take care of yourself Randall Price." Bella's dad walks over to Brandon. "You take care of him."

"You have my word, sir." Brandon shakes his hand. "I think he takes care of us though."

"Thank you all for coming." Bella's dad walks away from Bella's grave just it begins to lower in the ground. Once the casket has been fully lowered, we all leave the cemetery one at a time. Brandon and I are the last people remaining.

"I think It's time for us to go." Brandon says.

"Yeah." We head towards the car. "I'm going to miss you so much Bella, sleep peacefully beautiful."

SUMMER

RANDALL

August 5th 2:00pm

Brandon leaves for New York in a few days. His first day at Julliard is also my first day of senior year. We have been spending as much time as we can together. This summer has been a blast. I got to actually live and do all of the things I was so nervous to do because I was afraid that my body wasn't ready.

My hair is starting to grow back so it's been boosting my confidence more and more and I've been letting Brandon show all the PDA that he wants. I've truly been living the past couple of months. Each day has been a new adventure or experience with Brandon.

Jason invited us over to his house for a small get together. He wanted to send Kelly, Brandon, Shauna, and Sarah off in a sweet way. "I think I know my definition of a happy ending." Brandon and I are the only ones floating around in Jason's pool. "You wanna hear my thoughts?"

"Go for it." Brandon splashes.

"My mom defines it as whatever you want it to be...after Bella, she's changed her mind on happy endings. She told me that happy endings are self-defined because only you know what your ending is or what your ending should be." Brandon floats closer to me. "I've had many happy endings...when my mom and dad adopted me, when I beat cancer, when I reconnected with my birth mom and bonding with Shauna, growing closer to Bella, overcoming my fear of stepping outside of my comfort zone...?

Brandon pulls my float towards him. "I like that."

"I don't consider meeting you my happy ending. Even if in the future when we are married or whatever...I still won't consider it our happy ending."

"Why?"

"Because we fell in love...and true love never has a happy ending, because there is no ending to true love."

Brandon's lips are soft. "You're cute."

"I know." I lay back and float and stare up at the sun. "Alexander the Great said that by the way."

ACKNOWLEDGEMENTS

I'm going to keep it short and sweet, because I didn't have no big book company backing me for the releasing of my debut novel, so it's not ten thousand names of people to thank. I wrote this book partly based on a story my grandma told me from her time being a social worker in New York (read the author's note), and a lot of prospective agents told me that my story was great just that it reminded them of too many other books already out. I wasn't changing or shelving my story and thus self-publishing presented itself to me. Side bar, if you find anything else on the internet written by "me" no you didn't—this is my debut. The only book that matters.

On to the acknowledgements…

First and foremost, I have to thank my twin sister Aaliyah personally because if it weren't for her, there'd be no book. She isn't a big reader but her enthusiasm for my book matched my energy, and it kept me pushing for these past few years of trying to get this book out into the world.

I should also thanks to my family because…well, we're related but on a serious note, thank y'all for letting me be me. Grant it, I would have been who I was without the support (ha-ha) but having you all by my side has meant the world. I get to tell the stories I want in my voice and experience with no judgement and not many people in the world can do that. And for that, I love you guys.

On the professional side, thank you to Emily Klopfer—who edited and critiqued this story…twice. It is the story the world gets to read because of your honest feedback and honest notes. Also, thank you for putting up with me for the course of the year we worked together.

Lastly, thank you to Alana McCarthy. She's responsible for my BEAUTIFUL book cover. Funds willing, I hope to continue our collaboration on all of my future YA and New Adult books.

In closing, I'd like to thank you all for buying this book and getting me closer to my writer dreams. If you all didn't buy the book…you wouldn't be reading these acknowledgements. In seriousness, thanks again…and tell your friends and rate and review on Goodreads and Amazon.

Until the next story, Aaron.

AUTHOR'S NOTE

Firstly, to anyone battling any kind of unfortunate disease I hope I told an uplifting story—something you can hold on to even during those dark moments.

Next, I wanted to expand on a story my grandmother told me about a family she cherished when she first moved to New York in 1987. The way she told the story of the little boy, I felt like I had known him all of my life. Although, the boy ultimately passed away—I wanted to give him an ending the universe should have given him.

I did a lot of research for this story like with most things— we can leave out important information. I wanted to deal with Randall's diagnosis and treatment that way my grandmother (a former nurse) told it to me. So, if you are currently going through anything remotely close to what Randall dealt with in the book, I understand your plan was your plan—his treatment plan was a plan I wrote verbatim from old notes my grandma kept.

With all that being said, I cannot wait to continue to share the many characters that reside in Crestview and Westlake. They all have stories worth championing for and it's going to always be my goal to give and write a story some queer teen can look up and forward to.

CPSIA information can be obtained
at www.ICGtesting.com
Printed in the USA
BVHW081110071022
648929BV00014B/1692